ALSO BY LISA CACH

Have Glass Slippers, Will Travel
The Erotic Secrets of a French Maid

Available from Pocket Books

LISA CACH

A Babe in Ghostland

POCKET STAR BOOKS

NEW YORK   LONDON   TORONTO   SYDNEY

An *Original* Publication of POCKET BOOKS

 POCKET STAR BOOKS, a division of Simon & Schuster, Inc.
1230 Avenue of the Americas, New York, NY 10020

This book is a work of fiction. Names, characters, places and
incidents are products of the author's imagination or are used
fictitiously. Any resemblance to actual events or locales or
persons, living or dead, is entirely coincidental.

ISBN-13: 978-0-7434-7090-2
ISBN-10: 0-7434-7090-7

This Pocket Star Books paperback edition January 2007

10 9 8 7 6 5 4 3 2 1

POCKET and colophon are registered trademarks
of Simon & Schuster, Inc.

Cover design by Anna Dorfman
Cover illustration by Chris Long

Manufactured in the United States of America

For information regarding special discounts for bulk
purchases, please contact Simon & Schuster Special Sales
at 1-800-456-6798 or business@simonandschuster.com.

To Marilyn H.

A Babe in Ghostland

one

If she'd only had the right type of psychic abilities, Megan Barrows thought later that day, she would have sensed her doom when Case Lambert stepped through the doorway to Antique Fancies. Instead, when the bell over the door dinged and she looked up and saw him, her hands ceased work on the alabaster lamp she was rewiring, and her heart seized in her chest.

"Hello," she said, an uncertain smile on her lips, attraction turning her shy.

A tight smile briefly graced the man's face. "Hello." His gaze took a long trip over her tall body, and a frown formed between his brows as his gaze lingered on her chest. She moved sideways a few inches, hoping to hide her A-cups behind the inadequate lamp, her attraction to him fading as quickly as it had come. So he was one of *those*.

The man looked away, turning his attention to the late-Victorian tea table beside him, its top loaded with silver candlesticks. He picked one up and turned it over to examine the hallmarks on the bottom, then flipped it around, eyes narrowing as he scrutinized the plating where it had begun, ever so slightly, to wear off the copper core.

Megan pretended to turn her attention back to rewiring the lamp, just as the man pretended to examine candlesticks. He was a big guy: six-foot-three according to the height markings on the edge of her door, and with a solid broadness that hinted at years of laboring muscle; no youthful lankiness here. His squarely masculine face showed signs of weathering, and his short brown hair was mussed. She had a brief flash of him driving his pickup with the window down, elbow resting on the sill, wind in his hair, howling along to a country song about the cheatin' woman who done him wrong. His jeans and battered leather shoes, and the faded polo shirt with a breast pocket made lumpy by some object, all hinted at someone in one of the trades.

One thing for sure: he wasn't a cubicle monkey from Microsoft.

He set down the candlestick and wandered farther into the shop, pausing to stare into a lighted glass case full of small bits and pieces: thimbles, lorgnettes, spoons, figurines, vases. Perhaps he was looking for a gift for his wife.

She glanced at his left hand. No ring.

A gift for his girlfriend, then? Mother? Aunt Esmeralda?

He left the glass case and wandered closer to where she stood at her worktable/cashier's counter, his big frame feeling oversized in the crowded, feminine confines of her shop. The natural assurance of his stance, the silent assumption that he was master of his domain—master of *her* domain—grated on her, reminding her of the womanizing dolt she'd worked for while putting herself through college.

He made a show of casting his gaze over her shop. "You've got a nice place here—nicer than I expected. Judging from the outside, I thought it would be full of the usual thrift-store crap that passes for antiques these days."

Megan narrowed her eyes.

"I must have driven by a hundred times but never stopped," he went on, and ran a fingertip over the gracefully carved line of a chair back near the counter. He met her gaze, his gray eyes direct. "I should have. There are beautiful things here."

Attraction shot through her again despite her every thought against it. She blushed and looked down at the lamp beneath her hands, then away, not sure where to set her gaze, afraid he might see that his words had affected her. "The shop belonged to my mother. She started it when I was a child."

" 'Belonged.' Did she retire?"

She glanced up at him. "She died. Two years ago."

In his eyes, she saw empathy, the tightness around his mouth loosening. "I'm sorry. I lost my mother a few years ago, too."

She nodded, acknowledging the shared pain. "But I have the shop, so in some ways it feels like I see her every day."

He raised a brow and looked as if he were about to say something, then shook his head. A moment later, he asked, "So, can you make a living at this business? Doesn't sound like it pays too well, especially not in this economy. Haven't most of your colleagues gone out of business?"

She forced a smile. "I get by. Can I help you find something? Were you looking for something in particular?"

He ignored her question and made a show of again gazing around the shop. "You ever wonder what the long-dead owners of this stuff must be thinking, to see their things for sale?"

She rolled her eyes. The guy had one great question after another, didn't he? "I suspect the dead have better things to do than watch over their chipped teacups and sprung chairs."

His brows rose, and then he laughed, the loudness of it startling her, the whole room seeming to shake with the vibrations of his mirth. "What do you think the dead *are* doing with their time?" he asked when the storm had settled.

A wisp of suspicion floated into Megan's mind. A man like this, discussing the dead with *her*, of all people? "I'm sure they're fighting over the best dark hallways and attics to haunt, debating the merits of cemeteries on Halloween, et cetera, et cetera."

"You don't take it seriously?"

"Do you want me to?"

The small frown reappeared between his brows. "You must have been in a lot of old houses. You ever see a ghost?"

She tugged at the fresh wires coming out of the top of the lamp and began attaching them to a new socket. "In most cases, ghosts can be explained away rationally."

"So you've never seen one?"

She glanced at him. His expression was serious. "Have you?" she asked back.

He looked away from her, toward the front picture window and its display tableau of desk, chair, and leather library books, a bust of Dante on the floor. When he spoke, his voice was quiet. "Maybe I've experienced something. But nothing I'd swear to."

Megan felt the lure of the bait he'd just trailed before her, and with it, the small seed of suspicion that had been planted in her mind sprouted leaves. He'd heard something about her that made him come in and expect her to want to talk about ghosts.

His statement begged for follow-up questions, for her to lean forward and say, "Really? What happened?" But did she want to get involved in his problems? No, although he *was* shockingly good-looking for a dunderheaded brute. And there was always curiosity to satisfy.

She parted her lips to speak, and then caution laid hold of her tongue, forbidding her to take the tempting bait. "Was there something special you were looking for?" she asked, nodding toward the shop at large.

He stood straighter, her answer clearly not the one he was expecting. Then he shook his head and laughed again, the sound softer this time and strangely warming.

He dug into his breast pocket. "Would you be able to give me an appraisal on this, and maybe tell me something about it?" he asked, pulling a small gold pocket watch out of his shirt and handing it to her.

"I think so," she said, surprised he had a legitimate reason for visiting her shop. She'd convinced herself he wanted to pick her brain about ghosts. That's what she got for thinking too much of herself and her talents!

Megan took the watch and let it lie flat in her palm, feeling its heavy weight, the gold warm from his body. She ran her finger over the small dents along one edge and smiled.

"It's a lady's watch, meant to be pinned to her bodice. English—1910, 1915, I think." She wound it a few turns and heard the soft, regular ticking begin. "Still works. It's a lovely little thing." She started to hand it back to him.

"How much would you give me for it?"

She pushed her hand at him again, offering the watch. "You don't want to sell this."

"Sure I do."

She shook her head. "Someday you'll have a daughter who'd love to have a piece of family history like this."

"Family history?"

"I assume it belonged to your grandmother. Or a great-aunt," she added, wanting to make the ownership sound more like a guess than it was.

He stared at her a long moment, then nodded. "It was my maternal grandmother's. But I have no use for it, and I'm not one for holding on to something just for the sake of it. It's just a watch. And it's dented."

"But you know what those dents are from, don't you?"

He shook his head.

"They're the marks of a teething baby. Your teeth, perhaps? While your grandmother held you? You—or someone—used her watch as a teething ring." She shrugged, knowing she had sounded too certain. And she wasn't *that* certain. Her imagination often led her down the wrong path. "It's an educated guess.

She must have been a doting grandmother to allow it, if I'm right."

"Just a guess, huh? A pretty damn good guess!"

Megan crossed her arms over her chest. "You knew they were your teeth marks."

"You're the first antique 'expert' to know what those dents were from."

"You were *testing* me?"

"Just like to know who I'm dealing with," he said, grinning. "What else can you tell me about the watch?"

"What do you want to know?"

"I don't know. Surprise me. **Do some Sherlock Holmes**–like deducing."

"Sherlock Holmes?"

"Yeah."

"I'm not a detective."

"Come on. Try.

"He was fiction."

"You surprised me with the teeth marks. Do it again."

Was he serious?

Well, what the hell.

She enclosed the watch between her palms and closed her eyes. The trick was to let the images and snatches of sound come to her, not to force them. Not to think. She made her mind into a blank silver screen.

Bit by bit, a vague story began to emerge.

"I can tell you what anyone else might guess, given the probabilities," she said, opening her eyes. "Your grandmother's family emigrated to the U.S. She was moderately well-off, and she valued her family. She cared for people, both emotionally and physically."

That was what she said aloud, but in her mind a much fuller picture of a woman had emerged: a girl of thirteen coming across the ocean with her mother; the girl growing into a young woman who took up nursing and married a doctor; the young woman becoming a middle-aged widow who held her family together with every last ounce of her love.

"That's it?" he said. "'They were immigrants' and 'she valued family'? Anyone could have guessed that."

"Which is what I told you before I spoke, in case you've forgotten." She stared at him in silent challenge.

After a long moment, he reached out and took the watch back. "Sure you don't want to buy it?" he asked quietly. "A hundred bucks?"

"I wouldn't take it for five cents. Please keep it; I'm sure your grandmother would have wanted you to pass it down. Someday you'll be glad you still have it."

"Is that a prediction?"

"It's experience."

"My grandmother didn't . . . *say* that to you?"

Suspicion grew a bud and bloomed. "How could she?"

"I was told that you might have access to . . . *the Other Side,*" he said, hunching close to her, his eyes widening.

She stared at him.

He stared back. Then an easygoing smile cracked his composure, and he stood straight. "I call it that for lack of a better term. You probably call it the Sixth Plane of Ethereal Existence or something."

She set her jaw. "Just what is it that you want, Mr.—?"

"Lambert. Case Lambert," he said, sticking out his hand. "And you're Megan Barrows?"

She frowned at him.

"You *aren't* Megan Barrows?" His expression lightened, delight sparking the gray depths of his eyes.

"I'm afraid I am." She shook his hand, watching with her own delight as disappointment pulled at his features. Her amusement faded as she felt the warmth and strength of his hand surrounding her own, his calluses rough against her skin. A zing of a different delight shot straight down to her core. How long had it been since she'd been with a man, his body warming hers through the night? Too long.

His grip was firm but gentle, showing he knew it was a woman's hand he held, with finer bones than the meaty paws of men. No sixth-sense information came to her from his touch; it was not the way her gift worked. The living kept their secrets from her. However, if she could touch a frequently used personal object of his, she might get somewhere.

He released her hand. "What is it you're looking for, Mr. Lambert?" Megan asked, cradling her own hand against her stomach as if she could hold the warmth of his touch.

"I'm looking for you."

Her heart fluttered, and then reason reasserted itself. *"Why* were you looking for me?"

"I have a bit of a problem and was told you might be of help. I have to warn you, though, I'm a confirmed skeptic."

It was Megan's turn to laugh. "That's what everyone says."

He scowled. "I am not everyone."

"Of course not."

"I'm not. I really don't believe in ghosts."

"I never said you did."

"So, are you going to help me?"

"Given all you've said, I don't see how I can, unless it's an appraisal of antiques that you want. Is that what you want, Mr. Lambert?"

"You know it's not," he growled. "You're making this difficult."

"I am?"

"Eric said you were a piece of work, but—"

"Who told you about me?" she interrupted, laughter gone.

"Let's discuss that afterward. First, I'll take you to the house and see what you can make of it, if anything."

"Did you say *Eric?"*

He sighed. "Eric Ramsey told me about you."

"Ramsey! I should have known!" Rage suffused her

mind, blocking out all else. "Good day, Mr. Lambert!" she barked, and turned her back to him. She yanked a book off the shelf behind her worktable and opened it, pretending to look for some valuable piece of information. Her hands were shaking, and she could hear her heart pounding in her ears. *Eric Ramsey*. Anger shuddered through her.

"He warned me not to mention his name," Case said to her back, sounding annoyed. "I take it there's some bad history between you. He insists we need your help, though. He seems to think you're the only"—he paused and seemed to gag on his words—"*real medium* in the state."

With trembling fingers, she turned a page. "I said good day, Mr. Lambert!"

"Look, I'm willing to"—again the begrudging tone, as if forcing the words out went against every fiber of his being—"willing to *pay* you for your time. Not much, but enough to cover your lost hours here."

"Good day!" she screeched, and slammed the book shut. She jammed it back on the shelf and whirled around. "I don't want anything to do with Eric Ramsey or any of his crazy experiments!"

The bell over the door rang, and her friend Tracie, owner of the boutique next door, stuck her head in, face worried. "Megan, are you okay?"

"I'm fine." Megan flashed a strained smile to her friend.

Tracie stepped into the shop, her eyes running over Case's looming figure, his red face and tight jaw. "You sure? I heard raised voices."

"Case Lambert," Case said, turning to Tracie and holding out his hand.

Eyes still wary, Tracie shook it. "Tracie Thomas, Thomasina Designs."

"I was trying to hire your friend here, but she's having none of it."

"No? Why, did you ask her to do her famous go-go dance for you or something? She's trying to get out of that line of work, you know."

"Tracie!" Megan hissed.

An uncertain smile twitched at Case's mouth, as if he might believe she moonlighted as a dancer. "I want her to come look at a supposedly haunted house."

"Really? Cool! Can I come?"

"Tracie!"

"So, what's the problem?" Tracie asked them both.

"Eric Ramsey sent him," Megan said.

"Oh." Tracie made a duck bill of her lips and squinted her eyes at Case. "This is going to cost you."

"No, it won't," Megan said. "I won't do it."

"Sure she will," Tracie said to Case. "You've just got to pay her well enough to forget about Ramsey."

A cynical look settled over Case's features. "How much is well enough?"

Megan opened her mouth to answer, but Tracie's words were in the air first. "Three hundred an hour."

Megan gasped.

Case's breath burst from him. "That's criminal!"

Tracie shrugged. "You get what you pay for."

"He's not getting anything," Megan said. "Mr. Lambert, please be so kind as to leave. Now."

"Three hundred bucks, that's what you charge for an hour of your mumbo jumbo?"

"My *mumbo jumbo*? Why did you come in here if you're so convinced it's nonsense?"

"It wasn't my idea, believe me! It was Ramsey's. He insisted he needed you in order to do a thorough investigation, but he said you wouldn't come if you knew he was going to be there."

"Smart man! Although if you don't believe in *my* mumbo jumbo, why did you hire Eric?"

"I didn't. He's doing this for free."

"But why call a parapsychologist to look at a house if you don't believe in ghosts?"

"Because I don't think it's haunted. *Something* is going on there, but I'm sure there's a scientific explanation for it."

"And you think Ramsey will find that for you."

"With all that equipment he has? Yes."

Megan laughed. "A tool is only as good as the brain that uses it."

"His seems plenty sharp to me. He said he'd never once come across a supposed haunting that didn't turn out to be something completely rational."

"Did he, now."

"You saying he's lying?"

She arched a brow. "Yes."

"That's not kind repayment for his faith in *you.*"

"*I* don't lie."

"Ah. So you're one of the ones who believe their own gibberish."

"Gibberish!" Tracie blurted. "Megan—"

"Don't bother, Tracie," Megan said. "A ghost could climb into bed with him, and he still wouldn't take it as proof."

Case's face went pale. "I'd assume it was a dream."

Megan cocked her head. "Would you, now."

"Hypano-, hypannia-"

"Hypnagogic," Megan supplied. "The hypnagogic state right before sleep, when the brain plays naughty tricks on you—a feeling of presence in the room, paralysis, inability to breathe. Eric's been explaining things, I see."

"You don't believe that theory?"

"I believe it. But it's not the explanation each and every time."

"How could you tell any difference?"

"I use my magic fairy dust."

His lips tightened.

"I assume Eric sent you here because I'm the only person he knows who *can* tell the difference. His sensors and infrared cameras can't detect everything."

"So how much are you going to pay her?" Tracie

piped up. "Megan, you are going to do it, aren't you?"

Megan felt her determination slipping, pulled down by curiosity and a perverse attraction to the very things that scared her the most. How long had it been since she'd investigated a house? Two years? She'd sworn off doing it since that last disaster, but she wasn't immune to the lure. It was like an addiction, the promise of things that go bump in the night, pulling her toward an experience she knew to be dangerous. "I'll come look at the house *if*, and only if, Eric isn't there."

"How much?" he asked.

"Five hundred," Tracie said.

"Shush," Megan scolded her friend. "I'll do it for nothing."

Case looked suspicious. "And then you'll tell me that there are a dozen ghosts and I'll need to hire you for a six-month 'cleansing ritual'?"

"Fine. Never mind my offer. Good day, Mr. Lambert." She went back to work on the lamp.

Tracie scowled at Case and kicked his shoe. "What's the matter with you?"

Megan waited, watching from the corner of her eye as Case shifted his weight, distrust and indecision spelled out in every muscle of his body.

"You won't let me pay you?" he asked again. "Just for lost time at the shop?"

"No money. This will be a one-time thing, just to give you my impressions, and then that's it. No more.

No 'cleansing rituals' or séances or sitting up all night waiting for ghosts to molest you."

"I'd feel better about it if I paid you," Case said.

"So you don't have to stop thinking of me as a fraud who fleeces the innocent?"

He chuckled. "Yeah."

"Sorry."

"Will you accept dinner, then?" he asked, his voice dropping to a seductive rumble. "I'd love to take you out." The look in his eye said that wasn't all he'd love to do.

Megan blinked.

Tracie's jaw dropped open.

"N-no, I-" Megan stammered.

Tracie punched her arm.

"Ow!"

"Don't be an idiot," Tracie whispered. "Look at his ass!"

Case's mouth twitched.

Megan spoke through gritted teeth covered by a smile. "I can't *see* his ass from here."

"It's mighty damn fine!" Tracie punched her again. "For God's sake, say yes, you moron."

Megan's heart thumped. Dinner, with him? He might be a closed-minded jerk, but he wasn't like any of the other men—no, *boys*—she had gone out with in the past. Case Lambert was a man, full-grown and sure of himself, and that scared her. This was one man she would not be able to control.

But as with the dead, what scared her also lured her.

"Okay," she said finally.

"Okay?" Case repeated, surprised.

"Dinner. Okay."

Tracie clapped her hands in delight and did a boxing dance, faux-punching Megan's arm.

"Stop it," Megan said.

"I've got an appointment now, but I can be back at four to pick you up. We'll go to the house first, then eat," Case said.

"Wait, you mean *today?*"

"Yeah, why not? You've got plans?"

"But . . ." Didn't he understand that a woman needed more warning for a dinner date?

But that was just it. This wasn't a dinner date. No need to shave her legs or fuss with her hair.

"Okay, fine, four o'clock," she grumbled.

"See you then." He held out his hand to her.

She slipped hers into his broad palm. As he released her hand, he let his fingertips graze against the inside of her wrist. Her eyes met his, and he smiled, his gray eyes intent.

"Ms. Thomas," he said, turning to Tracie and shaking her hand. And then he was gone, the ringing of the bell marking his passage.

Megan sank down onto a stool. Her thoughts were scattered, her emotions a jumpy blend of fear and anger and arousal, all of it tinged with surprise at the scene she'd created. She could count on one hand the number of times she'd had as angry an exchange as the one she'd just had with Case Lambert. She was usually calm and collected.

She touched her upper lip, feeling the dew of nervous sweat. How had Case Lambert managed to have that strong an effect on her?

"Whooeee!" Tracie said, plopping down onto a Victorian fainting couch and throwing her arm over her brow. *"What* a piece of man-beef! I wouldn't mind getting a slice of that."

"Be my guest."

Tracie shook her head, smiling. "No, he's got the hots for *you.* "

"He does not. He can barely stand me. He thinks I'm a charlatan."

"Like a guy cares about that? He wants to jump your bones, I'm telling you."

"Delightful." Megan was silent a moment. "Do you really think so?"

"He wants you to take a ride on the ol' bucking bronco."

Megan rolled her eyes, a small traitorous part of her hoping it was true. "I don't care what he wants."

"Megan," Tracie said, her tone changing, "don't shut him down. Don't treat him like you treat all the other guys."

"How's that?"

Tracie waggled her head. *"You* know."

"I *don't* know!"

"You make yourself so unapproachable. No guy thinks you'll give him the time of day."

"I've had boyfriends!"

"Wimpy little guys looking for a mother figure to be their backbone for them."

"They've been smart men! Intellectuals! Artists! Scientists! And they've been empathetic and sensitive. Philosophical. Spiritual. Unlike that Neanderthal."

"They've been low-testosterone flakes, and you know it. Stop being a ball breaker, and give this one a chance."

Megan set her jaw. "That's the impression I give? A ball breaker?"

Tracie nodded.

"Well, never mind. It's not going to matter today."

"Heh. Right. You want to borrow a dress from the shop? I've got something that would look great on you."

Megan bit her upper lip. "I have no interest in Case Lambert."

"The dress looks innocent, but it's really very sexy. He'll have a hard-on the whole time he's with you."

"You're so crude."

Tracie grinned.

Megan sighed. "Do you have it in my size?"

Case headed across the street to his car, confounded by Megan Barrows. She had seemed so rational at first; so wry and levelheaded, and so unexpectedly sexy in her plain white blouse that showed the bumps of her nipples. He'd caught himself staring at them— a juvenile mistake he hadn't made in years.

But then he'd mentioned Eric Ramsey's name, and she'd turned into a hyperventilating banshee.

Which was what he'd initially expected of her: dramatics and hair tearing. From what he'd seen, "sensitives" came in limited varieties: you had your overly emotional hair tearers, you had your grandmotherly muumuu-wearing earth mothers, and then you had your foreign-accented black candle crowd. A pretty young woman like Megan was most likely going to be a hair tearer.

He'd seen plenty of frauds as his mother bankrupted herself by hiring them. It was beyond ironic that he'd now been put in a position where he had to hire one himself.

He opened the door to his old BMW and got in, welcomed by the familiar smell of spilled coffee. The leather on the driver's seat was splitting, and the car hadn't been detailed in at least two years, but Case never missed a tune-up. He sat behind the wheel now and stared at the glass windows fronting Antique Fancies.

Megan was either as loopy as the rest of her colleagues in the mediumship arts, or Eric Ramsey had done something to her that deserved her wrath. But what could Ramsey have done to so distress her?

It was hard to imagine. Megan was five-foot-ten if she was an inch, with a slim athletic build and a sharp attitude. It was difficult to imagine that Ramsey could, by force of either will or sluggish body, do anything to harm her.

Which left "flake and drama queen" as his explanation for her behavior. Not that that meant they couldn't enjoy a little time together, given the chance. Just the thought of those long legs wrapped around him . . .

He shifted in his seat and took a deep breath. His eyes roved over the facades of Megan's and Tracie's shops, then to the left of Antique Fancies to the hole-in-the-wall grocery. All three businesses were lodged in the same decrepit building, a single-story, flat-roofed, stuccoed rectangle entirely unsuited to the rainy climate or to the up-and-coming neighborhood. High up on the wall of the building was a For Sale sign.

Case turned in his seat and looked at the other shops nearby: an Irish pub, two popular restaurants, a quaint coffee shop, a pet grooming store, and an upscale hair salon. He looked back at the ugly stucco building and programmed the number of the real estate agent into his cell phone.

He glanced at the time. He was late for a meeting at one of his job sites. He started the car and pulled out into traffic, his mind ticking over the possibilities presented both by Megan Barrows and by the building that housed her shop.

"He'll know I changed clothes," Megan said, pulling at the low neckline of the sea-green halter top. It was edged with white eyelet lace, the bodice falling to an A-line skirt of thin cotton.

"Stop fussing with it," Tracie said. "You look divine, except for that cardigan you insist on covering yourself with."

"I'm cold," Megan lied.

"You're afraid to show your bare back."

"It's not appropriate ghost-busting attire."

"Yeah, yeah."

"Are you sure you don't want to come along?" Megan asked.

"And get between the two of you? No. I'll see the place the next time you go."

"There won't be a next time."

"Sure there will, and you'll make him pay for it, too."

"Tracie, you know how I feel about taking money for this type of thing."

"And I know how badly you *need* money right now. You're going to need a second source of income if you hope to pull off your big dream of buying the building."

Megan buttoned the cardigan. "I know, but there are safer ways to make a buck."

"You can't let one bad experience dictate your life."

"Can't I?"

A dirty BMW pulled up to the curb outside, and Case got out. Megan shut off the lights and locked up her shop, ushering Tracie out before her.

"Now, you keep your hands off her," Tracie said to Case. "At least until you've bought her a drink."

"Ah, come on, I'm a gentleman. I'll let her get through the appetizers." They both laughed, and Megan rolled her eyes.

Tracie winked and said her good-byes as Case came around the car and opened the passenger door. Megan started to get in, anxious to get away before Tracie did something else to embarrass her, but Case suddenly stopped her.

"Oh, jeez, wait a second. Sorry!" he said, slipping past her and bending down into the car. Loose papers and notebooks began flying into the backseat. "There!" He stood aside.

Megan gave him an uncertain look and got in, using her foot to nudge aside a thermos and a wadded-up Dick's Drive-In bag. Dirt and stains covered the floor mat, and the console between the seats had dust, fir needles, and sticky, fuzz-collecting spills embedded in every nook and cranny. The car smelled of old coffee and honey.

Case shut her door, and as he jogged around the car, she took the brief moment of privacy to close her eyes and let her mind take in what it could from the vehicle around her.

Stress. Always busy. On the move, no time to relax.

She opened her eyes as he got in, the atmosphere of the car filling with his vibrant presence. She watched him buckle up and start the car, his quick, efficient movements echoing what she felt from the vehicle.

"When's the last time you had a vacation?" Megan asked.

"Vacation? I don't take vacations. Why?"

"Just curious."

Curious, too, why a man who seemed as busy and hardheaded as Case Lambert should be so desperate as to call on paranormal investigators. She'd been so caught up in her troubling attraction to Case that she had barely spared a thought for that. Numerous dark possibilities began to fill her mind, and with them came a slowly growing sense of dread.

She tucked her hands under her thighs and crossed her fingers. She hoped Case Lambert was worried about something benign, like a noisy haunting that merely made a house difficult to sell and sent one's hairs standing on end. The last thing she wanted to face was a conscious spirit intent on harm.

She'd faced that once before and come out the loser.

Case snuck a glance at Megan as they cruised along Greenlake Way. The sun was fighting its way out from behind late-spring clouds, sending sparkling light across the surface of Green Lake to their right. The light highlighted Megan's delicate profile and turned her shoulder-length hair to spun gold.

Her beauty wasn't of the lush Victoria's Secret variety, nor was it the cold hauteur of a runway model. She reminded him of early-Renaissance portraits he had seen of fine-boned women painted in profile, their hair in braids twisted with pearls, their shoulders weighed down with gold chains, their breasts covered in scarlet velvet and fine gatherings of lace. As pampered as the portraits would imply the women were, there was nonetheless always a dark glint of intelligence in their eyes, a set to the jaw that hinted at the will behind the pretty face.

A hum of attraction buzzed in his blood, making his hands tighten on the steering wheel, his foot press a little harder on the gas pedal.

She had turned her face toward the window, watching the lake go by, and he suddenly had the sense that there was more sadness behind her features than he had recognized.

Was it the death of her mother, which he knew would still feel recent even at two years? It wasn't the type of question she'd answer, he suspected.

If he were honest with himself, the question he truly wanted answered was whether or not the two of them would end up in bed tonight. He didn't think she'd be in the car with him now—or that she would have changed clothes—if that thought wasn't also on her mind.

"Why don't you take money for what you do?" he asked. "I do hear of people spending three, four hundred dollars for an hour with a medium. Seems like it would be a lucrative career, if you're legitimate, or at least make a good show of it."

She shot him a frown, then looked back out the window. "I don't do consultations anymore."

"Why not? Help grieving people and such."

She turned away from the window and looked at him. "It doesn't help people. It does quite the opposite."

He thought about it. "What, do they hear their loved ones are suffering the fires of hell?"

A smile quirked her lips. "No. I've never gotten the least whiff of sulfur during a reading."

"Then what? My only guess is that it might make it harder for people to let go."

"Bingo."

He shrugged. "Maybe people aren't ready to let go." He thought about her and her shop, and the connection it must give her to her mother.

"No one is ever ready," she said, sitting forward. "It's only the utter, inescapable finality of death that pushes people to let go and move on with their lives. If they think there's a chance of talking to the dead person, they'll obsess on that instead of on grieving. They'll get stuck. They'll forget that they're here to live their own lives.

"A lot of the people who want a consultation with a medium are exactly the people who would be better off without one," she continued. "It's just not good for them." She made a wry face. "And it's not too good for the dead person, either."

Case blinked, struck by the image of ghosts being tortured by the grieving of their loved ones. "Well, how about helping the police solve murders?" he tried.

She waved her hand, dismissing the idea as she sat back, seeming to relax as she talked. "I've never had any information that would be of use to them. It goes against everything you see in movies or hear in ghost stories, but the dead care more about how they lived than how they died. The act of dying ceases to matter, once you've done it."

He smiled. "I kind of like that idea. Takes the pressure off. 'Dying? Aah, it's nothing. Not as bad as they say.'"

"Well, not so bad *afterward,*" she said with dry humor.

He laughed. "Fair enough."

They drove in silence a few minutes, crossing the bridge over the ship canal and turning off the main road to take a route up the back of Queen Anne Hill.

"You haven't given me much information about this house we're going to," she said before he could think of another question. "You own it?"

He nodded. "I didn't know how much I should tell you about it, if anything. I didn't know if you'd prefer not to be influenced beforehand."

"Or was it that you didn't want me making up stories to fit what you'd told me?"

"It's not that." He glanced at her. "Or, at least, I wouldn't expect you to do that intentionally. But the imagination can play its tricks." He paused. "Do you *need* to know something about the house or what's been going on?"

She shook her head. "No. But I warn you, there's a good chance I won't be able to give you more than a few impressions of your house. And they might be wildly inaccurate. I don't know what Eric told you, but for all I know, I'm just making up most of what I 'see.' It's rare to get concrete confirmation of my impressions."

"I'm not expecting much."

She snorted. "I don't suppose you are."

"You were right about the dents on my grandmother's watch."

"Are you trying to flatter me now?"

"Believe me, I could find better things to flatter you about than that."

She crossed her arms over her chest. "I'm not going to take that bait."

"You don't want to hear what I've been thinking about the curve of your lips?"

Her chin rose, and she gave him a dark look. "Case Johannsen Lambert, you will *not* be rude in the presence of ladies!" she said with the creaky voice of age, a tinge of England in her accent. "There'll be no chocolates for you, my good man, if you keep this up!"

Case gaped at her, a chill running down the back of his neck. He looked back at the street just in time to see a yellow light turn red and hit the brakes, skidding to a stop. His heart was pounding. "How the hell—"

Megan winked at him.

He swore under his breath.

"Sometimes the truth seems clear," she said in her normal voice. "Most of the time, no. As far as your house is concerned, a bit of vagueness won't matter if there's a scientific explanation for whatever is going on, or if all you have is a passive haunting. No danger there. And active hauntings are extremely rare, so you don't need to worry about that."

"Active? Passive? What's the difference?" he asked as the light turned green.

"A passive haunting is a recording of events,

embedded somehow in the environment. It plays over and over, seen or heard by some people, undetectable to others. There's no consciousness behind it, and it never varies."

"Like what? Give me an example."

"Okay, a lady in white who walks down a hallway every night at ten p.m. Ladies in white are pretty popular." She grinned. "The lady doesn't look at anyone, doesn't respond to voices. She's just a moving picture. Maybe she disappears into the wall where once upon a time there was a doorway. People see her, and a legend develops, but over the years fewer and fewer people encounter her. The recording fades. Eventually, no one sees the ghost at all.

"An *active* haunting is where true ghosts come in. Spirits of the dead, conscious of their environment and able to interact. Those are the ones that try to communicate or cause a bit of mischief. Make the lights flicker. Pinch women's behinds in bars."

He smiled, because it was expected, but he began to feel worried despite his disbelief. Hadn't she implied that active hauntings were trouble?

"And then sometimes a ghost isn't human; sometimes it's something else entirely."

Goose bumps rose on his skin. "What kind of something else?"

"I don't know. And I don't want to know any more than I do." She pulled the open neck of her cardigan closed, as if she were cold.

"You think you've seen such a thing?" he asked.

She gave him a quick, false smile. "Don't worry, I'm sure that's not what's going on here."

"Why don't I feel reassured?"

She shrugged, and a hint of impishness gleamed in her eyes. "Maybe I don't want you to be. Maybe this is part of my scheme to defraud you of your money."

"Good luck." He tried to sound tough, but Megan had freaked him out when his grandmother's voice had seemed to come out of her mouth. He even remembered when his grandmother had said those exact same words, when he'd misbehaved during one of her ladies' bridge club meetings.

And how did she know his middle name?

"So, what do you do in your free time?" he asked, moving back to firmer ground.

"Hang out at graveyards. Read the obituaries. Dust my collection of Victorian mourning wear. You know, the usual."

"Very funny. Seriously, though, do you have any hobbies?"

"That's such a strange word, don't you think? It's almost gone out of the lexicon. People have 'activities' now. 'Hobbies' always makes me think of middle-aged men in their basements building model airplanes."

"You're not going to answer, are you?"

"I don't really like to talk about myself."

"That makes you an anomaly of the human race."

"Just another part of the weirdness that is Megan Barrows," she said lightly.

"You think you're weird?"

"Don't you?"

"Not in any way that matters."

"Gee, thanks."

"I mean, you do everything else a woman your age does, right? You date, you go out with friends, you see movies. Don't you?"

She looked out the passenger window again, and some of the sadness seemed to have returned to her profile. "Are we almost there?"

Frustration surged inside him. The possibility of a night in her bed seemed more remote by the minute.

Maybe she was too troubled, and he should lay off. A pretty face wasn't everything.

He made the last turn to get to his house. "This is the start of the property, at this corner," he said, and slowed the car to a crawl. Enormous maples on either side shaded the street. His property was surrounded by a high stone wall overgrown with ivy, with a wrought-iron fence atop the wall.

"It's the whole block?" she asked, turning to him with her eyes opened wide in disbelief.

Proud, he nodded.

"It must have cost a fortune! Who can afford an entire block on top of Queen Anne?"

"I couldn't believe it was in my price range, either," he said, and turned into the driveway. He stopped the car with the nose barely inside the gate. Overhead, the iron fence atop the wall continued, making a massive arch over the drive, a coat of arms wrought in its center. The iron gates were propped open with rocks.

"That's it." He nodded toward the house.

She was silent, staring, then spoke under her breath: "Oh, Christ."

"Yeah, I know. I really hope you can help me."

Three

Megan took one look at the house and felt her heart drop. The decrepit house before her looked as if it belonged in a freakin' *horror* movie. How could it *not* be haunted? And haunted by something dark and troubled.

It was built in the Queen Anne style for which the hill had been named, back at the end of the nineteenth century. The house was a jumble of asymmetrical towers and gables, porches and wings, angled roofs and gingerbread trim, all adding up to a sprawling three-story building that could have housed a family of twenty in its day.

Now it looked as if it housed rats, bats, and all things creeping and crawling.

The exterior was nearly devoid of paint, the brown

wood smudged with faint traces of white. The roof was clearly new, but several windows over the facade of the house had been boarded over. The grounds were overgrown and thick with blackberry bushes, except for a wide swath immediately around the house that looked to have been cleared recently. The one element that should have been charming, the climbing roses, pink clematis, and wisteria, managed instead to be ominous, crawling up drainpipes and poking tendrils under the eaves.

In front of the main entrance to the house stood an enormous green Dumpster, plastered wood poking out above its rim. Several feet to the left of the Dumpster was a post made of fresh lumber, angled two-by-fours propping it upright. Heavy power lines swooped from the nearest telephone pole to the gray electrical box affixed to it, and wires from the box swung to the side of the house. A pickup truck was parked nearby.

"Who's doing the work?" Megan asked.

"I am," he said, and drove through the gate.

A sense of overwhelming claustrophobia descended on Megan. She gasped for air and twisted in her seat until she could see out the back window of the car. The street beyond the gate was like the air above the surface of the water for a drowning man. She could see it, but she kept moving farther away, sinking beneath it.

She started to panic. A low cry of despair started in her throat.

"Megan! What's wrong?"

She felt Case's hand on her shoulder, warm and strong. It cut through the panic, a touch of living energy anchored in the real world. It was enough for her to remember where and who she was.

"I'm okay, I'm okay, I'm okay," she chanted under her breath, trying to calm herself down. She closed her eyes and let the suffocating feeling wash over her, then drain away. She knew it wasn't her own emotion; it was something that belonged to the house.

She turned her face toward Case and opened her eyes. She was half lying between their seats, wedged into the opening to the backseat with her seat belt undone, her body touching his.

"What is it? What's going on?"

She righted herself in her seat and smoothed out her green cotton skirt, her fingers trembling. "I'll be fine. I was just taken by surprise. It was a feeling of claustrophobia; like I had to get out of here. I can't tell you what it was, exactly, that made me feel that way."

"Are you okay going on?"

She nodded. "It's okay," she said, laying her fingertips on his arm to reassure him. "Really. It was just an emotion. Nothing scary about emotions, right?"

"Spoken like a woman."

She laughed, although the humor did little to lessen the worry she hid underneath. She hadn't had such a strong reaction to a place since—

No, she didn't want to think about that.

As Case put the car in gear and moved forward, her gut soured with anxiety. She wanted to get this done and over with as quickly as possible and then get *out* of here.

He parked the car at the side of the house at the porte cochere, the covered area of the drive that had once allowed the residents to disembark from their carriages without getting wet in the rain. Megan opened her door and got out, looking toward the grounds, then froze as she saw something from the corner of her eye. At the corner of the house, where shadow met sunlight, a figure was standing.

A chill crept up the back of her neck.

"It's a mess inside, of course," Case said, getting out on his side. "I hope your shoes will be okay. I should have told you to wear grubbies."

The figure, indistinct in her peripheral vision, made of shadows and light, seemed to be watching them. Waiting.

"Megan?" Case said.

"*Shh.*"

Very slowly, she began to turn her head.

The figure vanished.

She turned her head fully toward the corner of the house, and there was nothing there. Disappointment and relief mingled inside her.

"What? What did you see?"

Megan shook her head. "Nothing. Peripheral vision can play tricks on you."

"What type of tricks?"

"Your brain likes to make faces and figures out of random shapes and shadows. You know, like how people are always seeing Mary in a potato chip or Christ in an oil slick."

"Great. Just don't tell me you see Satan in the water stain in the ceiling above my bed."

"I don't expect to be in a position to notice it," she said, then clamped her mouth shut. Where had *that* comment come from? Damn Tracie! She'd planted thoughts of sex in Megan's head, and now they were spilling out unbidden.

Case looked at her intensely.

She grinned brightly. "You're the one who wanted me here. Would you rather I try to keep everything I sense to myself?"

"Are you going to be seeing something every two minutes?" he asked dryly. "I'm not sure my heart can take it."

"I don't know, this house is . . . unusual."

He groaned softly. "I think we're going to have to have cocktails before dinner," he said. "The only way I'm going to get through this is if I know there's a dry martini at the end."

"A lavender cosmopolitan for me," she said.

"Lavender?"

"I'm a girl. I'm allowed." And no sense telling him that it was the only cocktail she'd ever had. She didn't want to seem like the homebody that she was.

"Shall we?" He gestured at the wood entrance doors.

She followed him up the three steps to the doors, waiting while he unlocked them. "You said you were doing the work on this house yourself?"

"Me and a few of my work crews, when they're between jobs."

"Your work crews? Wait a minute. Are you doing this work on the house for yourself or for someone else?"

"I bought the house about six months ago," he said, swinging open the door and letting her precede him inside. "I sold my very nice, very modern, very clean—let me repeat, *clean*—penthouse apartment downtown in order to move in here."

She stopped in her tracks. "Wait a minute. So that satanic water stain in your bedroom ceiling is *here*? You're living *here*?"

"Bright move on my part, don't you think?"

"Oh, dear."

The hall they'd stepped into smelled of dust, mice, mildew, and a faint, welcome whiff of freshly cut wood. The lath and plaster had been pulled off the walls on one side, revealing the wood studs beneath. Caged construction lights hung on a thick orange cord.

Ahead of them, light spilled across the floor from wide openings to both the left, where Megan assumed the main entrance hall was, and the right.

Doorways dotted the walls. The floor beneath her feet was made of wide wood planks, painted and worn.

"Why did you buy it?" Megan asked. "It looks like the type of place that could bankrupt anyone trying to renovate it."

"It certainly looks that way, doesn't it? But it's not *quite* that bad. The bones are good: it was built entirely of cedar, and the foundation is solid. The worst of the damage was done by water coming through the roof, but even that didn't touch all the rooms."

"But still, the cost of new wiring, plumbing, redoing all the walls and floors; it must be considerable. I get tired just thinking about all the work!"

His hands on his hips, he stared down the hall. "What can I say? I saw the place and fell in love." He met her eyes. "Can you understand that?"

She nodded. "I fall in love with furniture and antique jewelry. Light fixtures. Paintings. Textiles. Oh, yes, I know all about falling in love with inanimate objects." Only, to her, they were not without a life history of their own that she could share by running her fingertips across a surface or fastening a gold chain about her neck. But how could anyone feel a tie to a place that gave off as many bad vibes as this hulking wreck of a house?

Case led the way through the house and brought her to the entrance hall.

Megan gasped, suddenly understanding why the house had seduced Case.

Two stories of intricately leaded glass lit the main entry hall and the wood staircase that climbed up one wall. An enormous bronze chandelier hung from the box-beam ceiling above. Oak wainscoting with the dark patina of a century gave way at chest height to deeply embossed copper panels.

"It's like a museum!" Megan whispered in awe. "You *never* see places like this anymore, not unless they're historic houses with an entry fee."

"So you can understand how excited I was when I found it."

"Is the rest of it like this?"

"Nothing as impressive as this—it *is* the front entry, after all—but the original finish work is still in place. Even most of the furniture is still here. There were some unfortunate updates made to the house in later years, but much of it is still as I imagine it was when it was built."

"So, what's the story? It's obviously been empty for years. How did you get it?"

"Are you sure you want to know that right now?"

The question reminded Megan that she was there for a purpose, not just to sightsee. "I guess I should wait."

He laughed. "You sound so disappointed."

She thought he sounded delighted at her enthusiastic response to the hall, almost as if a compliment to the house was a compliment to him. Maybe it was. She looked at him now and saw not just a man but a man with a stunning Victorian mansion that he would rebuild to its former glory with his own two hands. Her inner damsel had palpitations at the thought. "Give me the grand tour."

"Any special instructions I should follow as we go through the house? Should I think positive, ghost-accepting thoughts? Burn incense? Spit over my shoulder?"

She wrinkled her nose, reconsidering. "Actually, maybe you should stay here while I walk around on my own."

His cheerful expression faded. "I don't think that's a good idea."

"You're going to be a distraction."

"The house isn't safe: it's a construction zone. You got badly frightened driving in the front gate. You were in a blind panic. I don't like to think of the harm you could do yourself if that happened again, in here."

"I know how not to fall through holes in the floor. And hey, if I break a leg, that's what your liability insurance is for."

"Megan—"

"Case, I know what I'm doing, so let me do it the way I see fit. I have more experience with this type of thing than you do, after all."

He threw up his hands. "Fine! Do it your way. But

I'm going to stay right here, and I want you to yell if anything happens. Yell, and stay right where you are. No running down the halls."

"But if I get really scared, can I throw myself out a window?"

"Sarcasm doesn't become you."

She felt a flush of embarrassment and pressed her lips together. Sarcasm was the defense of the weak, and weak was exactly what she was feeling. "See you in fifteen minutes," she said, and turned to go up the stairs.

"I'll be right here."

Megan looked up the stairs. The upper floor looked dark. Abandoned. Stuffed with evil spirits, no doubt.

You're a real idiot, you know that, Megan? she berated herself as she put her hand to the rail and began to climb. *A moment's injured pride because a man wanted to protect you, and now you're going upstairs alone. Dumb, dumb, du—*

She stopped, standing still. She clenched the rail more tightly and closed her eyes, an instant from another time filling her senses.

Joy. Such joy! Excitement. The sense of a thousand possibilities for the future.

Megan opened her eyes and looked over the rail, down into the entry. It wasn't Case she saw; it was the hall in another era. The doors were open, sunlight seeming to carry in on its rays a stream of finely dressed visitors. The men wore dark three-piece suits and sported mustaches. The women were corseted to pouter-pigeon chests, their skirts trailing behind them. Hats the size of turkey platters slanted across their heads, feathers and plumes set at graceful angles.

The image faded, the dusty, battered floor of the hall reappearing, Case standing and looking up at her with concern.

She gave him a quick smile of reassurance and continued up the stairs.

Case listened as Megan moved around on the floor above. Her footsteps went methodically down the hall and into one room after the other, pausing briefly in each and then moving on. With the floors bare of any carpet, her footsteps were as loud as if she wore taps on her shoes.

The deathly still quiet of the house helped carry the sound. It almost seemed as if the house itself were listening to her movements, holding its breath to hear her better.

A shiver flushed over Case's skin. It felt as if the house were waiting to see what she did, waiting to see if she was going to put a foot wrong and pry too deeply into its secrets.

The house, or whatever was in it, wouldn't like that.

Her footsteps continued on, easy and unhurried,

and then suddenly they stopped; then came a quick one-two dance of steps as if she were startled.

Silence again.

His heart pounded, and sweat broke out over his body. His muscles tensed, ready for him to fly up the stairs and drag her away from whatever was waiting for her.

He clenched his fists against the urge, forcing himself to stay where he was. It had never hurt him, whatever *it* was, so there was no rational reason to think Megan was in any danger. She was in her element. She knew how to deal with this type of thing far better than he did.

Didn't she?

There were no such things as ghosts. There was nothing here to hurt her but her own imagination.

He listened hard, waiting for her footsteps to resume.

A faint buzz started in his ears. He shook his head, trying to clear it, then felt a shiver go over his skin. He looked down at his arm and saw that it was rising in gooseflesh.

The buzzing sound grew louder, and through it he thought he heard the sound of running footsteps overhead.

He felt a cold touch on his cheek, as of a hand laid against his face. His eyes widened, his senses picking out the pressure of palm and fingertips, cold as frost. He froze in shock, then yelped and jerked back.

The cold touch came with him, and then it moved. The palm lifted, and icy fingertips trailed down over his jaw to his neck, dripping snow into the artery just beneath the skin.

He could hear his blood pounding, sending chilled fluid up into his brain. Terror seeped up out of his gut, flooding him with the urge to flee.

No! Not with Megan still upstairs.

He gritted his teeth and forced himself to stand still. There was no use trying to fight it off, no use in flailing or crying out. Such actions, he'd learned these past weeks, were like a starting pistol to the racehorse of panic. If he let himself move so much as an inch more, instinct would take over, and he'd run from the house screaming.

He wasn't a proud man, but for God's sake, he wanted to preserve some dignity.

And he didn't want *it* to win so easily.

God *damn* it, he wasn't some four-year-old scared of the bogeyman, crying for Mama. He was a grown man, and he didn't believe in ghosts!

"This is *my* house," he said in a low voice, barely audible over the buzzing in his head. "Whatever the hell you are, you're not welcome here!" he said more loudly, wanting to hear his own words. "If you're dead, then go toward the fucking light, will you? Leave me the hell alone!"

A shard of ice went through his chest.

His heart stopped, taking his breath with it.

A stunned surprise hit him first. *Crap, it's never done this* before!

His mouth gaped, seeking air that wouldn't come. All at once, his heart thudded to life, too fast. His breath came back in quick gasps. Sweat broke out all over his body. Numbness crept up his jaw and over his face.

Pain shot down his left arm.

A wild terror that he was having a heart attack swept through his mind. *Dad died of a heart attack . . .*

His vision swam, and he knew he wasn't getting enough oxygen. He felt himself beginning to separate from his body, and he grabbed for the newel post at the bottom of the staircase, clinging to it to stay upright and, if possible, to stay alive.

The goddamn thing is killing me!

And then, one brief, rational thought: *I've got to stop it from hurting Megan.*

He cast his gaze up the staircase, his mouth working as if to call out, the numbness preventing it. Stars danced before his eyes, the edges of his vision going black.

Crap.

Megan moved slowly down the hallway, her mind wandering to the moment in the car when she'd realized Case's hand was on her shoulder, her body touching his. A thrill shot through her, making her inner muscles clench.

Will he make a move on me after dinner? Maybe put his arm around me on the way to the car?

She imagined that, imagined being up close against his side. Another thrill coursed through her.

And if he puts his coat around my shoulders, because it's gotten chilly . . .

A faint gasp of sound reached her ears.

A thump of fear beat at her heart, chasing out her erotic thoughts. She stopped, turning her head, trying to pick up the sound again. Had that been a real-world gasp or an otherworld gasp?

Or had it been her own movements?

"Case?" she said aloud, wondering if he'd come silently up the stairs and snuck into a room, trying to keep an eye on her.

No answer.

A prickle of unease crawled up the back of her neck. The hallway, with its many doors and half-deconstructed walls, felt less empty than it had a moment ago.

There was a movement at the corner of her eye and a scratch of sound.

She jumped, drawing in a quick breath and turning.

A window was visible through the open doorway of a room, the cane of a climbing rose waving in the breeze, its thorns brushing against the glass.

Megan released a breath and shook her head. She was letting her imagination go to work on her. Never a good thing.

She waved back at the rose, then continued down the hall, glancing into rooms, finding the same thing in each: bare floors, faded and peeling wallpaper, a marble fireplace lost under layers of dirt, dusty dark-wood furniture stacked in a pile in the center of the room. She didn't spend more than a moment or two in each room, as there were no strong, obvious impressions they were giving off. She'd continue searching for something obvious, then come back to these rooms if she came up blank elsewhere.

She wouldn't mind coming back to take a closer look at the furniture, either. The place was a treasure trove of Victorian furnishings, and she itched to pull apart a few of those intriguing piles and see what goodies lay hidden. She'd love to claim first dibs for her shop.

The wide hallway came to a T at the end. To the left, the corridor ended a few feet later at a massive wooden door. To the right, the hall continued a dozen more feet, with a couple of doors to either side and one at the end.

She went left, to the massive door. The light was poor in the hall, and the patina of the wood was dark, so it wasn't until she was up close to the door that she saw there was a stylized border of flowers painted along the edges of the door, with a central decoration in the center of each of the door's panels. The flowers had been worn away around the knob, where hands must have repeatedly brushed against them. She laid her own fingertips against the painted flowers and closed her eyes.

For a moment, she was transported. Her hand now held a paintbrush, and the smells of linseed oil and turpentine were strong in the air. She painted the petal on a flower and then felt the touch of a loving hand on her hair.

Megan lifted her hand from the door and opened her eyes. It was the original mistress of the house who had painted that door.

She smiled. That Victorian woman had been a gentle spirit, a young bride much loved by her older husband. Megan turned the knob and pushed it open.

It was obviously the master suite. The large room with its tall windows was filled with natural light, and in the center of the room stood a massive tester bed, devoid of mattress or bedding but still with its original faded dusty fabric pleated in intricate folds and drapes on the underside of the tester.

Megan approached it in wonder: the thing was a Gothic monstrosity, a behemoth, a tumorous heap of grotesquely carved wood.

She loved it.

She loved it the way a wine critic might love white zinfandel: with full knowledge that her choice was awful. But she loved it. It proclaimed itself the king of beds. A place in which grand lovemaking could be done. It was a bed meant to see conception, birth, and death.

Drawn to it, she laid her hand against one massively thick, bulbous post.

The emotions rolled over her. *Loneliness. Loss. Never-ending waves of grief.*

Megan jerked her hand away, a sob in her throat, tears starting in her eyes. Sadness flowed through her, borrowed from the bed but finding its own channels in her grief over her mother.

It was a bed of mourning.

She stepped away from it and looked around at the rest of the room, but she had lost the heart to explore it. It seemed a place that had been built with hope and heart but had found only loss and pain.

She moved out of the room and on to the other end of the hall. One door led to an old-fashioned bath with a copper boiler mounted to the wall above the tub. It looked like it hadn't been used in a century.

Behind the second door she discovered an old woman's bedroom. Case hadn't cleared it out like the others, and it still held a faint powdery scent. The wallpaper was pink cabbage roses, the furniture a mishmash of Victorian, Art Deco, and bits of Danish Modern. The floor was covered in mustard-yellow wall-to-wall carpeting. A black rotary phone sat on the bedside table, and an enormous cabinet stereo in blond wood, with gold-flecked cloth over the speakers, squatted under a too-vivid painting of crashing waves.

Megan grimaced. *Yeesh.* What a charmless, tasteless room. Why on earth hadn't Case stripped it?

She took a couple of steps inside, but the room was so ugly she didn't want to open herself to it. The master bedroom was as much misery as she wanted to face for the day.

She stepped back into the hallway and moved toward the third door.

Something moved in her peripheral vision.

She shied, turning her head toward the movement. All was still.

She squinted at the shadows at the end of the hall, in the corner near the servants' stairs. Was that a shape? A shadow in shadows but the figure of a person?

The shadow moved, coming forward. Dark holes formed where the eyes and mouth would be.

Megan's arms tingled, and her belly tightened. Her eyes widened, and she held motionless, staring, too scared to do anything else.

It wasn't a thing any medium would want to admit, but she was afraid of ghosts.

And of the dark.

And of basements. And spiders. And all things that go bump in the night.

She'd only seen a true ghost, an active haunting, a handful of times, and most of those had been the recently deceased, lingering harmlessly before moving on.

This *thing* moving toward her was not dear old Grandmama saying good-bye.

Its mouth began to open.

She didn't know who or what it was, and with sudden, cowardly certainty, she knew she didn't want to know. She spun on her heel and took off running.

Her footsteps echoed in the long hallway, sounding as if there were someone following immediately behind her, breathing ghostly breaths down the back of her neck. The imagining was as bad as the real thing, and with a whining shriek in her throat, she upped her speed, sprinting to the head of the stairs.

She flew down them, her toes barely touching the treads. It wasn't until she was almost at the bottom that she saw Case, collapsed at the newel post, eyes closed.

"Case!" she cried. "Case!" A new fear tore at her heart, and she leaped down the last few steps, crouching down beside him and putting her hand to his shoulder. "Case!" She shook him.

He moaned softly.

Relief washed through her. Thank God! He wasn't dead.

"Wake up! Wake up!" She shook him again.

His eyes blinked open, confused at first and then with returning focus. As reality came back to him, he flinched and then quickly sat up, wincing as he did so.

"What happened?" Megan asked.

"I imagined that something attacked me," he said in a tight, gasping whisper. He lifted his left hand and winced again. "Oh, God, I think it did something to my heart."

A fresh sense of danger all around flushed over her. "What? How?" She cast a look over her shoulder, up the stairs. There was no sign of her dark ghost.

"I don't know." He described what had happened.

As he talked, some of Megan's alarm drained away. "You were pretty worried about me up there on my own, weren't you?"

"Hell yes!" he said, and got to his feet with her help. She could feel the clamminess of his skin and felt the shakiness of his muscles.

"You feel exhausted right now? Sore?"

He slanted a glance at her. "Yeah."

She dug into her purse until she found the small bottle. She tapped a couple of white pills into her palm and held them out to him. "Here. Take these."

"Aspirin?" he asked, taking them and tossing them back without water.

"Benadryl."

He frowned. "An allergy medication? Why? I thought aspirin was the thing to take for heart attacks."

"I'm not a doctor, obviously, but I think what you had was a panic attack. The Benadryl will take the edge off, help you get back on an even keel."

"It wasn't a damned panic attack," he said, and motioned for her to follow him as he stomped weakly back toward the hall. "I'm not a pansy."

Megan snorted.

He turned and glared.

She held up her hands. "Hey, it's not your manhood I'm questioning. You sounded extremely male right then."

He resumed walking. "It wasn't a panic attack," he grumbled.

"You'd rather it was a heart attack?" she asked, hurrying to keep up.

"No, I'm just saying. There's a history of heart problems in my family."

"Have you ever had any?"

"It *wasn't* a panic attack."

"So, you haven't had any heart trouble. If you've been living in this house for months on your own, you've been under a huge amount of stress."

"I can handle stress."

"Maybe you can, but your body has its limits. Look, I know something about this. When my mom was dying . . ." Her voice broke, and she took a moment to get her throat back under control. "When my mom was dying and I was taking care of her, I started having panic attacks. I don't have them anymore. It's just a stress reaction when you're overprimed for a fight-or-flight situation, that's all."

He was silent. They reached the door and stepped out into the daylight. Megan felt as if a cloud were lifted from her soul, the moment she was out of the house.

"But maybe you're right," she said as they moved to the car. "It could have been a heart attack. Do you want me to drive? Maybe we should get you checked out at an emergency room."

He looked at her, then went around to the passenger side and opened the door.

She raised her brows, surprised he'd taken her up on the offer.

He stared at her, then gestured toward the door. "My lady?"

She tried to keep the satisfaction from showing on her face. No emergency room. "Thank you," she said, and got into the passenger seat.

As they headed down the drive, her sense of satisfaction was drained away by the sight of a shadowy figure caught in the corner of her eye.

A shiver ran over her.

She hoped this was the last she would see of Case Lambert's house. She couldn't imagine him finding any way to persuade her to come back.

She glanced at him. His gaze was turned inward, his jaw set against the unmanly accusation of a panic attack. It was strangely appealing. A chink in the armor.

He needed help.

She clenched her jaw against the thought. *No, I can't give in! I've got to think of my own safety first.*

She wasn't going to go back to that house, no matter how badly Case needed her.

FOUR

Case drove and tried to digest the humiliating fact that he might have had a panic attack.

It was not the type of failing he wanted to admit to. He didn't care what the rational, underlying cause of it was; it still made a man seem like an overreacting sissy.

His frowned deepened. There he'd been, passed out on his own foyer floor, while Megan had been on her own upstairs. And then to have her find him like that. How embarrassing!

He could feel the trail of testosterone he was leaving behind him, like oil dripping from a car.

Dinner didn't seem like such a good idea now. He didn't want to see Megan's lovely face across the candlelight, gazing at him with concern, worried that he might start hyperventilating at any moment.

Crap.

But he'd said he'd buy her dinner, so he'd buy her dinner. Besides, he wanted to hear what she'd discovered, if anything, during her walk-through.

Five minutes later, he parked the car near a nice little restaurant he knew a dozen blocks from Antique Fancies. As they undid their seat belts, he turned to Megan.

"Not another word about panic attacks, okay?"

She gave him a look that said he was being a male of fragile ego.

"Just . . . don't," he said. "Please."

She gave a little shrug and nodded.

"Have you been to Eva?" he asked as they crossed the street to the small restaurant.

"I've always meant to, but it seemed an extravagance."

Her answer told him a lot about her financial status. Eva was not an expensive restaurant by his standards; it was a good restaurant, with a chef who experimented with seasonal local ingredients, but it wasn't a "Put on the fur and diamonds, honey, we're going to town," type of place. It had more of a "Wear your cashmere sweater" ambience.

They were seated at a candlelit, linen-covered table by the window. It was six-thirty, and the long days of a northern May meant that the sky was showing only the first signs of fading light.

"Would you like something to drink before the

wine?" he asked. "That lavender cosmopolitan you were talking about? Although I'm not sure they make one."

"How about you order for me? Something that doesn't taste too much of alcohol."

Another clue to Megan. She'd never been a party girl. It didn't surprise him, but he was beginning to wonder just how insular her life had been.

When the waitress returned, he ordered a Scotch for himself and a lemon drop for Megan.

He watched her as she perused the dinner menu, her face showing faint alarm, although whether that was for the prices, the esoteric choices, or the date-like atmosphere of the restaurant, he didn't know.

"They usually have a prix-fixe special, if you don't want to choose your courses," he offered.

She glanced up in surprise. "What, and take the fun out of it? I'm just trying to figure out how much I can eat, and whether it would be a mistake to order all the appetizers and call it dinner."

He laughed. "Be my guest, as long as you don't mind sharing."

When the waitress returned with their drinks, Megan surprised him again by asking a few knowledgeable questions about the dishes and pronouncing the occasional French word with a far better accent than he himself could manage. And she didn't order all appetizers.

"Cheers," he said, raising his Scotch glass.

She lifted her lemon drop, winked, and said, "Skoal!"

He shook his head, laughing silently, and took a much-welcome sip of his Scotch.

"For someone who doesn't go to expensive restaurants, you seem to know food," he said.

Megan tasted her lemon drop and licked a grain of sugar off her lip with a small dart of her tongue. "This is good. And not eating out a lot doesn't mean you can't cook well. My mom was a foodie, and she instilled the love in me. You should see the cookbook collection at the house. There's even a framed, autographed photo of Julia Child."

"You live in the house where you grew up?"

She nodded, taking another sip of her drink. "I really like this."

Maybe a little too much. The martini glass was already half empty. "Just because you can't taste the alcohol doesn't mean it's not there," he warned.

"Oh." She set her glass down. "I suppose we should talk about the house."

"Business before pleasure."

"Or at least before I drink myself under the table." She giggled.

He looked at her in concern.

She straightened up in her seat. "Sorry. I've found silliness to be an aftereffect of being scared out of my panties." She paused. "Not literally, of course."

He suddenly pictured her panties coming off and

cleared his throat. "So you did experience something upstairs?"

"Oh, yeah. Something I'd rather not experience again." She took another sip of her lemon drop.

"Tell me what happened."

Her description of the dark figure in the corner of the hall sent a chill down the back of his neck.

"I've never actually seen anything in the house—I mean, not an actual figure or ghost or whatever you want to call it. But I've seen things move. And heard them."

"Things like what?"

He barked a laugh. "Unfortunately, it's usually been the type of thing you talk yourself out of. Doors opening and closing when no one is there. Could just be drafts, right? A badly balanced door. A faulty latch. Some of my tools have disappeared, only to appear again somewhere I could not reasonably have left them. But still, maybe I did it. Or maybe a neighborhood prankster comes in and moves things. Periodically, the lights flicker and then go out, although the power usually stays on. Bad wiring? No electrician can find the problem. But even so, put almost everything down to the natural creakings of an old wooden house or to mischief on the part of an intruder. Almost everything."

"Almost."

"Yeah. There was a final straw that made me search out someone like Ramsey."

She waited, not saying anything.

He sighed and ran his hand through his hair. He didn't want to talk about this any more than he'd wanted to talk about the supposed panic attack. "Something seemed to get into bed with me."

Megan's eyes widened.

"Something cold and . . . curious."

"Wh-what did it do?"

"It didn't have a chance to do much. I felt hands on me, cold as stone. I shot out of bed faster than I knew I could move. I tried to light a candle but couldn't find the matches in the dark. When I finally found them and lit one, I saw nothing but my own rumpled sheets. Then, in the silence, I heard someone slide across the bed and a pair of bare feet softly hit the floor. I couldn't see anything: no movement to the sheets, no indentation on the mattress. But I was sure there was someone in the room with me.

"Then the bare footsteps started coming toward me where I stood by the door. And I'm afraid that my courage failed me. And the match, too—it singed my fingers and went out."

He smiled sheepishly and took another sip of Scotch. "I ran. Didn't even remember I was buck naked until I got outside. It was about the hardest thing I ever did, making myself go back in there to grab some clothes and my car keys. I spent the rest of the night in the backseat of the car."

Megan shook her head. "And yet you're still living

in that place. Why? I don't get it. I mean, sure, it's a great location, and the house has the potential to be beautiful, but at this point, I'd think you'd raze it and start fresh or sell it. Why put yourself through this? There are other houses."

He shook his head. "I've asked myself the same question more than once. I suppose the primary reason is that I'm a stubborn son of a bitch."

"So I've noticed. So, what is it? You don't want the ghosts to win?"

"Or whatever it is that's going on. I'm not going to let it beat me."

She tilted her head. "You're putting yourself through a lot of misery for the sake of pride. I'd think a businessman would cut his losses."

"This isn't about business for me." He didn't want to say exactly how personal an issue the house had become.

When he'd first laid eyes on it, it wasn't just a shattered beauty that he saw; it was his future. He had known in that instant, without understanding why, that if he was going to settle down and start a family, this was where it had to be. This was where he wanted to bring his bride; it was where he wanted to raise his children; it was where he wanted his grandchildren to come visit and be excited that they got to come to Grandpa and Grandma's crazy, enormous house on the hill.

He wanted summers with kids playing badminton

on a crooked net in the yard; Easter egg hunts enjoyed by all the neighbor kids; Christmas lights hanging from each and every angle of the roofline.

He'd seen the house on its private block and known it was the type of place a man could stay forever. Giving up on the house would mean giving up on his dream.

"Tell me what else you picked up about the house," he said.

She explained the rest of her experiences as they made their way through appetizers and soup. Scotch and lemon drop gave way to a Spanish rioja. Their entrées had appeared by the time she finished.

He shook his head. "I don't know what to make of it all."

"If you're willing to believe in ghosts for a moment, the simplest story would be that the thing that got into bed with you and that I saw in the hall—and that touched your face downstairs—was a widow who spent most of her life sleeping alone in that big bed. It would explain the loneliness I felt and why she seems interested in you."

"What about the feeling you had at the gate, of being trapped?"

"Maybe she was an invalid. Maybe that's why she couldn't leave and couldn't find someone else to marry. Her moving your tools around and opening and closing doors could be seen as a simple plea for attention," Megan said. "If you believed in ghosts."

"I might almost be tempted to. I'd rather have a lonely old lady ghost than think I've gone nuts."

Megan speared a sweet potato gnocchi with her fork and chased it through its sauce, grumbling beneath her breath.

"What?"

"Maybe your being nuts would make more sense." She set down her fork. "I'm not sure, but I got a vague sense that the shadowy figure I saw might be male."

"Oh."

"Which still might fit my story. I mean, if he was a gay Victorian, it's easy to imagine that he spent a lot of lonely time. And it would explain him climbing into your bed."

"Don't tell me I have a gay ghost coming on to me."

"Why are men always so upset by the thought of a gay guy finding them attractive? I never get that. You'd think it would be a compliment."

"First your talk of panic attacks, now this. I'm going to have to go beat someone up to feel better."

She laughed, then suddenly stopped. "You are kidding, right?"

"Of course. And I don't mind if someone's gay, by the way. Just so you know."

"Just as long as I don't mistake you for being gay, huh?"

"What heterosexual man wants a beautiful woman to think he swings the other way?"

She returned her attention to her gnocchi, her cheeks pinkening in the candlelight. The daylight had finally turned to dusk, and now a gentle darkness was falling, making it seem that they existed only in the small world of light thrown off by the candle.

"We've gotten off topic," Megan said. "There's another explanation besides that you're nuts or have a gay ghost haunting your house."

"Yeah?"

"You may have two ghosts."

"Your ideas keep getting better and better, don't they?"

"You haven't told me the story behind the house. What do you know about it and the people who built it and lived in it? Why has it been sitting empty for so long?"

"It was empty because the trust it belonged to required it to remain empty."

"Why on earth?"

"I don't know. Neither did the law firm that sold the house. The house was owned by sisters: Isabella and Penelope Smithson. They lived there until 1970, and both died there at the ages of eighty-eight and ninety."

"Good Lord. Great genes must have run in their family. They died the same year?"

"According to the records the law firm had. No one at the firm had been there when the Smithsons were alive and drew up the trust documents. I asked around the neighborhood, though, and found one old lady who remembered the sisters. Said they were the oddest pair of old birds, never out of each other's company. Bickering constantly but apparently devoted to each other. You never saw one without the other.

"This neighbor, Mrs. Gainsborough, said that it was a true tragedy when they died. The younger one, Penelope, had apparently fallen seriously ill, and instead of calling for an ambulance, Isabella—suffering from dementia, no doubt—tried to carry her sister out to the street for help. Put her on a blanket and pulled her halfway down the drive.

"Of course, a ninety-year-old woman doesn't have that kind of strength, and the effort killed her. They were found by each other's side, lying in the driveway."

"And the reason the house was to remain empty?"

"Like I said, no one knows. The Smithsons were well-off, never had to work. The trust declared that their investments were to be used solely for lawyer fees and to pay the taxes on the property and for a caretaker to make yearly checks that the house was sound. No provision was made for selling it or donating to charity. Conceivably, the house could have stood empty until it crumbled to the ground. If their investments had been better, it might have.

"As it was, though, bad investments coupled with rising property taxes and lawyer fees finally drained the trust. The law firm put the house up for sale, recouped probably more than its fair share of past fees, and the rest of the money went to the state."

"No heirs?"

"Neither sister was known to have married. Although who knows; if they *had* married, it could have been at the turn of the last century. There's a lot of time for love and loss between then and 1970, and lots of time for anyone else to forget it ever happened."

"Probably never long enough for the woman to forget."

He grimaced. "You think it's one of the sisters crawling into my bed?"

"Could be. Why not? But what about their parents? Were they the ones who built the house?"

"Their father, Jacob R. Smithson, had his fingers in both the lumber and coal industries and made a mint off them. That house must have been his statement to Seattle that he was now a member of the elite. It was built in 1880, when the Queen Anne style was cutting-edge. Isabella must have just been born, and Penelope was no more than a twinkle in her parents' eyes. I know nothing about their mother. The sisters obviously lived down the hall."

"I meant to ask you about that. Why didn't you clear out that room with the awful gold carpeting?"

He smiled crookedly. "Same reason you ran downstairs. That hallway gave me the creeps. I kept telling myself it didn't matter if I got to those rooms just yet."

"But you cleared out the master bedroom?"

"No, that had been stripped long ago. The other rooms, yes, I got rid of the rotted curtains and Oriental carpets. Sent a few carpets out to be cleaned, the ones that looked salvageable. I'd like to keep as much of the original character of the place as I can."

"Just not the otherworldly character."

He raised his wine glass in salute. "So, Madame Medium, what is your diagnosis of my house?"

She sighed and sat back. "I've never—ever—been anywhere that felt as if it had such a . . . *miasma* of activity. The place is seething with it, and that's not normal." She shook her head, a crease between her brows. "Not normal at all. It's as if something is seriously wrong there. I mean, neither battlefields nor hospitals have that degree of paranormal gunk floating around, and look at how many people died difficult, emotional deaths in those places."

"I thought you said that the manner of death didn't matter."

"It doesn't. I'm making a point. Places like your house just don't exist. We experienced as much in an hour as some famously haunted places have had happen in a decade. It's not natural, not even for the supernatural."

"Lucky me. You know, I've wondered if Isabella and Penelope knew that something was wrong with their house," Case said.

"You mean, that's why they set up the trust that way?"

"Yes. You didn't get a chance to go through the books in the house's library."

"No. Why?" she replied.

"The library's filled with books on the occult. I'm not talking dozens of books. I'm talking hundreds."

"Oh. Oh, dear."

"You know I don't believe in that crap, but I admit the damn things make me uneasy. They're just superstitious nonsense, of course, but I can't quite bring myself to touch them." He laughed at himself.

"I wonder what trouble those two women created for themselves, what sort of experiments they may have tried." Megan took a sip of her wine. "What sort of portal they may have opened and what may have come through it."

A shiver crawled up Case's spine. "Whatever they did, how are you going to fix it?"

FIVE

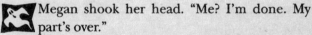Megan shook her head. "Me? I'm done. My part's over."

"What, you're passing up exploring the most unusual house you've ever seen?"

"Yup. Besides, why would you want me involved?"

"You're easier on the eyes than Ramsey."

She crossed her arms. "That's hardly a valid reason."

"Shows what you know about men."

She scowled.

"Ramsey seems to think you're useful," he added.

"But you don't."

"No, not with your 'powers.' But you've worked with Ramsey before and can help him with his equipment."

"And you'll pay me how much?" It had better be plenty, if she was going to get within ten feet of Eric Ramsey.

"I thought you didn't take money."

"I've had a change in policy."

"I won't pay you," he said.

"That's hardly fair!"

"Ramsey isn't getting paid. Why should you, as his assistant?"

"So, if we solved your little 'problem,' that would be worth nothing to you?"

"Ramsey thinks the investigation is its own reward. He would have paid *me* for this experience. If he fixes whatever is wrong with the house, though, I'll pay him."

"How much?"

"A few hundred."

"My time's worth more than that."

"It's your choice."

"No, I have a different proposal for you," she said.

He arched a brow. "Go on."

"If Eric and I 'fix' the house, and if it turns out that I was crucial to that success—if it wouldn't have happened without my abilities—then you will let me choose ten pieces of furniture from the house."

"That would be worth considerably more than a few hundred dollars."

"I know. I'll let you decide whether or not my actions are crucial, though. Consider this a bet: your skepticism against my 'woo-woo' talents."

Megan held her breath, waiting for his answer. Ten pieces of furniture could give her the financial breathing space she needed to make her dream a reality. That bed in the master suite could be worth $10,000 in the right circumstances. She could deal with Eric for the promise of a reward like that.

Case leaned back in his chair, eyeing her. "Cocky, aren't you? If you lose, what do *I* get?"

"What do you want?"

He thought a moment. "If I win, you have to clean and restore every piece of furniture in the house."

"That would be a year's work, at least!"

"Not so confident now?" he teased.

"Make it twenty pieces of furniture if I win."

He hesitated.

"Now who's not so confident?" she said triumphantly.

He held out his hand. "I'll take that bet."

"And I'll win it."

They shook, eyes meeting in mutual challenge.

Megan sat back, elated. Twenty pieces of antique furniture, hers for the taking! Of course, she'd win the bet. Eric's computers and sensors were nothing but toys against supernatural entities. Their best use was in finding natural causes for supposedly paranormal events, *not* in doing anything about a real ghost.

Case Lambert's house had a real ghost. Maybe two.

Her elation faded. She'd bet a year's worth of work that she could evict those spirits, but she had no idea how she was going to do it. She'd never done it before. In fact, the one time she'd gone head-to-head with something supernatural, she'd lost.

Case topped up her glass of wine. "Having second thoughts?"

"Why do I feel like I've just made a deal with the devil?"

"Because you let greed get the better of you."

She pressed her lips together, unable to deny it. Unable to deny, too, the small ball of panic growing inside her. That thing she'd seen in the hallway . . .

"When are you moving in?"

"What? I'm not moving in! No way I'm sleeping in that place."

"Afraid?"

"Yes!"

The waitress came with a dessert menu, and in her pique, Megan ordered the chef's dessert platter, which promised to be obscenely large and expensive.

"And tea," Megan added. "Earl Grey."

Case ordered coffee and smothered a yawn. "I don't know what's wrong with me. I feel ready to drop." He blinked at her.

She tucked in her chin, observing him with a frown. "You okay?"

"Exhausting day, I guess."

"Panic attacks can drain you."

He scowled.

"Oh, excuse me! *Heart attacks* can drain you."

"You should move in this weekend. I'll clean out the room next to mine and set up a bed for you."

"You're unbelievable. Didn't you hear me? I don't want to sleep in that place."

"Neither do I. But more happens at night than during the day. Isn't night the prime time for ghost hunting?"

"I don't think I could handle more."

"Twenty pieces of furniture . . ." He trailed it like bait. "The quickest way you're going to get there is to concentrate your time at my house. Eric's going to stay there. You wouldn't want him to beat you to a solution, would you? Close the shop and move in for a while."

"Closing the shop was never part of the deal!"

"Consider it a vacation. When was the last time you took one?" he asked, turning her earlier question back on her.

"Staying at your house will *not* be a vacation."

"Think of it as a rustic B and B, with a congenial host who'll tuck you in every night." Beneath the table, his leg touched hers, sending little shivers up her thigh.

She swallowed hard. "I don't need tucking in."

A slow, seductive smile spread across his face. "Sure you do."

"Ha!" she protested, but it sounded weak even to her ears.

The waitress set down the dessert platter and two

spoons. Megan dug into a wedge of torte and tried to marshal her defenses while Case smothered another yawn.

"Why do you care if I'm there?" she asked.

"Frankly, because you'll be better company than Ramsey."

"I thought you liked him."

"I do. That doesn't mean I wouldn't rather look at you across the dinner table."

"Even if you think that everything I say is gibberish?"

"What's that got to do with it?" he asked, grinning.

Megan growled and scooped up the last of the mango sherbet. She sucked her spoon clean and pointed it at him. "I'm going to make you eat your words, you know."

His eyelids drooped, his gaze on her lips. "Please do."

The bill came and was paid, and they both stood to go.

Case swayed and sat back down. "Whoa."

Concern swept through her. "What is it?"

"Almost blacked out." He shook his head as if trying to shake it off. "Wine doesn't usually affect me like this." He smothered another yawn.

Megan bit her lip. "Er . . . but wine and Scotch plus a couple of Benadryl might."

He stared up at her, eyes barely focused. "Oh, that's right." With visible effort, he rose to his feet. He swayed a bit, and Megan grabbed his arm.

"Um, I don't think you should drive home," she murmured.

He yawned again, and his eyelids began to lower. "Would you feel comfortable driving my car?"

She shook her head. "I've probably had too much myself. You could take a taxi home."

They moved together to the front door and out into the fresh air.

"I'll call a taxi for *you*. Me, I don't really want to spend the night alone in the house in this condition," he replied.

"I can walk home; it's less than five minutes on foot. Why don't you stay in a hotel tonight?"

"Pay money for a bed when I have my car right here?"

"But the backseat of your car isn't big enough for you."

"I don't think I'm in any condition to care."

"But . . ." She hesitated. She felt bad about the Benadryl, since she was the one who'd given it to him. "You could sleep on my couch, then walk back and get your car in the morning."

"You sure? I'm quite fond of my car."

"It's no place to sleep. Take the couch. Just knock before you go into any bathrooms. I've got a few housemates, and they're going to be pretty surprised to find a strange man in the house."

"Is there a familiar man who appears in the house?"

"Are you asking if I have a boyfriend?"

"Maybe."

"Not that it's any of your business, but no. Not at the moment. Not for any of us, actually. It makes for dispirited talk around the dinner table. Come on, this way," she said, leading him down the sidewalk.

"I go to slumber amongst virgins."

She laughed. "I never said *that*. And you'll be slumbering with Kelly's cat, most likely."

"I'm allergic."

"Then thank goodness you took the Benadryl."

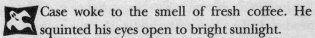Case woke to the smell of fresh coffee. He squinted his eyes open to bright sunlight.

Something warm and furry was wedged between his neck and shoulder. A black tail flicked across his face, and purring started, loud as a lawn mower in his ear.

Cat.

He shuddered and sat up, the feline falling away from him and mewing once in displeasure. Case spit cat hair from his lips and shuddered, tossing aside the quilt that had covered him.

What was it with women and cats?

He had slept in his underclothes and saw his other clothes neatly laid out over the chair where he'd left them. He dressed quickly and popped his head into the kitchen.

Megan was already up and dressed, looking depressingly like sunshine and springtime all wrapped up in one tall blonde. She must be a morning person.

"Hi," he croaked.

She turned from the counter, where she was fixing breakfast. "You're alive! I was beginning to wonder, but I thought the cat would have left you if you'd grown cold."

"Thanks for your concern."

"You might have had a heart attack in your sleep."

He grumbled a response. "Which way is the bathroom?"

"Upstairs, first door on the right."

"Thanks."

The trip up the stairs gave him a chance to clear his head and take a look at the house. He took in the trim work, the leaded glass windows, the built-in cabinets and drawers. The floors were old-growth Douglas fir, not the inferior new stuff they sold. The light fixtures overhead had to have dated to the time the house was built, but he doubted they were original. They were too ornate for what appeared to be a two-story farmhouse.

Case remembered Megan's warning about roommates in the bathroom and knocked on the door. No one answered, and he pushed the door open.

An older woman stood in front of the sink, staring at him.

He jumped.

"Oh, jeez, sorry! I didn't hear you!" He backed out of the room, closing the door behind him, and stood to the side, waiting.

A young woman in a pink bathrobe came out of her room and smiled tentatively at him. She scooted past and went down the stairs.

Case waited. And waited. He didn't hear any movements or water running. Was there another exit from the bathroom?

The girl in pink came back up the stairs, a mug of coffee in her hand. She sidled by, then stopped. "Are you waiting for the bathroom?"

He nodded.

"I don't think there's anyone in there."

"No, I think—"

She went past him and knocked on the door, then pushed it open. "See? No one."

Case peered in. No one.

A chill went down his back.

"Thanks," he said to the girl, and she nodded and disappeared.

Case closed the door after her and warily looked around the room. It was tiled in black and white hexagons and had a pedestal sink and clawfoot tub. He felt a superstitious unwillingness to look into the mirror. Who knew, the devil might appear.

Maybe it was the aftereffects of the Benadryl, he told himself, deeply unsettled.

He washed his hands and dared a look in the mirror. Nothing faced him but his own unshaven mug. He rubbed his hands over his hair, trying to tame a bad case of bed head.

He gave it up. There was no saving the face that looked back at him.

Megan had most of breakfast on the table by the time he returned. Coffee, toast, eggs, orange juice, and a few choices of yogurt and cereal.

"I didn't know what you'd like, so I'm going for the hotel buffet effect," she said from the stove.

"More than I deserve," he said, sitting down where she directed. "Thanks. You eat like this every morning?"

"I'm not much of a breakfast person. Raisin bran and a cup of tea usually do it for me."

"Coffee and a danish are usually as far as I get."

"You've got to take better care of yourself."

"Interested in my welfare, are you?"

"I have to be. You're going to specify in your will that if you die, I get all your furniture, right?"

He gave her a dark look.

"In case you have a heart attack, you know." She grinned.

"If I have *another* one, I'll be sure to live through it again."

"Good." A kettle began to whistle, and she shut it off and poured steaming water into a waiting mug.

"Do you rent this place?"

"I own it free and clear. My mother left it to me."

"Ever think of selling it?"

"With all the work she and I put into it? No. Besides, I love the character of the place: the wide trim, the ceiling medallions, the built-in storage and odd nooks."

"If you own it, why do you have housemates?"

"I don't much like living alone. The extra income pays for taxes and insurance, upkeep, et cetera. An old house is never a cheap house to live in. As you know."

"Don't I," Case said. "I don't suppose *this* house is haunted?"

Megan shook her head and picked up a spatula. "Not to my knowledge."

"Huh. Really."

Megan arched a brow at him. "Did something disturb you? You were upstairs quite a while."

He laughed self-consciously. "I don't think I'm awake yet."

"What happened?"

"I thought I saw an older woman in the bathroom. Short, overweight, fluffy brown hair. Glasses."

Megan dropped her spatula with a clatter. *"What* did she look like?"

His stomach fluttered. "Round, short, brown hair. Why?" he asked with trepidation.

Megan shook her head, her lips tight, and turned back to the stove. She lifted the skillet and transferred eggs to a bowl.

"What?" he asked again.

Megan mumbled something.

"Megan, what?"

"My mother."

A quiver went through him. "Your deceased mother?"

She nodded and brought the bowl over to the table, plopping it down with a clatter.

"You look upset," he observed.

Megan slid into a chair and stared at the breakfast she'd prepared. "She's never appeared to me. Why would she appear to you?"

"I have no idea. I wish she hadn't. You know, before I bought that house, I never so much as heard a set of unexplained footsteps. What the hell is happening to me?"

Megan took the bag out of her teacup and set it in a small dish. "If I had to guess, I'd say that house is opening you up to the Other Side."

"I don't want to be opened up."

"Maybe you're a natural medium."

He shuddered and looked at her. "You're joking, right?"

Her lips quirked. "You don't like the idea?"

"No. Nor do I believe it. I've never had the least unusual thing happen to me. Am I going to start seeing things everywhere I go now?"

"Do you know what confirmation bias is?"

He shook his head.

"It's where you have an idea in mind, and everything you see you interpret in a way that confirms your idea. It's sort of the same with the paranormal: with some people, every noise becomes a ghost, even if it's just the wood in the house creaking because of a change in temperature."

"This wasn't wood creaking. I *saw* someone whom you recognized."

"A corollary of the confirmation bias is that the more you think about something—however outlandish—the more possible you think it is. By thinking about ghosts, you begin to believe they might exist."

"You're saying I imagined it!"

"I thought you'd rather hear that than the more likely explanation."

"Which is?"

"For some people, being exposed to the Other Side in one place opens up the pathways for them to see it elsewhere, at times they don't expect. It's like when you learn a word you've never heard before, and suddenly you notice it everywhere. Because it wasn't in your sphere of knowledge, you couldn't recognize it. But once you know it, it's easy to recognize."

"So I'm going to start seeing ghosts everywhere I go? That's not good for someone who works with a lot of old houses."

"Active hauntings are rare, like I said before. You probably won't come across any."

"Except in your bathroom."

"It could have been a passive haunting. A recording."

"She stared right at me."

She didn't answer.

"You sure it was your mom?" he asked after a minute.

"I don't know what other short, brown-haired woman would be lurking there."

"She didn't look like you."

"No."

"Do you look more like your father?"

"I don't look much like either," she said, and there was a secretive smile on her lips. "The eggs are getting cold."

He dug into breakfast.

"What exactly is it that you do, anyway?" Megan asked after a bit. "You never did say, although I've guessed that it's something to do with construction."

"I have a company that buys houses, renovates them inside a month, then sells them."

"You flip houses."

"Yes. Although it wasn't something I intended to get into to this degree. Through college, I worked as a carpenter, then got a real estate license and became a broker. I did renovations on the side on houses I found cheap, then discovered it was a hell of a lot more satisfying to rebuild a house than to run around showing homes to buyers who made choices based on paint color and insisted on spa tubs in the master bath."

"The type of people who say they want their bedroom to feel like a hotel room."

"Exactly! Why the hell would anyone want to live in a hotel room?"

She smiled over her tea. "I'm not sure our way is so much better. Just different."

He took another bite of toast, liking the sound of that "our." Megan's sensibilities were in sync with his, and it felt good to be with someone who spoke the same language of old buildings, someone who had the same appreciation for character and craftsmanship and thought the costs were worth it.

"You're lost in thought," she said.

He smiled. "Yes."

They talked about the house and the work that she and her mother had done on it. He noticed she'd avoided mentioning her father.

"And your father?" he asked at one point.

"Left when I was four. I barely remember him. He moved back east somewhere, and we lost contact. Mom thought it was for the best; they fought all the time, and he drank too much."

"I must have made you feel just great last night with my bleariness."

She shook her head and put her hand on his forearm. The unexpected contact sent a shock of warmth through him.

"It was the Benadryl," she said. "And that was my fault. I counted, and over the course of a long meal, you only had your Scotch and one and a half glasses of wine."

"You counted?"

"I knew you intended to drive me home."

He laughed and shook his head. "You're a funny one, Megan."

"I don't think that's particularly funny," she said, sitting back and removing her hand.

"No, I just mean, you're surprisingly proper in some ways."

"And that's bad?"

"Not at all. Because you're also delightful company."

She blushed and turned her face away.

He settled back into his chair, feeling strangely at peace. The kitchen was light and bright, and there was a homey feel to it that he hoped he'd be able to capture in the kitchen he was planning for his house.

It was only while he was pouring his fourth cup of coffee that he thought to look at the time.

"Ah, *cr*—"

"What?"

"The time! I was supposed to meet my crew two hours ago." He dashed into the living room and dug his cell phone out of his jacket pocket. The ringer was off, and there were six messages. He made a couple of quick calls.

"I've got to go," he said, coming back into the

kitchen. Megan was still looking relaxed at the kitchen table, her mug of tea held in both hands.

He wanted to stay. God help him, he wanted to take her hand and lead her up to her bedroom and show her a different way to say good morning.

She said, "I've been thinking about your unreasonable insistence that I stay in that hell house while working with Ramsey on exorcising whatever wraiths are fouling the place."

"You make it sound so inviting."

"Believe me, I could make it sound worse. Anyway, I've been thinking about it, and I've decided I'll do it."

"You will?"

"It'll get me my furniture that much faster."

Ah, yes. How could he have forgotten the mercenary nature of all "sensitives"? "You'll only get it if you win the bet."

"Oh, I'll win it."

Her confidence gave him pause. Would she cheat? She *seemed* sincere, but no man was a good judge of character when a pretty face and a set of long legs were involved. Not for the first time, it crossed his mind that his "haunting" may have been set up somehow by Eric Ramsey, and all of this was an elaborate scheme to bilk him of thousands of dollars.

If so, he intended to catch them in the act and see them thrown in jail for fraud.

"I do have one condition to my staying at the house, though," she said.

"Yeah?" *Here it comes. Hazard pay? An expense account?*

"If I ask you to, you'll get me out of there."

"You can leave whenever you wish," he said, surprised.

She ran her finger over the edge of her mug. "I know. I'm just saying. If somehow I let you know that I need to be *taken* from there, I want you to do it."

"Of course. But what could—"

"I don't know," she said, cutting him off. "But that feeling of being trapped when we drove in . . . I don't know what that meant. Maybe I won't be able to leave of my own volition." She threw up her hands. "I guess what I'm asking for is your reassurance that you won't sacrifice me for the sake of that house."

"God, Megan! How could you even think that?"

The smile on her lips was bitter. "Not everyone behaves as one would wish."

seven

Megan steered her old Chevy Astro van into Case's driveway and stopped, leaning forward over the steering wheel to stare up at the iron arch overhead with its coat of arms. She couldn't see it clearly from this angle and couldn't make sense of the lines and blobs of iron. There was a family motto above the crest, written in Latin.

She looked ahead at the house, sitting in its clearing amid the chaos of the garden, trees grown up around on all sides and obscuring the stone wall she knew was there. It might almost have been a house in the middle of the countryside, so little could be seen of the neighborhood around or of the city of Seattle. If Case cut down the trees on the south and west sides, he would have a panoramic view of the city, Mount Rainier, Elliott Bay, and the Olympic Mountains.

No wonder he was fighting so hard to claim the place as his own. There must be less than half a dozen houses in the city that had as much space, view, history, and character as this one.

She braced herself for any psychic zings and drove through the arch.

Nothing happened.

Relieved, Megan released a pent-up breath and continued around the driveway. Case's BMW was parked over near the Dumpster, but his pickup was gone.

A small thread of anxiety pinged in Megan. Was he not there yet?

When he'd left her house the other morning, they'd agreed that she would spend a few days putting things in order with the shop, then meet him at the house today at four p.m. That would allow plenty of time for her to settle in before darkness fell. Eric Ramsey would arrive with all his gear tomorrow.

Megan was secretly glad she'd have tonight alone with Case, and not just because she loathed Ramsey. There was no denying that her body said *yes yes yes* to Case, even while her mind said *no no no*. He was bossy, blunt, and closed-minded, and yet she felt tingles all over her body when she stood close to him. She'd never been excited like that by her past boyfriends.

They *had* been gentle men, with a deep spiritual

side, and not much going on in the bedroom. Sometimes she felt as if she had to do all the work in bed, which left her feeling lonely and unfulfilled after sex.

Maybe Tracie was right. She didn't want to be bowed to by a man. She wanted to be *taken*.

Just once. Maybe twice. If only to see what it was like.

As she parked the van and went around to open the sliding door and haul out her stuff, she chided herself for letting the animal half of her sway her decision to stay at the house. She might think raunchy thoughts, but she'd never act on them. She'd never slept with a guy she didn't love, and she could never love Case Lambert. She could never love anyone who didn't understand her and believe in her.

After unloading her bags, Megan stepped up to the front door and knocked. "Case? Hallooo! Case, are you there?"

She didn't expect an answer and didn't get one.

A breeze picked up, and she felt the chill of a shadow passing through her. She shivered, suddenly feeling very alone on the doorstep.

She turned around and shaded her eyes from the sun with her hand. She looked out at the tangle of the yard. It looked as if Case had beaten a path along the perimeter of the lot—investigating the stability of the stone wall, no doubt. She couldn't tell how far the path went, but a bit of exploration was better than standing there waiting, letting her fears go to work on her.

She was determined that she wasn't going to let herself become panicked by anything. Whatever was going on in the house, those two old ladies had lived to ripe old ages, hadn't they? There was no reason to think that whatever was there had the ability to harm her.

Okay, not much of a theory, but it was all she had.

She started down the rough path into the tangled yard, glad she was wearing jeans. Blackberries plucked at the denim, and nettles lashed at her legs. Mixed in with the tangle were massive rhododendrons and volunteer saplings from the fir and maples. It wasn't long before the growth blocked out all view of the house, and Megan found herself in a leafy, vine-choked wilderness. It was slow going, the tall grass underfoot trampled partly flat but grabbing at her toes with each lifted step.

She started to sweat. A bee found her and was intrigued, circling in annoying, buzzing sweeps. Something moved in the undergrowth to her left, and she jumped sideways into the blackberries.

Curses flowed beneath her breath as she carefully unsnagged each thorn, the vines resenting her efforts and springing back at her, trying to catch her anew.

A thorn caught her in the back of the hand, and she swore aloud. The adventure of the walk was wearing off. She figured she had to be at least halfway around the yard by now. Better to continue than to turn back.

The path kept going, bending around trees and shrubs, the stone wall out of sight except for a few glimpses of vertical walls of ivy that she assumed covered it. She began to get the creepy sense that the path was never going to end, that somehow it would continue its snaking turns into eternity. Or worse yet, maybe something was leading her down this path as into the mouth of a trap. Maybe something was waiting for her, glad to have her alone, glad that she could not run with the brambles and grass catching at her every movement.

A trickle of fear started in her chest, and she cursed again. She'd promised herself not to get freaked out!

But the trickle was still there, and it seemed to be whispering to her, "Hurry, hurry, you've little time."

She hurried her steps, moving heedlessly now, the blackberries ripping at her legs. She felt the needle tips of their thorns piercing the skin of her thighs through her jeans.

Through the leaves and shadows, she saw something gray and motionless, tall as a person.

Startled, she stumbled away, her knees weak. Something grabbed her head from behind. She shrieked and jerked away, turning to see the bouncing branch of a maple tree.

Panting, heart racing, she forced herself to stand still and get a grip.

From the corner of her eye, she saw that the gray thing was still there. A sinking sensation went through her, a terrible sense of dread.

She forced herself to turn her head.

It came more clearly into view. A head, its features unintelligible. Shoulders. A body beneath, almost totally obscured by vegetation.

Megan stared fully at it, her eyes trying to make sense of what she saw. It seemed to shimmer in her vision, perspective changing.

And then she understood.

A laugh burst forth, and she doubled over, hands on knees in relief.

It was a statue: a stone statue of a woman, facing away from her. Algae and lichen obscured part of its dirty surface, camouflaging it among the overgrowth.

If that wasn't a lesson for her not to let herself get carried away with her own imagination, she didn't know what was.

With a firmer step, she continued down the path and soon found the growth thinning, and then the house came into view above the blackberries. A moment later, she came out behind the house near a big maple tree. She saw Case standing with hands on hips, staring at the tangle of yard.

"Hi," she called.

He turned around. "There you are!" He walked

toward her and took in her appearance. "Looks like the blackberries got the best of you."

"Not the leisurely amble I'd expected," she admitted. "Did you know there's a statue in there?"

"It's still there?" he asked in surprise.

"You know about it?"

"I'll have to show you some pictures I found of the house at the turn of the century. There was a formal garden here, complete with reflecting pond and statue."

"I wonder if the pond is still here."

"At the rate work is progressing, I'll probably get around to the yard in about six years. I'll let you know."

"You made that path?"

He nodded. "Just wanted to see what was out there. I see you have all your stuff. You ready to unpack at Case's House of Horror?"

"Ready as I'll ever be."

He unlocked the door to the house and scooped up most of Megan's things. She grabbed the few odd bits that were left and followed him inside.

The house was as dim, dusty, and forlorn as it had been the day before, but familiarity made it easier to walk down the hall and follow Case up the main stairs. Sunlight streamed through the leaded glass windows, and once again Megan found herself awed. It was so spectacularly beyond her expectations of what a normal person's home could be, it was hard to imagine living there herself.

If not for his ghost problem, Megan doubted that Case would ever have given her the time of day. He was too busy with work and probably dated aggressive businesswomen who were just as busy themselves, with no time for serious entanglements. They probably took ski weekends together or went to Mariners games and then to a noisy pub with friends. Loud places, with beer and shouting. Places she would never go. Now that Case was living in this wreck, he probably slept with the women at their places.

Her mood darkened as she followed him down the hall, contemplating his possible dating life. The two of them could never be a match. She liked quiet and thought staying home at night was a delight. She spent her weekends gardening and riding her bike all over the neighborhoods of Seattle, stopping at estate sales to peruse the contents, biking home again to fetch her van if anything looked worth buying.

"I thought this might do for your room," he said, pushing open a door at the opposite end of the house from where she'd seen the shadow in the hall.

Megan stepped past him and into the chamber. It smelled of new paint, the walls an antique white. A full-size bed with a six-foot-tall headboard was set against one wall, a brand-new mattress on its slats, bedding folded neatly at its foot.

Megan put her things down and went to the window. Curtains still with the creases from being in a package hung on an iron rod and outside was a view of trees.

"I'm tempted to cut the trees down now, before doing anything else," Case said behind her. "It would make working here more cheerful."

"It wouldn't feel so claustrophobic," she agreed. "I wonder why they let them grow so tall?"

"Too expensive to remove them, perhaps. Or maybe they just got used to them and had seen enough of the view over their lives. Maybe they preferred the privacy."

Megan shook her head. "Makes me wonder what oddness I'll get up to in my old age, assuming I make it there."

"No reason to think you won't, is there?"

"You never know. You painted?"

"I had a quick coat done on a couple of rooms, so there was someplace bright and clean and not so depressing. It's temporary, as are the curtains. As is everything at this point."

He gestured to a bureau and a wardrobe against one wall. "Those have been cleaned out of bird nests, mice, and so on. There's a toilet room across the hall and a bathroom next to it with hot running water. It must have been cheaper for the sisters to update this bath, two floors directly above the electric hot water heater, than the one at the other end."

"Does that copper boiler still work?"

"God knows. I was afraid to try it without the fire department standing by."

"Where are you and Eric going to be sleeping?"

"I'm through here," he said, opening a door close to her bed that she had assumed went to a closet.

"Connecting doors?"

"I thought it might make you more comfortable if you knew someone was close by. I promise not to peep."

She smiled.

"Eric's room is on the ground floor. There's better access to electricity down there for his equipment, and I figured you didn't want him too near. Oh, and sorry I didn't get the bed made up. Ran out of time. If you want to unpack and settle in, I'll go unload the groceries and make dinner later. Although after our discussion last night, I'm afraid it's not going to be up to your standards."

"Any dinner made for me by someone else is up to my standards. It'll be a treat."

"I'd reserve judgment if I were you." He grinned and headed for the door. "After you unpack, check out the library. There are some things in there that you might want to see." He looked at her, a crease of worry forming on his brow. "Are you going to be okay up here on your own?"

"I should be fine," she said, and meant it. "No more running scared for me—too, too tiresome."

He smiled. "Now, there's a tack I haven't tried:

obvious ennui with the spectral performance. We'll humiliate the ghosts out of the house."

"I wonder if that would work," Megan mused. "Treat them like children having a temper tantrum. Ignore them until they behave."

"Easier said than done," Case said.

"I'm sure any parent would tell you the same. But don't worry, if you don't have faith in me, at least I'm sure Eric has some grand plan in mind for taking care of your problem."

"I'm counting on it." He smiled and disappeared out into the hall.

Megan went to work unpacking and making the bed and found herself hoping that Eric really did have something planned. Because the thing about children behaving badly when ignored was that the behavior usually got a heck of a lot worse before it got any better.

Megan made her way downstairs and explored a bit until she found the library.

Case sat on a wooden chair at the one big table in the room, the table's surface covered in papers and folders and rolls of blueprints.

"Hey. Everything okay upstairs?"

"All clear, chief, and in tip-top order," she said, and touched her forehead in salute. "No signs of ghosts. Maybe they wore themselves out with yesterday's display."

"Does that happen?"

"Heck if I know. Neither I nor anyone else has enough experience with active hauntings to say what's normal and what's not."

He dragged another chair over to the table, putting it beside his. "Sit. I have some stuff to show you."

Megan's eye was caught by the books on the shelves. "I assume this is that library of the occult you were talking about?" she asked, moving toward the books and examining their covers. Many of them were leather or cloth and looked as if they'd come from an earlier time, but there were just as many that still wore faded dust jackets, as well as dozens of spine-creased paperbacks mixed in with the rest. "How's this organized? Or is it?"

"Haven't thought to look."

Megan scanned over a few titles:

The Encyclopedia of Witchcraft
Witchcraft through the Ages
The ABCs of Witchcraft

A different shelf offered:

Demons
Demons II
Demonology for Beginners

By subject, apparently.

"Feel free to read whatever you think might be useful. I was going to clear them all out of here, but when strange things started happening, I decided to put it off, in case there was something I could learn in those books. I read a few and can't say I was impressed. I even tried a few of the things they suggested, for what that was worth."

"Like what?"

His face colored. "Burning a sage smudge. Having the house blessed. Sprinkling holy water around the place and telling the spirits to leave, that it was my house now."

"Any effect, good or bad?"

He shook his head. "No, of course not. If there really are ghosts, I imagine they thought it a very good joke." He frowned. "But come to think of it, yesterday, while I was having my heart attack, something seemed to get mad when I told it to go to the light."

Megan giggled.

Case cracked a smile. "It worked in *Poltergeist.*"

"A doctor would tell you that the dark tunnel and the light are an effect of oxygen deprivation on a dying brain."

"Is that what you think?"

"Pretty much. I imagine it's the last thing the living consciousness sees before reaching the Other Side. It's not that they're going into the light; it's that the light is a sort of Last Chance for Gas for Eternity signpost they go by, then *poof,* they're dead."

"*Poof?*"

"Well, you know."

"What about all the loved ones meeting them there?"

"I hope that's true. But even I sometimes wonder, is it again just an effect of the brain dying? Maybe emotion and long-term memory are the last things to go, as they often are in people with dementia. My mother knew someone who had Alzheimer's, who lost everything except the ability to say 'I love you.' She would say it again and again and again to her husband when he came to visit her."

"Christ, I don't know whether that's a happy story or a painfully sad one."

"I think it's both."

"Remind me not to get old."

"Maybe you'll be lucky."

"And die young?" he asked.

She laughed, sitting down in the chair he'd pulled over for her. "No. Maybe you'll have a healthy old age."

"You ever get a sense about that with people? I mean, whether or not they'll have a long life? Whether death is imminent?"

Megan saw the edge of a photograph under a stack of papers and pulled the picture out. "Sometimes."

"Is there a dark cloud hanging over them or something?"

The photo was of the house sometime before the turn of the century, judging by the horse and buggy.

"No cloud. When I first meet them, there's a sort of flicker when I look at them, like a lightbulb about to go out. It's just for a moment, and then they seem like everyone else. I saw it in my mom, before she was diagnosed with cancer." Megan looked up at him. "I tried to persuade myself I was wrong. I thought I had been, when months went by and nothing happened."

She looked back down at the photo. "The garden was lovely."

"You can just see that statue," he said, and pointed to a small white spot in the background. "Er . . . I didn't flicker when you met me, did I?"

"I thought you didn't believe in that type of thing."

"I don't. Never mind."

She laughed. "No, you didn't flicker."

"Good. I plan to be a grumpy old fart someday, arguing politics with bored whippersnappers on the back porch. And you? What will you be doing?" he asked.

"Baking cookies and nagging my husband to take his heart medication."

"You'll marry a man with heart problems?"

Embarrassment flooded her. She hadn't been thinking, she just said what popped into her mind, only Case was obviously on her mind. "Or nagging him to take his prostate medicine."

"That's no good. He'll be waking you up every two hours when he gets out of bed to go to the bathroom. You'll be better off with the heart problem guy."

"Mmm. Are there any more photos?"

He pulled over a file and opened it. "These are the ones I came across while cleaning out the rooms. There are probably ten times as many hidden around the house. There are several locked chests and desks and no sign of the keys. I didn't want to force them."

Megan opened the folder.

The first photo looking up at her was a formal portrait of two teenage girls, hair down in ringlets, big bows on the sides of their heads. One was slightly taller than the other, her features more well defined, her body showing the curves of womanhood. She had a lovely face and bright eyes and an eager curve to her slightly parted lips.

The other girl, a bit younger, was just as pretty or even more so, but her eyes had a narrow look, her lips set in a straighter line. She looked like a troublemaker, although perhaps also more intelligent than the older girl. The older girl looked like the type who needed a father's watchful, protective eye to stay out of harm's way—that harm's way being lustful young men. The younger girl looked as if she'd castrate any man who tried to take advantage of her.

Megan flipped the photo over and read the inscription:

Easter, 1896
Isabella, 18
Penelope, 16

"The sisters," Megan said.

"Quite a pair, eh?"

"They were beautiful."

A draft rustled the papers on the table, then died away.

Megan and Case exchanged glances. Megan set the photo aside and went on to the next. It was from an earlier date, a married couple, the large bearded man sitting, his tiny, doe-eyed young wife standing beside him, her head topping his by only a couple of inches. Her tightly laced corset made her look as if all her soft parts were being extruded out of a metal form. She didn't seem to mind it, though; the same soft, eager smile that played on Isabella's lips played on hers. *Mr. and Mrs. Jacob Smithson, 1880,* the back said.

"He's the one who built the house," Case said.

"His wife's a doll."

"They look a bit like a bear and a chipmunk, don't they?"

Megan giggled. "I really don't want to picture how their daughters were conceived."

He groaned. "Thanks for the image."

She grinned, but then the grin faded. "It's probably their bed upstairs, don't you think?"

"Unless one of the sisters married and moved in there after their parents were gone. And the bed could have belonged to someone else before that."

Megan shook her head. "I'd guess it belonged to these two, almost exclusively."

She set that picture aside and went through the others. There was one more of the house from the outside, this time taken from the backyard, facing the back of the house. As with the other picture of the house, everything looked strangely clean and stark, because the vegetation had been no more than low shrubs and an occasional spindly young tree, all separated by expanses of shorn lawn. No vines clambered up the drainpipes; no ivy obscured the walls of the yard.

"It all looks so new and raw," she said.

"I've seen pictures of this hill when all the development was going on, in the 1880s. It looked just like housing developments do now: scraped earth and houses sticking up out of it like tree stumps. The garden may be a mess now, but at least the tall trees soften the house's presence in the landscape."

She nodded and thumbed through the rest of the photos. There were several of people, their names and the dates written on the backs. None of the names meant anything to Megan. Some of the pictures gave intriguing hints into what the house was like in its glory. There were no newer pictures, though, no snapshots of later eras. "You didn't find anything more recent?" Megan asked.

"No, not yet. I didn't go through the sisters' rooms, though."

"It's like time stopped in this house," Megan mused, spreading out the photos in front of her. "It seems there should have been so much more life lived here than this."

"Maybe you'll find hints of it elsewhere. God only knows what's stuffed in those other two bedrooms. One thing I did find was a set of original house plans." He unrolled a large tube of paper and weighted its corners with books. "Found it in the newel post of the main staircase. Lots of home owners put their house blueprints in the newel post. I don't know why."

"Maybe so people who come along later, like you, know where to find them."

"Maybe." He put his index finger down on a square on the paper. "This is where we are." He traced a route down the other hallway, the one she'd not yet explored. "Kitchen is here. Dining room here. Grand salon." He pointed out all the main rooms.

"Can you imagine the housework? I wonder how many servants they had."

"There were servants' quarters up on the third floor. The attic is something else, too. There's a cistern up there for rainwater, but it's empty. Someone must have shut it down once city water was put in. If it's solid and not lined with toxic metals, I plan to put it back into use for yard irrigation."

"Going green?"

"Only to avoid going broke. Anyway, I'd better get dinner started. You'll find me here," he said, pointing again to the kitchen on the map, "when you're done going through this stuff."

"Okay."

She watched him go and listened to his footsteps move down the corridor. The room fell quiet, and her senses heightened, picking up the slight drafts of air on her skin, the shadows on the walls, the distant creaks and pops and groans of the old wood house. She could feel the heat of the big light on its stand and imagined she could hear it buzzing; or perhaps that was the buzzing in her own ears.

A tingle crept up Megan's neck, an awareness that there might be someone else in the room with her. She looked slowly around but saw nothing unusual in the shadows and the glare of light.

"I want to know who you are," Megan said softly. "Who are you? Why are you here?"

A draft rustled the papers and photos again.

"Is the answer in these?"

She waited, but there was no answer, no breeze of affirmation.

She picked up a handful of papers and glanced through them. Tax statements, work orders and receipts for the house, insurance documents, letters from a law firm, papers pertaining to businesses the family had owned or in which they'd held stock. It was all jumbled together, mid-century papers mixed among those that were older.

What a mess. Investigating the past was going to be a full-time job.

She sighed and put the papers down, then turned to

the books on the shelves. To her delight, she found a
battered copy of William Hope Hodgson's *Carnacki the
Ghost Finder.* They were delightfully spooky ghost detective tales from the turn of the last century, with half—
but not all—of the ghosts turning out to be fakes, much
like the villains in an episode of *Scooby-Doo.* She'd take it
up to her room for bedtime reading, and to remind
herself that not every draft was a ghost going by.

Half an hour later, tired of the dust and mildew of
old books and their naive discussions of ectoplasm
and rappings on tables, Megan left the library with
Carnacki in hand and made her way to the kitchen,
following the sound of a baseball game on the radio.

The kitchen was a surprise. She'd been expecting
peeling linoleum and sagging cabinetry, maybe a
range that looked as if it belonged to some time
before the First World War. Instead, she saw a room
stripped down to the studs.

A few functional pieces sat like islands in the lath-
and-plaster gloom: a refrigerator and a propane
range, both about ten years old, and a freestanding
commercial stainless-steel sink with drain boards to
either side. Pots, dishes, and nonperishable food
were crammed onto freestanding metal shelves. The
farm-style table in the center of the room was plainly
office desk, food prep space, and dining table. An oil
lamp was burning in the center of the table.

"Wow. You're really camping out here, aren't you?"
Megan asked.

Case turned around from the sink, where he was peeling potatoes. "What? Oh, yeah." He gestured at the walls with a half-peeled potato. "It's not so bad. I've got what I need, and it's not as filthy as it was before I tore everything out. I don't think anyone had cleaned the place since the fifties." He grimaced. "It wasn't appetizing."

"Can I help?" she asked.

"No, you're my guest. Have a seat. Would you like a glass of wine?"

"Are you having one?"

"Sure. Red or white?"

"Either."

He opened a bottle of red and poured out the glasses. Megan twiddled the stem between her fingertips as the glass sat on the table in front of her, feeling uneasy. How had she gone so quickly from having met him only once to staying in his house?

"You ever go to Mariners games?" she asked.

He glanced over his shoulder at her. "Maybe once a year. Why?"

"Just wondering. Do you ski?"

"Used to, downhill. But then I messed up my knee. I've been meaning to try cross-country but never get around to it. You?"

She shook her head.

He carried his potatoes to the table and the cutting board there, chopping them into cubes.

"I bike," she offered. "Not racing. Just cruising around."

"You ever try that old railroad grade over along the Cedar River?"

She shook her head, and they talked about routes they liked and favorite places around the city. They chatted like strangers at a party, filling time, being sociable and avoiding personal and ghostly topics.

Case opened a box of curry concentrate and broke the cubes into the large pan of vegetables and meat he now had cooking on the stove. "Gourmet bachelor fare," he told her, holding up the box.

"It smells good."

"Thanks." He turned the heat off under a pan of rice, and a few minutes later, the food was on the table, and they tucked in.

"It's not bad," Megan said, trying to be kind.

"Good. I have fourteen more boxes of it."

"I could cook dinner if you'd like."

He laughed. "No, you're free to make anything you want for yourself, but you're not here to be my chef."

She shrugged, happy enough to have her offer refused.

"How did you get into being a medium, anyway?" Case asked, serving himself a second helping of rice.

The lights flickered and went out. The refrigerator kept humming, the baseball game continued softly, but they sat now in a pool of light cast by the oil lamp.

"It happens every night," Case said softly. "I try not to notice."

Megan nodded, eyes wide. She *really* did not like the dark.

"Did you 'see dead people' from the time you were a child?" Case asked in his normal voice.

Megan shook her head, doing her best to follow his lead despite being unnerved. "It's not like in the movies. I don't suddenly see dead people standing in front of me. I don't hear them say things in plain English.

"My mom told me that the first time she knew there was something different about me was when I was three. She'd taken me to an estate sale at a big house in Laurelhurst, and I picked up a silver hairbrush and said I wanted it for my kitty.

"Mom told me that was silly, that the brush was for a lady, but she says I kept insisting that no, it was for kitties.

"An acquaintance of the deceased was at the sale and overheard us and told my mom—in some shock—that the woman whose brush it had been had indeed used it exclusively for her cats. It had been thoroughly cleaned, of course. There was no sign of cat hair on it."

"Quite a story."

"Not all that much of one. It could have been coincidence. If old people sometimes become like children, it's no wonder we both would have wanted to brush cats with a silver brush.

"But it was a strange enough occurrence that my mom started paying attention to things I said about items at estate sales. It was a hobby for her then, going to the sales. She'd do some 'picking' for antique shops, but other than that, she stayed at home with me.

"Well, the rest is history, as they say. She found out that most of the time when I talked about an object or piece of furniture, the 'stories' I told were true. Even better, the items I was most drawn to because of the happy stories tied to them were items that fetched the highest prices or sold the quickest. They weren't always valuable in an objective sense, but they felt good, even to people who didn't know why they liked the things."

"It wasn't just good lines? Artistic balance?"

She shook her head. "There has been some pretty ugly stuff over the years. But people laugh instead of grimacing when they see the ugly items I've chosen. They think they're unique and have character."

"And thus Antique Fancies was born?"

Megan nodded and sipped her wine. "Mom was setting up the shop when Dad left us. I think he resented the time she spent on it, and when he threatened to leave, she gladly let him go."

"So you grew up without a father."

"I had an uncle who filled in."

"Not the same, though, is it?"

"I wouldn't know," she said with false lightness,

and poked her fork at a mushy carrot smothered in brown sauce. The curry had been bearable for a couple of bites but was an inedible, gloppy mess after that.

"Where did this ability of yours come from?" he asked, apparently unaware of her change in mood. "Does it run in your family?"

"I really couldn't say." She chewed the mushy carrot and tried to swallow. "I was adopted. I have no idea who my birth mother is."

"Really? You ever get curious to find out?"

"Not really. I wonder sometimes what she looks like and whether she has an ability like mine. But other than that, no, I've never been curious enough to do anything about it. And frankly, I wouldn't have wanted to hurt my mother's feelings by doing that. I have too much loyalty. I figure my biological mother was an unwed teen who made the wisest choice she could, and I've always been grateful that she did. My adoptive father might not have turned out so great, but I loved my mother deeply. We were closer than a lot of mothers and daughters ever are and surprisingly similar for two people who weren't related. We understood each other."

"But you've never seen her since she died, not even on the night she passed?"

Megan remembered the scene. It had been past midnight, and she'd been sitting at her mother's bedside in the hospital, her mother unconscious, her limbs beginning to bloat because her heart was no longer beating strongly enough to move the fluids. She'd held her mother's limp, chilled hand and watched the slow rise and fall of her chest.

And then her chest fell and did not rise again.

Megan's uncle Charlie had been reading a magazine in a chair on the other side of the bed. Megan made a sound, and he looked up, then at his sister. He had understood as quickly as Megan had and put down his magazine. He looked into his sister's still face, her mouth hanging open, and touched her cheek. " 'Bye, Sis," he whispered.

Megan let go of her mother's hand.

Uncle Charlie had come home with her and spent the night, but despite his presence, the house had felt empty and silent. Her mother had been in the hospital for more than a week, but somehow the house had not felt as empty of her presence then as it did now.

Now, Megan knew for certain that her mother would never come home.

She'd lain awake the rest of the night, waiting for her mother to come to her and say good-bye.

When dawn peeped through the windows, Megan had wept and finally fallen asleep, even then hoping that her mother would come to her with some message, some hint that she was okay, all was well, life would go on, Megan would never be alone.

She'd woken at noon, and the house had been just as empty.

"No, I never saw her after she died," Megan now said softly, swallowing against the tightness in her throat.

He looked at her, and she dropped her gaze, not wanting him to see the sheen of tears in her eyes.

He reached across the table and put his hand over hers. "I'm sorry," he said.

"Why did she appear to you?" Megan asked, the injustice of it still hurting. "How did she look? Angry? Happy? Worried? Was she trying to tell you something?"

He shook his head, releasing her hand. "It was only for a moment. She was looking at me, that's all. Maybe you'll see my mother, then we'll be even, huh?" He tried a smile on her.

"Yeah, maybe." She sniffled, trying to regain control of herself. "Would she tell me what a wild boy you used to be, or would she sing your praises?"

"She'd say I had a good heart under all my wildness, but she'd be disappointed I hadn't married yet. She thought that no one could be truly happy unless they found their soul mate."

"And do you believe that?"

He met her eyes. "Yes."

Something upstairs fell over with a crash. They both jumped.

Her heart pounded. "What was that?"

Case slowly pushed back in his chair and stood, head cocked to listen.

There was a slow scrape of something being dragged across the floor above their heads.

A moment of silence.

Then *crash,* something else fell.

Megan's heart jumped to her throat.

Case simply topped off his wine.

"Case?"

"They do this all the time."

"Every night?"

"Off and on."

"But . . . don't you want to go see what's happening?"

"I've looked before."

"And?" she asked.

"The rooms always look pretty much the same as when I last saw them. There's never anything broken. No chairs lying on their sides or stacked in an improbable manner."

"So no evidence that anything moved."

"Right." He took a sip of wine. "It can make you crazy wondering if you imagined it all, if you don't have someone else to say, 'What the hell?'"

Above them somewhere, a door creaked open.

"I showed my old friend George around the place a few weeks after I bought it. He heard the floor show, ran to investigate, and ended up doing the same thing I did the very first time: dashing from door to door, jerking them open looking for the culprit. He didn't find anything, of course, but I was perversely glad he'd been given such a fright." He grinned. "Made me feel better. I wasn't crazy, and I wasn't any more a coward than he was."

Overhead, the door slammed. Case merely glanced at the ceiling.

"What did he think of your plans to hire me?" Megan squeaked.

The door slowly creaked open again.

He smiled crookedly. "He thought I should sell the place. Get out before I sank any more money into it. Let someone else worry about the ghosts, and certainly not let myself get sucked into a world of séances and Ouija boards."

"A reasonable man." Megan waited tensely for the door to slam. Waited, waited . . .

"He's a good guy. When this is all cleared up, we'll have to have him over for dinner and show him how harmless the house is."

Megan was distracted from the door by the "we" and wondered what it meant. She'd once dated a man who peppered his talk with "we" and mentions of things they'd do in the future, even in the far future. Then he'd dumped her.

Wham! The door slammed.

Megan jumped. She took a gulp of wine. "Once the house is renovated, you'll probably get more visitors if you say the house is still haunted. People don't really believe it, but they like the thrill of maybe seeing a ghost. Sort of like the thrill of a roller coaster:

fun because you know there's not really any danger."

"Only roller coasters sometimes go off their tracks," Case said.

"And sometimes the ghosts are real."

They sat in silence for several seconds, both listening to the house around them. She raised her brows in question.

Case whispered, "They might be done for now." He grinned. "Maybe this 'Ignore them and they'll go away' approach has some merit."

"Maybe."

"Have you had enough to eat?" Case asked in a normal voice.

She nodded and picked up her plate. "I'll do cleanup."

"Nonsense." He took the plate from her hand, then went to the sink, grabbed a sponge, and threw it to her. "We both will."

She laughed and tried not to think of what might happen tonight in this house as she lay alone in her antique bed.

EIGHT

Megan snuggled down in her freshly made bed and opened *Carnacki the Ghost Finder*. A small candelabra burned on her bedside table, throwing just enough light for reading a spooky book.

She wished that the fireplace had a steady flame warming the room. The house had grown cold with the coming of darkness, there being no insulation to keep the heat from wafting out between the boards.

She was two-thirds of the way through a ghastly tale of a room that dripped blood when three soft raps came on the door near the head of her bed.

"Yes, ghost?" she said.

"Are you decent?" Case asked from the other side, his voice muffled by the heavy door.

"Relatively." She tucked the sheets a little higher up over her nightgown to avoid giving a cold nipple show.

The door inched open. "Everything okay?"

"Everything's fine. How about you?"

"Fine. I just wondered if you'd feel better if the door was left ajar."

She considered. She'd feel braver knowing he could easily hear anything in her room, but at the same time, she didn't know what types of noises she made in her sleep. Worrying what unattractive sounds she might produce would keep her from getting to sleep at all.

"I'm told my snoring isn't too terrible," he said.

That clinched it. "I'll be fine with the door shut."

"Okay. Good night."

" 'Night."

Megan watched him close the door and heard it snick shut. She listened for any other sounds he might make, but either he was silent on his feet, or the door did an extraordinarily good job of blocking sound.

Megan scooted a little lower under the covers, feeling very much the only living thing in the room.

She finished the Carnacki story—it was smugglers making fake blood drip from the ceiling—and blew out the candles.

The brightest spot in the room was the window,

filled with the gray light of a moon behind clouds. Megan curled onto her side, staring at the window, listening to the house creak around her.

A faint creak came to her from Case's room, and she guessed he had rolled over in bed.

The house seemed to sigh and settle down for sleep.

No shadows moved, no hairs on her arms rose. Gradually, her vigilance weakened, and she felt her eyelids grow heavy. She shut her eyes against the light of the cloud-shrouded moon and slept.

Megan.

"Mom?"

Megan, the voice of her mother said again, her name spoken without inflection.

Megan's heart rose. "Mom? Are you here?"

Megan.

Megan looked around her. She was in the center of the tangled garden, in a clearing that did not exist. "Mom?"

Right here, Megan.

Megan turned around. Her mother was scrubbing the white statue, a bucket of soap at her feet. "Why are you cleaning that?" she asked.

"I'll bet it would sell quickly in the shop. Garden art is getting very popular nowadays."

"I don't think Case wants to sell it."

"Oh, he'll give it to you if you ask nicely," her

mother said, and scrubbed at lichen on the statue's neck. Only this wasn't the statue Megan had seen; instead, it was of a young, handsome man.

Part of Megan's mind protested at the scene. *Mom's dead. I know she's dead. I'm dreaming this.*

But then a hope started in her heart. "Are you visiting me?"

Her mother blinked at her. "Do you think we can get this into the van ourselves? Or is it too heavy?"

"I don't know. It looks heavy. Maybe Case will help."

Her mother looked at her watch. "Oh, dear. I hope he's strong enough. I need to get going. The boat leaves in an hour."

"What boat? Where are you going?"

Her mother handed her the wet sponge. "Be sure to get all the algae off. I'm sure he's got a good heart under there somewhere."

Megan looked again at the statue. He looked like no one she knew. When she looked back at her mother, she was disappearing down the pathway.

"Mom, wait! It's not really you, is it? I mean, you're not really you—you're just in my head, right?"

The dreamscape dissolved as Megan's distress woke her. She opened her eyes to the empty room.

"Mom?" she whispered.

The house was silent.

Megan closed her eyes, and a tear spilled onto her pillow. She snuffled quietly and dabbed at her nose with the edge of her sheet. After a few minutes, her breathing calmed. She lay still, eyes closed, waiting for sleep to claim her again.

A hand gently brushed the hair from her temple. *Mom.*

She smiled, not wanting to wake from her dozing state to find it wasn't so.

The hand gently brushed her hair again, then with a feather touch took hold of her hand and tugged, as if urging her to come along.

Megan opened her eyes a slit, trying to keep herself in the half-dozing state. *You want me to come with you?* she thought, rather than saying it aloud. *I'll come with you.*

She closed her eyes again and slipped out of bed, trusting her mother to guide her. *Where are we going?*

No answer came, but the gentle pressure on her hand continued, leading her toward the door. Megan felt for the knob and opened it slowly, flinching when the hinges creaked. She passed out into the hall, the floor dusty beneath her feet. A board groaned when she stepped on it, and by reflex she opened her eyes.

There was nothing to see, the hallway dark. Eerily dark, unnerving her. She could "see" it better in her imagination, with her eyes closed. The only thing dimly visible was the pale glow of her own hand and white gown-clad arm, held out for her invisible guide. She could still feel the slight pressure grasping her hand, although it was so faint she could almost be imagining it.

She closed her eyes again, focusing on that touch. *What do you want to show me? Or is it that you want me to leave?*

The hand seemed to grip hers a little more tightly, pulling with more urgency. Megan hurried her steps.

Soft footsteps started behind her, slow at first, then with increasing speed, growing louder as they descended upon her.

Fear shot through Megan, and with imaginings of the black shadow foremost in her mind, she broke into a run. Her hand was suddenly jerked to the right, and she followed it.

An arm wrapped around her from behind, grabbing tight and lifting her off the ground.

Megan's whole body flooded with terror, and she screamed, limbs flailing, eyes flying open.

"Megan! Wake up! It's me!"

It took a moment for the familiar voice to penetrate her fear and for her to recognize that it was a solid, warm body that restrained her. Case.

He'd chased her mother off. "Let me go!" she demanded angrily.

"Not until I'm sure you won't go running off again."

"I was being guided! Why did you interfere?" she wailed.

He pivoted, turning her toward a tall wall of windows. "Are your eyes open?"

Inches from where they stood was the top of the stairs. Horrified understanding washed through Megan.

"One step more, and you would have fallen down the stairs." He squeezed her a little more tightly, anger entering his voice. "What were you thinking?"

Megan stared at the void into which she'd almost run headlong. "I was being guided," she said softly. "I thought . . ."

"Guided by something that wanted to kill you."

She shook her head. "It didn't feel malevolent. It was gentle."

"It almost killed you."

Megan looked again at the staircase, remembering the jerk on her hand that had almost sent her down it, and sagged, heartbroken. It hadn't been her mother guiding her. The dream had just been a dream, like so many others before it that had nothing of her mother in them except Megan's own memories and imagination.

Case released her. "You can't trust anything in this house," he said gently. "I don't know what it is that's messing with our minds, but something is. Don't believe anything you see or hear."

Megan felt embarrassed. She was the one who should have been giving Case such simple advice. She shouldn't have let wishful thinking take over. "This was careless of me."

"Well, no harm done, right? Maybe a couple more years taken off my life, but I've stopped counting."

She started to turn around to face him. "I'm—"

"Er, you might not want to look at me."

"What?" she said, completing the turn and looking at him. He was faintly visible in the light from the staircase, but it was enough for her to see his naked chest and the dark shadow of his groin. "Oh!" She looked quickly away, embarrassed.

"A scarier sight than a ghost, huh?" he said with a laugh in his voice. "I'm getting a little chilly. Let's head back to our rooms, where I can put something on."

She preceded him back down the hall, aware with every nerve of his naked self immediately behind her. A flush went through her as she realized that when he'd caught her and scooped her off her feet, only a whisper-thin layer of white cotton had separated her squirming backside from his groin. "I'm surprised you heard me in the hall," she squeaked. "You weren't asleep?"

"Something woke me. Maybe the sound of your door. I checked your room and didn't see you in bed. Then, when I saw you in the hall, there wasn't time to grab my bathrobe."

"Not a problem. Really. So, you, uh . . . always sleep in the buff?"

"Getting dressed for bed has never made any sense to me. Do you always sleep in ten yards of white cotton?"

"In winter, I switch to flowered flannel."

He groaned.

"What?" she asked, knowing exactly what.

"Did your last boyfriend put up with that?"

"None of your business! But yes, he did. Wouldn't you?"

"Hell no! I want to feel a woman's skin against mine all night."

A tingle raced over Megan's shoulders and down her breasts as she imagined his hands enjoying the softness of her own skin.

They reached their rooms. "I think it's best if we leave the connecting door open," Case said. "Don't you?"

"Yes, I guess so."

They went through their separate doors, and Megan could see by the faint light from the window that the connecting door was still open. "Good night," she called softly into the next room.

"Good night."

"And Case?"

"Mm?"

"Thanks. For keeping me from a bad tumble."

He was silent for a moment. "Anything for my lady. Good night, Megan. Sweet dreams."

"G'night."

NINE

Megan woke to sunlight streaming through her window and that most familiar bird sound in Seattle: crows. A caucus of them had taken up session in the trees of the garden and were raucously debating the state of the Crow Union.

Megan snuggled a little deeper under the covers and smiled. Some people hated crows and their noisy mischief and their stark black color that looked like ragged mourning wear. To Megan, the crows were a link to the past, to the local tribes and their legends about the clever birds. The crows belonged there as much as the salmon and the killer whales.

A crow landed on the thin ledge outside her window and cocked its head, staring in at her.

"Hey, crow," Megan said softly, waving her finger-tips. "How're things?"

The crow blinked its shiny eye, walked the length of the ledge, and cocked its head at her again.

Curious thing!

Amused, Megan sat up. "What are you looking for, huh? You think there's something to eat in here?"

The crow cawed, one short cry.

"Is that so?"

Curious herself, she got out of bed and walked to the window. The crow fluttered its wings at her approach but held its ground.

"Caw yourself, you nutty bird! What are you doing here?"

The crow started cleaning its beak on its toe, or vice versa. She couldn't tell which.

Megan tapped on the window glass.

The crow jumped and stared at her, as if to ask why she had to do that.

"Sorry," Megan said.

The crow flew off, disappearing into the trees.

Disappointed, Megan watched it go.

"Fucking crows!" came a familiar male voice from outside. *Eric Ramsey.*

Megan's heart sank. She pressed her face to the glass and could see Eric down below, running and waving his arms over his head as an angry crow swooped at him, cawing. It landed on a branch, cawing still, and Eric pointed his hand like a gun and pretended to shoot it.

A lovely morning ruined.

Then Megan noticed the sun was well up in the sky, and she checked her watch: 11:50.

She'd slept more than twelve hours! Who would ever think that a house as haunted as this one would end up giving her the longest rest she'd had in two years?

Once she was showered and dressed, Megan trotted down the stairs and headed for the kitchen, her stomach reminding her that she needed to do some grocery shopping if she didn't want curry for dinner.

As she approached the kitchen, she saw that new electrical cords were taped down on the floor, crossing from the kitchen to two rooms on the opposite side of the hall. Sounds of movement came from one of the rooms, then a soft curse. Eric popped out into the hall.

Megan stopped in her tracks, feeling as if a rabid possum had just appeared in her path. The nasty creature had put on a few pounds since she'd seen him last, and his black hair was longer, almost reaching his shoulders. His earlobes with their plugs were stretched wider, too. The Elvis Costello glasses were the same, as was the goatee. An uncertain smile was twitching on his lips.

"Hi," he said.

"Hi," she answered, her momentary good mood draining away.

He stared at her and fidgeted.

Megan tightened her lips and stared back, silently daring him to say anything more to her.

"So, hey," Eric said, and lapsed into silence.

She raised one brow. He wouldn't try to act like her friend, would he?

"Some house, huh?" he tried brightly.

"Yeah."

"Megan, I'm really sorry, you know. For what happened. I really didn't think that you were in any danger. I mean, when had there ever been a *real* entity to deal with?"

"But you thought it was possible. Otherwise, why put all that time and money into SPIRIT?" SPIRIT was the Seattle Paranormal Intensive Research and Investigation Team, Eric's pet organization. There were about twenty active members, the majority of them women, and for a short time Megan had been one of them.

"I was just hoping, you know? Like everyone else on the planet. Hoping for proof of life after death, or at least for proof of something beyond the world we see."

"Despite what you did to me, you didn't get the proof, though, did you?"

He took a step toward her and gazed at her with puppy-dog eyes. "No. And I lost you."

Megan snorted. "Lost your chance to use me."

"No, I mean more than that. We were good together. We really had a connection."

"Is that why you persuaded me to go to the O'Neill house even after I told you about the bad vibe I was getting, and then changed the equipment settings without telling me?"

"I know, I know, the whole thing was a mistake."

"I suspected you were up to something. It was only that poor O'Neill woman and her fear for her children that made me stay."

"It was crazy of me. And stupid! So stupid! Especially because . . ." He trailed off, looking down. After a moment, he looked up again, eyes shining behind the heavy-rimmed glasses, brows pinched together in wistful meaningfulness. "Because I think I love you, Megan."

She turned on her heel and headed back down the hall.

She had to get out of the house, away from him. He was making her skin crawl. Why couldn't he do her a favor and go drown himself in the bay?

She hurried upstairs to her bedroom to grab her purse.

It was two years ago. More important things have happened in your life since then. Eric doesn't matter anymore. You're beyond that.

Somewhat calmer, she left the house. Eric's old yellow Toyota pickup with canopy was parked next to her van, the back open to reveal a bed half full of electrical equipment. It brought back a wash of memories of her brief time with SPIRIT: riding with Eric in the cab; listening to his excitement over the pending investigation; unloading and setting up equipment and usually discovering a crucial piece had been forgotten; the feeling of embarrassment while setting up overly technical equipment in a shabby home the residents thought was haunted— and wasn't.

Not all the memories were bad, but they left her feeling vaguely unsettled, as if there were something she should be ashamed about. Maybe the shameful part was that she *had* been a bit attracted to Eric at one point, flattered by the attention he gave her and his encouragement in regard to her gift. She'd even let him kiss her once, let him put his hand on her breast as they sat in the cab of the Toyota.

A shudder went through her at the memory. How starved for male attention could she have been to have allowed that? And worse yet, to have put her hand over the bulge in his jeans and smiled at him when she felt the thickness of his erection?

Thank God it hadn't gone farther than that.

She was opening the door to her van when Case called to her.

"Megan, good morning!"

" 'Morning," she said in surprise, seeing him over

near the Dumpster, where a load of fresh lumber had been delivered.

Case jogged over to her. "When did you get up? I checked on you at ten, but you were still out."

"Half an hour ago. I thought I'd go get a few things from the store," she said, gesturing at the open van door. "Do you need anything?"

He shook his head. "You okay?"

She forced a smile. "I'm fine."

He didn't look as if he believed it. "You see Eric inside?"

"We said hello."

"Everything okay there? Any problems?"

Nothing cement shoes and a trip to the pier wouldn't fix. "Everything's fine. How did you two find each other, anyway?"

"Match.com. I enjoyed candlelight dinners; he was looking for quiet nights at home."

She punched his arm.

He grinned. "I went to a local conference hosted by SPIRIT and sat in on a talk he gave. He impressed me. He has a thousand explanations for why people think they see ghosts, and none of them involves dead people or evil spirits."

"He said what you wanted to hear."

"He was rational. And yeah, I wanted to hear that."

She shook her head and clucked her tongue. "My, my, but you are going to have a hard time when you have to pay up on our bet."

"I'm stocking up on rubber gloves and brushes for your year of furniture restoration. What else will you need? Paint stripper? Linseed oil? Wood glue?"

"Your entire worldview is going to crack apart."

He snorted.

"Anything else happen while I was asleep?"

"The house has been quiet."

"Good."

He looked at the house and frowned with worry. "I'd better go check on Eric, though. God only knows what mischief the ghosts may be trying on him."

"He doesn't spook easily, I'll say that much for him. He'll be okay with whatever goes on, as long as he gets it on tape."

"A cool head isn't a bad thing to have around. Keeps the rest of us from overreacting."

She took the comment personally. "I'll try to keep a better grip on myself."

He looked back at her in surprise. "What? Oh, hey, I wasn't talking about *you*. I meant myself." A pained grin curved his mouth. "You know. The heart attack thing."

"Oh! I'd almost forgotten about that."

"Brilliant of me to remind you," he grumbled.

Megan laughed and got into the van. A few minutes with Case, and she was feeling much better about the day. "I won't be gone more than an hour. Will that interfere with your plans? What *are* the plans, anyway?"

"I was counting on you and Eric to figure that out."

Megan looked back at the pickup. "He probably has another couple of hours of setting up. I'm sure he has something in mind for us after that. This place is a jackpot of paranormal activity, and he always has multiple things in mind for what he wants to do." Unfortunately, he didn't always share those plans with his companions.

"So we'll be busy tonight."

"I'm sure we will be."

She shut the door and started the van. Halfway down the drive, she stopped and stared up at the iron arch over the gate. Just what *did* that Latin motto say?

She grabbed a piece of paper and a pen off the floor and hopped out of the van.

"A problem?" Case called from back by the porte cochere.

"You haven't translated the coat-of-arms thingy, have you?"

"No."

"Okay." She walked up closer to the scrolled gate. The coat of arms had a shield with an X through it and was supported on either side by animals that could be bears or lions, something four-legged and snarling. Atop the shield was an eaglelike bird gripping a lump of something in one of its claws, a piece of vegetation in the other. Coal and timber? Mr. Smithson had made his fortune in those industries.

The motto was in an arch underneath the coat of

arms. Letter by letter, she copied it down: *Ingenio experior funera digna meo.*

Case walked up beside her. "Any idea what it might mean?"

"I can only guess. *Ingenio* sounds like 'ingenious.' I have no idea what *experior* might mean."

" 'Experience'?"

"Yeah, maybe. The rest sounds like 'funeral dignity me.' Our amateur translation leaves us with: 'Ingenious experience funeral dignity me.' "

"Doesn't sound too bad, sort of a 'dignity in death' theme. But I think we may have lost some of the finer points in translation."

"Hey, I never said I was a Latin scholar. Where's the branch library? I'll go see if I can get some help," she offered.

He gave her directions, and she drove off, feeling as if unseen presences were lifted from her shoulders the moment she passed beneath the gate.

TEN

"What *is* all this?" Case asked, surveying all the electronics covering the grand salon of the house. He'd been tearing out moldering lath and plaster upstairs, but curiosity about Eric's truck full of electronics had drawn him from his labor. Watching Eric amid the power cords, screens, and light-blinking boxes, Case felt as if he were walking into a mad scientist's lair.

"The rational applied to the irrational," Eric said, attaching connectors between a computer and a black box.

Megan's dislike of Eric had planted a seed of doubt in Case's mind. In high school, it was always the smartest and most marginalized boys who created explosions in the chemistry lab.

Eric bounced on the balls of his feet and began pointing around the room in proprietary glee. "EMF meters, infrared cameras, regular cameras, digital video camera, digital video camera with night vision, motion sensors, infrared thermal scanner, regular thermometers, digital audio recorder, computer, monitors, air ion counter, barometer, electromagnetic pulse generator, EM blaster, temporal lobe stimulator—"

"Whoa, slow down! EM blaster?"

Eric grinned proudly and hefted up a one-foot black cube with vertical handles on either side. A black cone protruded from the front, looking like a part from an old-fashioned movie camera. "One of my experiments. She's a beaut, isn't she?"

"What the hell does it do?"

"It produces an enormous burst of electromagnetic energy, aimed at whatever you wish."

"And what does that do?" Case asked with some trepidation, stepping out of the aim of the thing.

"Well, there are all these theories about active ghosts thriving on electromagnetic energy. My thinking is that if you give a ghost a blast of it, it might get strong enough to appear before everyone. We might finally get proof that they exist!"

The last thing Case wanted was for the ghosts to get stronger. "Are you sure that's a wise idea?"

"How could it not be? If the power of a ghost's manifestation was increased, we could capture evidence on our equipment that would leave no doubt

about their existence. And we'd get multiple wit-
nesses to the event. Think of it! We might have *repro-
ducible* evidence of the Other Side! It's the Holy Grail
of parapsychologists everywhere."

"I thought you were a skeptic," Case said, his heart
sinking. Was Eric as full of loony ideas as Megan?

"Oh, I am. Being a skeptic doesn't mean that you're
completely closed to the idea of something paranormal existing. It means that you want solid, irrefutable
proof that it's real. Unfortunately, no one's ever gotten
that."

"Why do you need Megan's help to get it?"

Eric gave a lopsided grin. "Can't find anything to
aim my equipment at without her. Active spirit presences being as rare as they are, it would be like going
hunting in the woods and firing randomly. Not a
good idea."

"I thought that even an 'active presence' could be
explained away. Electromagnetic forces working on
the brain, sleep states, all that."

"Ah, but that's where the EM blaster comes in,"
Eric said, stroking his hand over the black cone.
"When I set it off, if Megan goes nuts and you and I
have a couple of unrelated hallucinations, then
we'll know that the 'haunting' is not an active presence with its own identity. If the same ghost appears
in front of all of us, though, and if we can gather
physical evidence of its presence, then we're in
business!"

Case frowned at the blaster. "Is Megan in any danger from that?"

"Nah. It might give her a temporary freak-out, but that's all. It's not like she has a pacemaker."

"And if she did?"

"The blaster can scramble anything electrical. Blow a few circuits, maybe."

"Is this thing going to piss off my neighbors?"

"You mean, is it going to blow up their TVs?"

"Scramble cell phones. Turn on microwaves. Crash computers. Set off security systems. Kill cars."

Eric giggled. "Maybe."

"Christ." He scowled at the box. "You said that it was just a theory that it would make the ghosts stronger. What else might it do to them?"

"Well, it occurred to me that a blast of EM might feel to them like an electric shock does to us. So it *might* chase them away. Sort of cattle-prod them out of here."

"I like the sound of that."

"But either way, we should be able to get rid of the ghosts, if that's what's going on here. 'Cause if the blaster makes them stronger, then it's more likely we or Megan can communicate clearly with them and help them figure out that it's time to go."

"And if it's not ghosts? You *will* be looking for other explanations, won't you?"

"Yeah, of course. If we find something physically wrong with the house or the land it sits on, chances are it can be fixed."

"Good." Case's eye was caught by a battered yellow motorcycle helmet with wires dripping from its bottom. "And what's that?"

"That!" Eric picked it up, grinning. "This is my temporal lobe stimulator. The inspiration came from the work of Dr. Persinger, a neuroscientist up in Canada. He's been pioneering the study of what happens when you apply electromagnetic pulse patterns to the temporal lobes."

Case remembered Eric talking about Persinger at the conference. "Ah. The scientist who makes you see God."

"The helmet may provide access to even more than that. Look at this thing," he said, bringing it over to Case and showing him the inside of the helmet, either side of which was covered in metal bumps, wires trailing from them. "These are the electromagnets, which in turn will be hooked up to *this*"—he said, nudging a black box on the floor with his foot—"for power, and then that will be connected to my computer, where I adjust the intensity and the pattern of stimulation, depending on what results we're getting."

"You won't be getting any results," Megan said, stepping into the room. "I'm not using it!"

"I've refined it since you last used it. There won't be any problems this time," Eric said, undisturbed.

"I don't care what you've done to it," she said. "I'm not letting that thing anywhere near me."

"Oh, don't be stupid. It can't hurt you—any more than it hurt you last time, if you're honest about it."

Case put his hand on Megan's shoulder and felt her trembling.

"You think nothing happened last time?"

"You got freaked out. It was the fault of the helmet, but nothing serious happened. I mean, it's not like you were physically injured. It was like a bad drug trip, that's all."

Megan shook her head. "No, it was much more than that."

Case squeezed her shoulder, and she looked at him, her eyes wide. "How about you tell me what happened?" he asked.

She shuddered.

"Megan? Tell me what happened."

"The helmet gave her the wrong type of stimulation," Eric said. "She thought some sort of demon was attacking her."

"I didn't *think* it," Megan barked back.

"Tell me," Case repeated.

"A woman phoned SPIRIT, asking if we could come investigate her house. She said that her two little girls, ages eight and ten, were being tormented at night by something, something that she herself had seen as a dark shadow in the hallway at night, and once in the corner of the girls' room."

"First thing we did," Eric interrupted, "was make sure there wasn't a man living in the house, or even spending the nights. The woman hadn't been seeing anyone since her divorce three years earlier; there were no male visitors to the house. Also, the bedroom was on the second floor, and the windows were locked. We knew it wasn't a pedophile getting the girls.

"The woman was religious, though. Superstitious as well. Lots of junk around the house for 'good energy' and 'protective spirits.' I'm always suspicious of that sort; they're the most likely to interpret a bad dream as a visit from an evil spirit, or to think a ghost moved their car keys and that's why they can't find them. We went into the woman's house thinking that she was misguided and had transferred her fears to her daughters."

Megan broke in, "But the moment I set foot inside the house for our preliminary interview, I no longer thought the woman was a nut. It felt wrong. Bad. That doesn't always mean there's something sentient and evil in a house. A house can feel terrible just because of an awkward layout and not enough windows, a lack of natural light, a traffic flow that goes contrary to human instinct, too low a ceiling. These things make people unhappy. They feel caged and uneasy.

"But there was something in this house that I didn't like. It was a feeling of something large and dark pressing down on you. Watching you. Waiting for its chance at you. The woman was genuinely frightened. She begged us to clear the house of spir-

its for her daughters' sakes. She couldn't afford to
move, but staying in the house was destroying her
children. She didn't know what to do.

"I felt bad for her, but after that preliminary interview, I knew that I didn't want to go back." She smiled
wanly at Case. "Being able to sense the unseen
doesn't mean you're not afraid of it. I didn't know
what it was in that house—human or nonhuman—
but I did know that it would be attracted to me. If
there is a presence in a place, it goes to the person
best able to perceive it. It wants attention." She
paused. "I didn't want it anywhere near me. I refused
to go back."

"Which was unfair to that woman and her kids,"
Eric said. "I mean, if those kids could endure it, then
surely a grown woman with a talent for mediumship
could face it. It would have gone against everything
SPIRIT stands for not to try to help. I couldn't have
lived with myself."

Megan's face betrayed subtle signs of disgust. She
wasn't buying Eric's protestations of nobility.

"So, you talked Megan into going back," Case said
to Eric.

"Yeah. She has a generous heart. I knew she
wouldn't be able to live with herself if she didn't try to
help those kids."

Megan glowered.

Eric continued. "A few days later, our whole team
went back for a full-scale investigation. The woman

and her kids had gone to a friend's house for the night. This was going to be the first really good test we'd have of the helmet. In my enthusiasm, I made some adjustments and forgot to tell Megan."

"You deliberately didn't say anything." She looked at Case. "He knew that I wouldn't use it if I hadn't first tried out the changes in a safe environment."

"I didn't think anything bad would happen!"

"Anyway," Megan went on, "I was willing to use the helmet because I didn't—and still don't—have a very clear idea of how my abilities work. If the helmet was able to alter or magnify my abilities, then I might learn something about myself. I might learn something about just how real my abilities are."

"You *don't* think they're real?"

"I've never been a hundred percent convinced that I have contact with the Other Side. There's always a tiny part of me that follows Occam's razor."

"That the simplest solution is the correct one?"

She rocked her head from side to side. "That's almost it, but that translation misses an important nuance. Occam's razor says that you should employ no more assumptions, or entities, than necessary in looking for the solution to a question. For example, if you put a shallow dish of milk on the floor and the next morning it's empty, you'd be employing Occam's razor if you said that your cat drank it or that it evaporated, rather than claim that fairies drank it. Employing fairies in your solution requires adding an entity, or assuming that they exist, when you have no proof. Therefore, the other explanations are preferred.

"So, in my case, it makes the most sense to say that I'm imagining what I 'see.' Or even saying that I somehow 'pick up' details about a dead person *from the mind of someone living* makes a better explanation than that I somehow pick up details about a dead person *from a dead person himself.* That last explanation requires two assumptions: that the dead still have an existence, and that I can get in tune with it.

"I thought the helmet could somehow make the choice clearer. Was everything a hallucination, or was everything I saw real? I wanted to learn something about myself and wanted to learn something about the 'reality' of an existence beyond that which we see."

"We'd all tried using the helmet in neutral places," Eric broke in. "Testing it out, seeing what it could do. I didn't have any reason to think something would go wrong. Some people got a trippy feel from it, some got nothing, some people had an out-of-body experience. Megan usually just felt really relaxed."

"But that was when there were no entities around. It wasn't someplace where children were being terrorized. And those test runs had been at settings a quarter the strength of what you threw at me that night!"

"I've tried to explain to you a hundred times, I

thought it was just some minor tweaking I'd done—"

"Without warning me!"

"I didn't think anything was going to happen."

"Then why not tell me? Why didn't you run some baseline tests to be sure there wasn't something screwed up in your little invention, before sticking it on my head?"

"Because I was excited about the entity and wanted to get on with it, and I didn't think there'd be any problem."

Case looked with disapproval at Eric. He had been careless of Megan's well-being, and that wasn't how a man was supposed to behave toward any woman.

"What happened when you put the helmet on?" Case asked her.

"Nothing, at first. I was lying on a bed in the little girls' room, lights out, SPIRIT's night-vision and infrared cameras aimed at me while the rest of the crew watched the monitors in the kitchen. Everything was quiet. The helmet began its pulses, and I felt myself sinking into the same free-floating, relaxing oblivion as when I'd tried the helmet before."

"Oblivion?"

"An aware sort of oblivion. It was a loss of a sense of self or individual identity. As if your bodily sensations are no longer coming to a unified whole to be processed but instead are happening in scattered elsewheres. It becomes nearly impossible to concentrate. You just disperse into the void, even your emotions feeling distant. It's a little eerie but not at all unpleasant.

"But then Eric turned up the power. And the feeling of peaceful floating ended, as did any sense of who or where I was. Everything was washed away by a tidal wave of anger and terror—a violent rage seeking destruction, but at the same time shot through with lightning bolts of fear. Whatever it was, it wanted to hurt something. I felt like I was part of that horrific angry darkness for an eternity."

"It wasn't any more than a minute, though," Eric said. "She started screaming, and we shut it off. She got freaked out, was all. She wasn't hurt."

Megan was shaking her head. "It didn't stop. The entity, whatever it was, had gotten inside me. It didn't go away when the helmet was shut off. It was still there. In me."

Case felt a chill go down his neck. Megan's eyes were haunted as she looked up at him.

"That's impossible, Megan," Eric said. "It left a powerful imprint on your memory, that's all."

"No, that thing got inside me, like an infection. I could feel it. I didn't know what it wanted, and I didn't want to wait to find out."

"What did you do?" Case asked.

"I went home and holed up in my room and went through every paranormal book I had, looking for ways to get rid of it. Much like the Smithson sisters appear to have done here," Megan said, inclining her head toward the library across the hall. "But nothing I tried worked. No Hail Marys, no holy water, no blessings from any of five dozen cultures, no burning sage. And all the time, I felt it roiling around in me, as if assessing its new tool.

"Sometime well after dawn, I finally sat down in the center of my bed and put myself into a light trance state. One of my books suggested that dark entities cannot abide feelings of love and joy, so I concentrated on those emotions, thinking of my mother. How much she meant to me, how close we were, and how lucky I was to have her. And bit by bit, I felt the thing's presence shrinking.

"I must not have heard my mom knock on my door or call my name. But then I felt her hand on my shoulder, and all at once the dark presence was gone from me. I opened my eyes and saw Mom looking at me, worried.

"Everything seemed okay at first. I took a nap, then joined her at the shop, and we had lunch together. She didn't have much of an appetite at lunch and said she was tired. Remember when I told you about seeing the flicker?" she asked Case.

He nodded, having a sick feeling where this story was headed.

"I saw it then. A few months later, she finally went to the doctor for a checkup, and they found the cancer. They thought they'd been lucky and caught it early, but no matter what they did—surgery, chemotherapy, radiation—it never completely went away. It kept popping up again. It metastasized. And then it killed her."

Megan's voice grew hoarse. "She was healthy up until that night I brought the entity home with me."

Case shook his head, his heart wrenching. "Megan, no. You aren't blaming yourself for your mother's cancer, are you?"

Her eyes were filled with pain. "It saw that I cared about her, and it destroyed her."

The room fell silent. Megan sniffled.

Case wrapped his arms around her, her slender body surprisingly soft as she allowed herself to be gathered into his embrace. "There's no way this could be your fault," he said softly into her hair, which smelled of jasmine. "If you've been carrying that thought around in your head since your mother got sick, you've got to release it."

"How can you know that thing didn't do it to her?" Megan whispered, her voice creaking.

"I don't. But even if it did, it's still not your fault. It would be the entity's fault. Don't play the 'what if' game with yourself. You'll never win it." He could feel the soft swell of her breasts pressed against him, and his body started to react. *No! Think of Nixon, potatoes, the IRS long form!* "And as harsh as this sounds, do you think your mother would have preferred that the entity stay with you and kill you?"

Megan shook her head against his shoulder.

He had an almost unbearable urge to slide his hand down to her butt. He let it move down her back, over the ridge of her bra strap, and settle at the top of her hip. "She wouldn't even have wanted it to stay with those little girls, would she?"

"There should have been another way to get rid of it."

Case looked at Eric, who was watching them with an unreadable expression on his face. "Did you know all of this?"

Eric's face twitched. "Not really. And I don't think anything followed Megan home. Her wearing the helmet had nothing to do with her mom getting sick."

"Did the haunting at that house stop?" Megan moved against Case, and he gritted his teeth, arching his back to get his erection out of contact. *Don't think about her breasts, don't think about them, don't!*

Eric didn't respond, then tightened his lips and nodded. "But it could have been the placebo effect."

Case released Megan and picked up the helmet, holding it strategically in front of his crotch. "I don't blame Megan for not wanting to wear this. I wouldn't, either, in her shoes."

"But you can't judge by what happened then!" Eric cried. "This is a completely different helmet. The electromagnetic pulse patterns are different. I have deliberate patterns this time, instead of the random crap I was throwing at her last time. I can get precisely the effect I want now. I've tested the thing on my own brain a hundred times, and I'm okay!"

"You can't know what effect you'll get," Megan said. "What it does to you is not what it'll do to me."

"Look, I've tested it on dozens of people. That's how I figured out the patterns to begin with. I know how to create fear, euphoria, know how to trigger childhood memories. I can make someone feel like they're floating or like someone else is in the room with them. I even know how to give a guy a boner."

"What?" Case said.

"Yeah, there's one pattern that creates sexual arousal in people, male or female. It's not strong, but it's there. Makes you think about those people with their stories of alien abduction and all that probing, eh?"

"But what you don't know," Megan said, "is whether that machine opens up a doorway in the mind that something from the other side can step through."

"It hasn't happened to anyone else."

"Have you tried it on anyone who had a sixth sense?"

Eric set his jaw and glared at Megan. "A couple of the sensitives with SPIRIT tried it. Nothing happened."

"The 'sensitives.' Ah, yes. I remember the type," Megan said dryly, then arched an eyebrow at Case. "Highly imaginative, emotionally unstable people. If you think *I'm* bad, you need to meet one of these pieces of work."

Case looked at Eric. "Do you think they have any ability, these sensitives?"

Eric made a face. "Not really. It's fun to watch them freak themselves out sometimes, though." He laughed. "They make themselves sick with fear; you should see it when they faint. Only they're pretty careful about it, making sure they have a safe place to fall."

Case felt a twist of dislike for the man. Had Eric been similarly amused while Megan was screaming in terror? "I don't think she should use the helmet."

Megan shot him a look of gratitude and relief.

"You can't be serious. You can't let what happened two years ago eliminate useful tools for us today! Christ, we'd never have airplanes or medicine or anything if people gave up after the first disastrous failures. Failure is part of the process!"

"I think Megan's made a good case for not wanting to be your guinea pig."

"I'm past the guinea pig stage! I wasn't lying. I've used the thing on dozens of people, including myself. It's safe. It's way more controlled now. Besides, if we don't use it, how the hell are we going to find out what's haunting this place?"

"We'll do it the old-fashioned way," Megan said. "We'll have a regular séance and see what we discover. We'll see what the monitors pick up through the night. And if we don't pick up any information at all, then maybe—*maybe*—I'll consider using the helmet."

"Are you sure, Megan?" Case asked. "You don't have to do that."

"I think we'll get something tonight. But . . ." She trailed off. She sighed. "As much as I hate to admit it, it *isn't* fair to shut off a possibility just because of one bad experience. If we don't get anywhere without it, maybe we'll have to try using it."

"I'll use it myself before I let you put it on," Case said.

"Would you?" she said in obvious relief.

"Oh, so you'll trust it if he uses it, but not me?" Eric complained.

Megan shot Eric a look. "Do you blame me?"

He stared at her a minute, then smiled with his mouth only, his eyes flatly on Megan. "Nah, I don't blame you. I have to earn your trust after what I did. I'm just glad you're giving me the chance."

Megan opened her mouth as if to speak but then shook her head and said nothing.

Case clapped his hands together to break the tension. "So, the plan is for a séance tonight?" he asked lightly. "I'm suddenly imagining old aunties wearing costume jewelry and conjuring ectoplasm."

Megan laughed. "No ectoplasm here. I'll put myself into a light trance, and you'll ask the 'spirits'— if there are any—questions that they might answer to me."

"And this works?" he asked doubtfully.

"Who knows? You've heard all my doubts already,

but if I'm going to get my furniture, I'm going to have to come up with something, aren't I?"

"Furniture?" Eric interrupted.

Megan looked over her shoulder at Eric with a saucy, taunting flip of her hair. "Case will give me twenty pieces of furniture if I'm the key to making his house habitable, not you."

"And all I'm getting out of this is free meals."

"It's a bet," Case clarified. "If she loses, she has to clean and restore all the furniture in the house."

Eric laughed. "I'll bet you're hoping I do a good job. So, where are the hot spots in this place? I should set up cameras there, and we're going to want to use one of them for the séance."

"The upstairs hall at the north end of the T seems to be one." Case looked at Megan for confirmation.

She nodded. "But I haven't been all through the house yet. There might be others. Looks like it's time for an expedition."

Eric gathered a few pieces of equipment, and the three of them left the grand salon. Case led the way upstairs, the staircases growing progressively narrower as they went up.

"The most water damage was up here," Case said as they reached the servants' floor with its low ceilings.

Eric pointed a handheld electric thermometer down the wall-less hallway of studs, his eyes on the digital display. "I'm not getting any cold spots." A moment with another instrument, and he declared,

"No energy fluctuations in the electromagnetometer." He whacked its side with the palm of his hand. "The power's going!"

Megan laughed softly. "You sound like Scottie on *Star Trek*. 'I'm not getting' any readin's, cap'n! The warp drive's down!' " she said in a bad Scottish accent. " 'We've got no ghoosts!'"

Case chuckled, and even Eric cracked a smile. They took a quick tour of the empty floor, then Case opened the door to the attic stairs.

As with the rest of this part of the house, he'd had to remove the rotted lath and plaster in the stairwell. "I had to replace half the floor due to rot, but it's safe now," he explained as he flipped a switch. Bare fluorescent bulbs down the length of the space flickered on. "I shoved all the furniture and trunks over to the other side while I did it. The water storage tank, for runoff from the roofs, is back there in the corner." He pointed beyond the pile of furniture.

"Ohhhh," Megan warbled as her gaze fell on the furniture. She made a beeline for the dusty mass. Her hands hovered over a chair and then a dresser, as if not knowing where to start. She looked back at him, hope in her eyes. "May I?"

"Be my guest."

"Did you have any encounters up here while you were repairing the roof and floor?" Eric asked, walking slowly down the attic space, pointing his instruments at nooks and crannies. He looked in puzzlement at the electromagnetometer. "Huh. Working now."

"No encounters I could swear to," Case said, following Eric's slow exploration. Behind them, Megan shifted furniture and made soft sounds of delight, talking excitedly to herself. Case felt as if he'd just given her a well-chosen birthday present.

"What type of stuff happened?"

"Electrical problems for no apparent reason," he said, looking pointedly at Eric's misbehaving device. "Tools disappearing and then reappearing elsewhere. Nothing that couldn't happen in normal circumstances due to shorts and a lapse of attention or memory."

"But you don't think that's what it was."

"I'm not careless with my work."

Eric glanced at him.

"Ever hear any noises up here?" Eric asked.

"Footsteps and doors closing. But the footsteps were probably the crows on the roof. The wood amplifies the sound."

"And the doors could be drafts. Gotcha." Eric raised his digital camera and snapped off a few shots of the empty half of the attic. He turned and took a step closer to Case and lowered his voice. "You know, there are some things you should know about Megan."

Case narrowed his eyes, suspicion roused. "Oh? Like what?"

"Well, she puts on a good act of being an innocent victim, but—"

"Case! Come look at this!" Megan cried out.

They both turned. Megan had dragged a small occasional table away from the pile and was kneeling beside it with a wide grin on her face.

Case turned back to Eric, his curiosity about what Eric had been about to say overwhelmed by distrust of his motivations. His own voice low, Case leaned forward and warned him, "Watch what you say about Megan, Eric. I judge people on their actions, not on hearsay."

"Case!" Megan implored.

"Coming!" He looked back at Eric. "Are we clear?"

Eric touched his brow in mock salute. "Crystal. And I trust you'll give me the same benefit of judgment."

Case nodded curtly and went to join Megan. "What have you found?" he asked, trying to set aside the ill temper that Eric's words had stirred up.

"All sorts of stuff! The Smithsons must have shipped a lot of furniture from back east at some point. This table, it's from the 1700s. It's got some minor damage, but if I'm right about it, it could bring ten or twenty thousand at auction."

"For *that?*"

Megan laughed. "That's probably what the Smithsons thought when they put it up here to make room for all their spiffy new Victorian furniture."

Case looked at the pile. "Good Lord. That little table could pay for new cabinets in my kitchen."

Megan's glee faded. "I wouldn't feel right about taking this as one of my twenty pieces."

He looked at her in surprise. "No, the table's fair game, if you win."

"Really?" Megan ran her hand slowly over the carved leg of the table. "It's beautiful, but jeez, I think of what ten or twenty thousand could do for me and the shop . . . . You wouldn't think that a tiny table could matter so much in a person's life, would you? But it'll change everything."

"How?"

"I want to buy the building my shop is in. I have some money saved for a down payment but not nearly enough."

Case's stomach turned. "How long have you been saving up?"

"Mom and I together started saving about eight years ago. We knew the owner was getting old and would sell sooner or later. The building's actually on the market now, and I've been worried sick that someone would buy it before I could raise the money."

Case closed his eyes for a long moment. He'd taken a couple hours to talk to the Realtor, review the preliminary financial information, and put in an offer on the building yesterday. It was a good deal in an improving neighborhood, and he'd needed to act fast to beat out the three other potential buyers sniffing around. "Why didn't you get a loan on your house for the down payment?"

"It would have stretched me too thin. And I thought I had more time. But now, if I win the bet, I can get enough money from the furniture for the down payment. Thank God there are people out there willing to pay obscene amounts of money for side tables!"

Maybe he didn't have to tell her about the offer. She wasn't going to win the bet, anyway. There was always the chance his offer would be refused, too, or that the deal would fall through for other reasons. Telling her about it now would piss her off for no reason.

Business was business. The building was a good investment, and he wouldn't let her unrealistic hopes of owning it herself stop him from buying it.

"Maybe there's more like it in the pile." She grinned. "It's like a treasure hunt, isn't it? But so far, the only other thing that intrigues me," she said, going over to the pile and tugging a trunk away from the other furniture, "is this thing. It's hard to resist a locked box."

"We could break it open," he said without enthusiasm. The fun had gone out of this game.

"Break the lock? No! I have a drawer full of old keys in my shop; something in there ought to open this. I could probably open any locked piece of furniture in the house, come to think of it."

"There's nothing up here, far as I can tell," Eric

said, joining them. He noticed the trunk. "What did you find in there?"

"Nothing yet," Megan said, and got up off the ground, brushing fine sawdust off her knees. She didn't want to include Eric in the delight of discovery she was enjoying with Case.

She immediately felt bad for the selfish thought. Maybe she was being too hard on Eric. She glanced at him with his sloppy clothes on his marshmallow frame. He hadn't ever been malicious toward her, after all. He was just . . . Eric, lost in his own obsessive world, and even less skilled than she at dealing with people. "Shall we continue the tour?" she asked brightly, giving Eric a quick smile. They'd be working together, and his horrible helmet might help her win the furniture.

She still didn't feel quite right about taking the colonial table. Maybe she and Case could split the profits. She smiled at the thought and followed Case back down the stairs.

ELEVEN

"I've seen everything on this floor except for that one room," Megan said, eyeing the far end of the corridor with a trickle of apprehension. She didn't want to see Ol' Hollow Eyes again.

"Then let's go visit it," Eric said. "I went in all those rooms earlier, and there wasn't any activity, but maybe it will be different with you present."

"Delightful."

Case put his hand on her shoulder, giving it a squeeze. She turned her head and smiled at him. It was good to have him there; it seemed that nothing would be able to hurt her.

The master suite was just as she remembered, only the strong emotions she'd gotten from it before were muted now. It was often that way for her: the first impression of an object or space was strong, but, like a noise she'd grown accustomed to, the sense of a thing faded into the background on subsequent encounters.

The bedroom with the hideous gold carpet told her nothing new, either.

Somehow she'd become the leader in their small expedition, and she found herself standing in front of the one door she hadn't opened before, Case and Eric waiting behind her.

"This is when the shadow appeared at the end of the hall," she said.

Eric jerked a glance over his shoulder, then, seeing Megan watching him, pulled himself up a little straighter and turned, aiming one of his meters down the hall. A moment later, he said, "I'm not reading anything."

"Small mercies," Case murmured.

"Amen," Megan agreed under her breath. She put her hand on the knob but was reluctant to turn it. The room behind the door had taken on unknown horrors in her imagination, all the worse for her not having been brave enough to go into it on her first tour of the house.

It wasn't going to get less scary for standing there, though, she grumbled to herself, and twisted on the knob.

It refused to turn.

A moment of surprise went through her, then relief. She didn't have to go in!

She twisted again and rattled the knob, just to be sure. "It's locked."

"It can't be," Case said.

Megan stepped aside, confident.

Case put his hand to the knob, twisted, and then a clear click was heard and the door swung open. "See? Just a little sticky."

Megan frowned, then cast a glance at Eric. He raised a brow at her. They'd come across this type of thing before, and it wasn't always a sticky latch at fault.

Megan followed Case into the room. It was nothing like the kitsch monstrosity next door. It was like stepping back into time, to the world of a hundred years ago.

The walls were covered in faded paper of violets and ribbons. The wood floors were graced with a single large area rug, moth-eaten now. The bed, wardrobe, washstand, and nightstand were all of heavy dark wood, carved with stylized floral patterns. Several framed charcoal drawings and watercolors adorned the walls.

"It's charming!" Megan said.

"And undamaged except for the usual insect and rodent problems," Case said. "I saw no reason to clear it out. None of the other rooms was as nice."

Megan walked over to the wall and leaned close to the largest of the pictures. The dirt of years obscured the glass surface, making tantalizingly vague the features of a male face drawn in charcoal. She reached up and rubbed the side of her hand against the grit.

A wave of sexual desire washed over her. She sucked in a breath and staggered back.

"Megan?" Case said, putting his hand on her shoulder.

His touch was like a bolt of lightning to a summer field, setting her on fire and burning out all restraint. She turned and threw herself at him, her arms wrapping around his neck, her mouth seeking his.

Case staggered under her assault, losing his balance and falling back onto the ancient mattress of the bed. Megan stayed on top of him, her fingers digging into his hair, her body grinding against his. He was too stunned to protest, and too stunned to enjoy it for a moment. But then his body took over, his hands sliding down to cup her buttocks and pull her against his firm arousal.

Her lips took hungry possession of his, her tongue delving deep as she made whimpering moans of frustrated desire. Her kisses trailed down his neck to the opening of his shirt, and she parted her legs over his thigh, rubbing her sex against him.

"For God's sake, get a room," Eric said.

The words brought Case back to the brink of sanity. Eric was standing three feet away, watching them with his arms crossed.

What the hell?

Megan moaned again and slid her hand down the front of his pants.

Case grabbed her by the shoulders and lifted her off him. "Megan! Snap out of it!"

Her pupils were wide black pools of desire, blank of awareness. She puckered and made kissing noises, stretching toward him.

Eric bent down and examined her face. "She's in a trance."

"Get her out of it!"

Eric shrugged and slapped her.

"What the f—!" Case cried, even as Megan twisted in his hold and sent her foot flying into Eric's gut.

Eric doubled over and fell to the floor, gasping.

Megan's body relaxed in Case's hold. He watched as consciousness flooded back, her eyes widening as she took in her position. She scrambled off him, and he sat up.

"What happened?" Megan asked, her voice shaking. She touched her fingertips lightly to her lips, as if wondering what she still felt upon them.

"You went freaking *insane!*" Eric gasped from the floor.

"Case, did you hit him?"

"You don't remember?"

She shook her head, but then her head stilled and her eyes went wide, her face turning scarlet. "Oh."

"You *do* remember."

She leaned away from him. "I'm so sorry! I wasn't

in my right mind. I never would have jumped on you like that if I had been."

"I'm not complaining."

Megan put her hands over her face, mortified.

"What about me?" Eric asked from the floor, sitting up and holding his gut. "I think you rearranged my internal organs."

"Sorry."

Eric rolled his eyes and got to his feet. "It was that picture that set you off." He picked up one of his fallen instruments and aimed it at the picture. He shook his head, plainly not getting any readings. "Useless piece of . . ." he muttered, then grabbed the hem of his T-shirt and rubbed it on the picture glass. He stood back to take in his handiwork. "Decent-looking guy, if a little smarmy."

Megan and Case got off the bed and moved beside Eric. Megan was careful not to look at Case, her embarrassment still fresh.

Attraction again stirred in Megan as she looked at the man in the drawing, but along with it was instinctive mistrust. The face was that of a young man, early twenties perhaps, his hair parted on the side and plastered into place with macassar oil or something similar, one rakish curl draped over his left brow. The artist had captured an insouciance to his appearance, his lips faintly quirked, his lively dark eyes a little too familiar with the viewer.

"I wouldn't trust him as far as I could kick him,"

Case said darkly. "I'd keep one hand on my wallet, too."

"Oh, I don't know," Megan said. "I could think of worse ways to spend an evening than sitting on a balcony, having him whisper sweet nothings into my ear."

Case scowled, and she laughed.

"Frat boy," Eric said, frowning with dislike at the picture.

Megan shook her head. "If this picture were in my shop, it would sell to the first woman through the door."

"And her husband would return it the next morning," Case said.

"I suppose it's a credit to the artist's skill that we're all having such a strong reaction," she said. "I mean, separate from *my* reaction. That was something else." She leaned closer, looking for any hint of a signature. "Not signed." She stepped back and examined the other pictures on the walls. "Did you find any art supplies in the house?" she asked Case.

"No. But that doesn't mean there aren't some shoved into a desk or trunk somewhere."

"Or maybe she gave up art," Megan mused.

"You think one of the sisters drew it?"

Megan nodded. "I think all this art is hers. If these two rooms belonged to the Smithson sisters, then what an opposite pair they must have been. One with artistic talent, taste, and passion; the other tasteless but open to modern life, willing to buy a record player and put some wall-to-wall carpet on her cold floor."

"So, what's the story?" Eric asked. "Sister One is in love, gets jilted, goes insane, and refuses to admit that time is moving on. Sister Two sacrifices her own life to take care of nutball Sister One, and they live here miserably ever after. When Sister One finally bites it thirty years ago, her dead spirit still can't bear to leave—after all, her lover might return—and thus the haunting."

"It doesn't explain that library full of paranormal how-to books," Megan said. "Not unless they were trying to conjure the spirit of the lover, if he was dead. Besides, it's just as possible that the haunting has to do with the sisters' mother or father, or someone else entirely. There could also be more than one spirit."

"You're sure we're dealing with a some*one* and not some*thing*?" Case asked.

Megan paused. "It *feels* human. I don't have much to base that on, but yeah, I'd bet this was something human going on, whether in our own minds or a real ghost." She looked around the room. "I really expected to encounter something more direct by now. Any other places we haven't seen?"

"Just the cellars."

"Oh, delightful."

"Megan doesn't like cellars and basements," Eric clarified.

"I'd like to know who does." Megan sniffed. "Low

ceilings, dark, cold, damp, full of rodents and spiders—why would I like them? They're like dungeons. Dank, miserable dungeons." She cast a woeful look at Case.

He grinned. "These aren't so bad." He led them out of the bedroom and to the central staircase. "They're rather pleasant for Victorian cellars. There was a lot of garbage down there when I bought the place, and raccoons had been living in it all—and God knows what else—but I had one of my crews clean it all out, and they've been largely wildlife-free ever since."

"Largely?"

"Spiders can't help liking cool, damp, dark places."

Eric chimed in, "That's why you've got to check under the toilet seat before you sit down."

Megan groaned.

"Are you really afraid of spiders?" Case asked.

"It depends on whether they're running toward me or away from me."

"You ever find one in your sheets?" Eric asked. "I did once. One of those big fat blackish-brown ones. Now I check between my sheets before I put my feet down to the bottom of the bed. It is *not* nice to feel those quick little legs running over your belly in the middle of the night."

"Will you *stop* it?" Megan cried.

"Look, it's an old house, you know the place is crawling with them—"

"Eric, *enough,*" Case ordered, with the sternness of a grade-school teacher. "Megan, in the course of my work, I've stuck my head into more cobwebs and spider nests than you will ever see in your life, and I've never been bitten. You've got nothing to worry about here. All my tearing down of walls has driven them outside for the summer. The crows have probably eaten every last one of them."

"I'll try to keep that in mind. And speaking of crows or whatever bird is on that arch over your gate," she said as they reached the bottom of the stairs and made their way down the hall toward the kitchen, "I found out what that motto means."

"Motto?" Eric asked.

"Above the gate," Megan explained. "It's part of the family crest."

"What does it say?" Case asked, stopping.

Megan didn't answer for a moment, her attention captivated by his mouth. Had she really been kissing him only a few minutes ago? Her body flushed in response to the thought, her loins feeling the pressure of his leg against her.

Megan blinked and shifted her gaze. "The librarian at the local branch called a friend who knew Latin to be sure, but as far as we could tell, it translates as 'I experience the end worthy of my nature.'"

Case and Eric were silent, staring at her.

"Basically, it means 'I get what I deserve' or 'I earn my final fate.' "

"That's pretty dour," Case said. "It sounds like Smithson was a puritanical sort."

"Or he thought he deserved all his riches both on this plane and the next, because he was a good guy. It really could be read as either, though it's hard to take the cheerful view when you're standing in a haunted house."

"He was probably a control freak," Eric said. "Bet he read the Bible to his daughters every night, warning them of eternal damnation if they masturbated."

Megan rolled her eyes. "You've got a seriously twisted mind, do you know that?"

Eric was unfazed. "Hey, the girls never left home. Bet he wouldn't let them. Maybe *he's* one of the ghosts."

Megan hated to admit it, but the idea wasn't without merit. "It might explain the library. Maybe they were trying to get his spirit out of the house. Although why they wouldn't just sell the place after he died, I don't know."

"Maybe that would mean their father had won," Case said. "It might have been a battle of wills."

Megan looked at him, wondering what he might know of such battles, firsthand. Then she shook her head. "We don't have enough information. I've got to get those keys from my shop and start opening up desks and trunks."

They went through the kitchen to a small hallway with doors leading outside, to storage rooms, servant stairs, and the cellars. Case plugged in another string of construction lights, and the stairway lit up, the lights leading the way down.

Megan sighed silently and followed Case down the stairs. As they descended, a cold tingling began in Megan's feet, rising slowly up her legs and into her torso. Puzzled, she traced its progress up her body. She wasn't *aware* of being frightened, but was she? She staggered when she reached the bottom of the stairs, the cold tingling creeping up her neck and filling her head, disorienting her.

"Megan?" Case said, gently grabbing her arm and steadying her.

She blinked, the brick-walled room of the dim cellar swimming around her. The sensation began to frighten her. "I don't feel so good."

"Told you she was afraid of cellars," Eric said, his voice sounding as if it came from the other end of a tin tunnel.

Megan felt her knees sag. Shadows moved in the corners of the room, her vision tilting the world sideways. She felt as if she were sliding off its edge into an abyss and grabbed Case for support. Fear shot up her spine.

"Megan!"

"Slipping . . ." she gurgled, and the edges of her vision began to go black.

She was vaguely aware of being scooped up into Case's arms and carried quickly back up the stairs, Eric's questioning voice following them upward.

Her vision began to clear and the racing of her heart to slow as they reached the kitchen and Case laid her on the floor. She was like a drowning person returned suddenly to land, the danger past. She blinked in surprise and started to sit up.

Case gently held her down. "No, you almost fainted. Keep down for a minute."

She looked up into his worried eyes, and the last of her fear ebbed away, replaced by warmth and a feeling of safety. She smiled, hoping to soothe his worries. "It was a heart attack, I tell you."

A smile twitched at the corner of his mouth, the concern smoothing from his brow. "How are you feeling?"

"Fine." She sat up, and he sat back on his heels.

"What happened down there?" he asked.

She frowned. "I don't know. There was no feeling of a presence. It was just . . ." She shook her head. "I don't know. Is Eric still down there?"

"Hasn't come up." He looked back over his shoulder, toward the doorway. "I'd better check on him."

Megan waited while he went through the door. She heard him call out to Eric and receive an affirmative reply. A moment later, Case reappeared.

"He's fine."

"None of your work crews ever had a problem down there?"

He shook his head. "Not to my knowledge. They

didn't *like* it down there, but that's normal when you have raccoon nests and rat droppings to deal with."

With Case's help, Megan got back up onto her feet. Curiosity plucked at her, overwhelming her uneasiness. "Let's give it another look, shall we?"

His brows rose in surprise. "That's not wise, is it?"

It probably wasn't, but she wasn't going to leave the mystery unexamined and Case thinking she was a fainting sissy. "It shouldn't strike me so hard the second time. And you can always rush me to safety, right?"

"I don't think—"

She moved past him, squaring her jaw. "This house has too many mysteries. I'm here to solve them, not to faint."

Case made low grumbling noises but led the way back to the stairs. She followed him down, being careful to hold tight to the handrail. The tingling sensation started again but with less force, and she did her best to block it from her awareness, like deliberately ignoring an itch or an ache.

"You okay?" Case asked as she reached the bottom of the stairs.

"Never better."

"Mm. That doesn't say much for what qualifies as good in your book."

"Megan, look at this!" Eric said before she could reply. He came over to join them, holding his EMF meter out so she could see it. "It's going crazy!"

Megan saw the needle bouncing between the middle zone and its top limit.

"Something is definitely going on here!"

Case looked at the meter. "What's it mean?"

"I don't know what it means," Eric said, breaking away from them to take photos of the empty cellar. "It could mean we're surrounded by spirits at this moment."

"I don't feel them," Megan said.

"Or it could mean that there's something about this room that encourages their existence. That feeds them."

"But what?" Megan said, looking around. Floors, walls, and ceiling were brick, and a wide archway in the far wall opened into another space. Massive wood beams spanned the low ceiling, small windows were set high in the walls, and a manhole-sized drain was set in the center of the floor, the bricks sloped toward it. Megan went to the arch and peered into the next room. It looked identical to the first one, only with no drain in the floor. The lights ended just past the doorway, but she could see another arch in the shadows, indicating yet another brick chamber beyond.

Eric joined her at the arch. "The readings aren't half so strong in that room, or the one beyond."

"Huh." Megan turned back to the room and looked at the drain cover. "Is that a sump?"

Case went to the drain, bouncing the edge of it

with his foot and making a metal-on-metal clanging. "Either a sump or a drain. I haven't found the outlet to it yet, but it probably comes out somewhere down the slope of the backyard, in that mess of a garden."

"Outdoors? It looks big enough that someone could get into the house that way."

He shook his head. "The outlet drain is probably much smaller. You probably couldn't get anything bigger than a dachshund through it."

Megan came over to the drain and stood beside it, looking down. A cold, damp draft came up out it, smelling faintly of earth and rock. The lights dangling from the ceiling reflected off the metal, leaving the hole itself lost in blackness. Megan was about to dig her fingers into the grate and lift it out of its place, but then she remembered spiders and dark, damp places.

"What is it about this room?" she mused aloud.

Eric said, "There must be something about the surrounding rock, maybe a streak of magnetized iron. Or it could be specific stresses in the earth. I believe Queen Anne Hill sits on a fault line."

"If all it took was a fault line to cause this type of thing, the entire West Coast would be haunted," Case said.

"Whatever the reason for the high EMF readings, this is obviously a good place to set up some remote cameras to see what happens at night," said Megan.

"Good place for a séance, too," Eric said.

Megan's stomach sank a few inches. "I'd really rather not . . ."

"Hey, you said it yourself. This is the place where something might happen."

Megan felt Case's hand on her shoulder. "She wouldn't feel comfortable down here," he said. "Would you, Megan?"

She shook her head, grateful for the support. Of course, Eric was right that this would be a terrific spot, ripe with the potential for contact with spirits, but her whole inner self revolted at the idea of making herself vulnerable in such a place as this. "I wouldn't be able to relax."

"Christ," Eric swore. "We'll be here five years if we have to wait for you to relax and feel *comfortable* before we can get anything done! There's so much friggin' potential all around here, but I'm being held back from it."

"I thought you wanted me to trust you," Megan said, her voice quiet. "I thought you were going to put people above your experiments."

Eric glared at her, his nostrils flaring, then he puffed out a breath and let his shoulders sag. A smarmy smile stretched across his mouth. "Of course. Sorry. Thanks for the reminder."

"Why don't we have the séance in one of the bedrooms obviously used by the Smithson family?" she suggested. "Perhaps the master suite—go right to the head of the family and see what we can see."

Eric pretended to fiddle with his equipment, not meeting her gaze. "Sure, whatever you want. You're the medium." His lower lip protruded.

Megan held her exasperation in check and turned to Case. "That sound all right to you?"

"Yup. Are we doing it now?"

Megan glanced at the high cellar windows, noting that the daylight was beginning to fade. "It's better to wait until after dark. Maybe we should have dinner first." She started for the stairs.

They emerged back into the kitchen. Realizing she was getting hungry, Megan headed for her stash of groceries and got out the ingredients for a taco salad.

Case pulled Tupperware containers of curry and rice out of the refrigerator. He popped the top off the curry, looked in at the glop, then looked at Megan's fresh, crisp ingredients with longing.

Eric sulked into the room. Case offered him curry.

"Is it vegetarian?"

"No."

"I'll pick out the meat." Eric plopped himself down in a chair.

"So, what is it about the dark that brings out the ghosts?" Case asked, getting out plates and sticking the curry and rice into the microwave.

Eric leaned back on the back legs of his chair, his hands folded behind his head. "It goes with my theories about electromagnetic energy, if you think about it," he pontificated. "The sun emits EM radiation in a wide range of frequencies, and I think there are some of them that cause interference with ghosts, just like sunspot activity can cause interference with radio signals. Put the sun on the other side of the earth, like at night, and your EM interference goes way, way down. Now, if I just knew which frequencies caused interference and which boosted the signal, so to speak, we'd be in business with my EM blaster."

Megan shrugged one shoulder. "I'm sure Eric's theory is part of it, but I doubt it's the whole story. As far as my own role as a medium, I think nighttime is better because there are fewer distractions. I can focus better. And circadian rhythms might help: when we're falling asleep, our bodies stop sending as much information about our environment to our brains, and our brains themselves go into a theta brain-wave pattern before descending all the way to delta for sleep." She rinsed lettuce and set it on paper towels to dry, then turned toward Case. "It's the theta pattern that gives you active dreaming. You also get there when you're doing something repetitious like driving on the freeway. There's a noncritical free flow of ideas, a lot like what hypnosis does. And for me, it's easier to intentionally get myself into that state at night."

"So, you're more or less dreaming during a séance."

"More *and* less. I'm more self-aware, but my memory doesn't function quite right. You know how you wake up in the morning with a dream crystal-clear in your mind, and then a few seconds later it's totally gone? It's like that for me when I go into a trance. That's why I need other people to ask questions, take notes, and so on."

"Or record it," Eric said. "I'm just waiting for the day I get a video recording of Megan in a trance and see a ghost standing right beside her, whispering into her ear. Can you imagine?"

Megan shuddered. "I don't think I'd like that."

Case looked at her in surprise. "Why not?"

"If I see them, I want to see them while it's happening. It's too freaky to think of a ghost standing right beside you, and you never saw it, but the camera did."

"Megan likes the lights on," Eric said, a leer in his voice.

Megan ground her teeth.

"Yes, I've already established that," Case said.

Megan raised a brow, but he just raised one back. She shook her head and smiled, not sure if he'd meant that as a double entendre.

Eric was scowling at Case, not sure himself what was going on.

Megan tucked her chin down and sliced a tomato, a smile on her lips.

TWELVE

Had she really been so confident only two hours earlier? Megan wondered as she sat in the dark master suite, with Case and Eric somewhere off in the shadows. She could hear them breathing, could hear Eric fiddling with recording equipment, yet the dark space between her and any other living human was becoming a chasm in her mind, filled with nameless monsters.

The darkness took on an almost physical thickness, tingling against her skin, breathing on her, exploring her face. Reaching out to touch her with its long-fingered claws.

Eric belched. " 'Scuze."

"You're not helping!" Megan barked.

"Hey, it's a sign of appreciation in some cultures."

"Not ours."

"Calm down. You need to concentrate."

"Okay. Time to get serious." She took a deep breath and closed her eyes against the darkness. She used a visual script to get into a trance. She imagined herself sinking slowly to the bottom of crystal-blue tropical waters, needing no air, the sunlight above her darkening with the water. When her feet hit sand at the bottom, she walked through an imaginary black cave in a reef, and when she came out the other side, she was *on the Other Side.*

Or at least, that's the way it usually worked. Usually, she came out of the cave into a charcoal void through which images, sounds, and emotions would appear to her in a confusing rush with occasional moments of clarity. The closest thing she'd ever heard to it was Tibetan Buddhism's Bardo, the hallucinatory place one visits after death and before rebirth. It could be a frightening experience, making her feel that she was without identity or an existence of her own, lost and drifting in chaos. While there, she always tried to keep one part of herself centered on who she was in her own life.

This time, she came out to a gray nothingness where all the spirits seemed to have gone on vacation. There were a few glimmerings of distant movement, a few whispers of sound and emotion, but basically the place was deserted.

A few long, silent minutes passed, and she realized she wasn't getting anything.

Perhaps their laughter had spoiled the ghostly mood. Or maybe she was clinging too tightly to reality, afraid to let go and experience whatever was there for her in the house.

Eric shifted in his seat, the sound distracting her more than it should. She was too aware of both men in the room, too aware of their expectations that she perform.

If she *didn't* get something, it would mean wearing that evil helmet next time. She took another deep breath and concentrated on the charcoal void.

Minutes passed.

There were still movements and sounds in the distance but nothing she could make out. And then, softly but distinctly, she heard the sound of weeping.

"Someone's crying," Megan whispered. "A woman."

"What's her name?" Eric asked.

Megan let the question flow through her, knowing it was easier to remain in the trance if she channeled questions instead of composing them. She rephrased Eric's words in her mind: *What's your name?*

"Te . . . Te . . ." Megan said, searching for the sound. It came to her as if heard through a wall, the syllables barely audible. Usually, she heard sounds much more clearly; this time, it was as if something were interfering with their communication. It was like trying to yell to someone at the other end of a football field. "Something that begins with the letter *T.*" She paused, listening carefully. "Theresa?"

"Why is she crying?" Eric asked.

Megan saw a brief, distant flash of what looked like a broken window, plastic taped over it. A wall with a square hole, the pipes showing. A gutter half torn off the roof. "Her house is falling apart."

Case made a sound.

"Is it this house?" Eric asked.

"No, I don't think so."

"Why is she here?"

Megan asked it, *Why are you here?* It took a few moments to get a response. Again, it was unusually hard to decipher, the image faint, the sense of it brief. "I think she's showing me a hammer, an old hammer with a red wooden handle and a wedge-shaped top."

"Christ," Case said under his breath, his voice shaky. "I think it's my mom. That's the hammer I made for her in shop class when I was thirteen."

The moment he said the words, a flood of warmth filled Megan, the love so strong that it brought tears to her eyes. That, at least, came through loud and clear. She nodded, then remembered that Case couldn't see her in the dark. "Yes. She loves you very much."

"Does she have a message for Case?" Eric asked.

The answer came in a spoken sentence that Megan could not decipher. *Again?* she silently asked. The sounds came a second time, and then a third. "You couldn't . . ." Megan made out. "You shouldn't have . . . something." She listened again. "You shouldn't have tried to fix it."

"Does that make any sense to you?" Eric asked Case.

"I don't know. Not really." Case shifted again in his chair, and when he spoke, there was a crack in his voice. "Megan, is my mom . . . is she okay?"

"I think she's fine. And she's saying it again. 'You shouldn't have tried to fix it.' She seems to really want you to know that. And now she's fading, she's pulling away . . ."

There was quiet in the room, and quiet in the charcoal void.

This was the strangest séance she'd ever attempted. She'd never had such a lack of response before. It was as if she were isolated there, as if no spirits could get to her.

Long minutes passed. Megan felt herself pulling out of the trance, and as she did so, her memories of it started to fragment. She could still see pieces, but she had to struggle to repeat them in her mind, trying to lock them into her memory as she emerged into full consciousness.

"I'm done," Megan said, and opened her eyes.

"Is that a message?" Case asked.

She laughed. "No, that's just me." She reviewed in her mind what she had cemented as well as she could into memory. "This didn't work very well, did it? They couldn't get to us?"

"Well, obviously, they *can* get to us, given what you two have said goes on in this house," Eric said.

"There was activity until Eric arrived," Case pointed out. "Do you think it could have something to do with all the equipment?"

Eric answered. "It does seem sometimes that all activity stops when a SPIRIT crew arrives to document events, but I always assumed that was because the people in the 'haunted' house were distracted and not in the frame of mind to let their imaginations run away with them."

"That can't be the case here," Megan said. "Not with what I've heard and seen. Maybe it *is* something about the equipment. Maybe it's sucking too much power?"

Case moved, and a moment later, a construction light on a tripod went on. Megan blinked against it, strangely surprised to find herself in the stark master suite. Everything looked so solid and plain in the artificial light, as opposed to the richer appearance it had held in her imagination while the lights were out.

"So, what we have are more questions," Eric said. "Case, why do you think your mother thought it was so important to tell you that you shouldn't have tried to fix it?"

He shook his head. "I don't know."

But Megan got the feeling he did know, or at least had been thinking about it enough to form a few suspicions. "Shall we pack it up for the night?" she suggested.

Eric went to shut off the digital night-vision camera that was perched in a corner and had filmed their séance. "At least I've got some footage to go through, although I doubt I'll find anything. You two go on; I'm going to finish setting up cameras and motion detectors for the night. Maybe we'll get something while all the ghoulies think we're snug in our beds."

Megan followed Case out of the room.

"Do you want some coffee?" he asked.

"Sure."

Down in the kitchen, she sat at the table while Case got some decaf going. There was something companionable and cozy about the sounds of coffee being made at such a late hour, the oil lamp glowing on the table.

"Apparently, mothers like to visit you," Megan said. "Your second one in as many days."

Case pulled out a chair and sat down across from her. He shook his head. "I don't quite believe it."

"The hammer and the decrepit house, those meant something to you. Your mother showed them to me so you'd know it was her."

"I can't figure out how you'd know about that hammer."

"I didn't," Megan said.

"Lots of guys take shop class and make hammers. It could have been a lucky guess."

Megan felt a spark of annoyance. "Why are you so set against the possibility that what I do might be real?"

"If it *is* real, I don't know whether a visit from Mom is frightening or comforting."

"She's your mother. Why would you be scared?"

The corner of his mouth pulled back in a wry smile. "Maybe *unnerved* is the better word. Have you found, since your mother passed, that apart from the grief, there's a certain sense of freedom and relief?"

"Relief?"

"Maybe it's just me."

She shook her head. "No, tell me more. What type of relief?"

"That you're not being watched anymore by a parent. You no longer have, in the back of your head, the fear of disappointing them. The choices you make can be yours alone, not made with a nod to what your parent would think best."

Megan sat silent, letting what he was saying soak in. She'd never considered it before, but was there any of that in what she'd been going through since her mom had died? "I think I still feel like she's watching. Maybe I'll never get away from that, given my psychic ability."

He grinned. "You could always revert to adolescence and rebel. But somehow I doubt you were a wild thing in your teens."

"Nope. Goody-two-shoes all the way. I was incredibly boring."

"Is that what you're still doing now? Behaving as you think your mother would want?"

Megan thought of the shop and her struggle to buy the building, and she felt a familiar spurt of desperation at the thought of possibly losing it all. She couldn't let her mother's work of twenty years go down the drain. "She wouldn't have wanted to close the shop. But . . ." She trailed off, thinking.

"But what?"

"I don't know. She always enjoyed having me work with her at the shop and said it was as much mine as hers. I don't think I'd be doing it now if I didn't enjoy it. But . . ."

"But . . . ?"

"But I don't know that she ever expected me to make it my life's work. She was a big one for encouraging me to follow my dreams. I think she thought they lay elsewhere."

"Do they?" he asked, getting up to fill two cups and bring them back to the table.

"That's a bigger question than can be answered on decaf."

"Fair enough."

They sipped, and then Megan set her cup on the table. "So, what do you think your mother meant with her message, 'You shouldn't have tried to fix it'? Do you know? Was it the falling-down house?"

"That was the house I grew up in."

"Buckled countertops?" Megan asked, pulling the image from her fragmented memory.

He stared at her. "Yes."

"Your dad wasn't much of a handyman."

Case laughed, the sound dry and without humor. "He was a carpenter."

"Then why—"

"He was also rarely home. He spent his time with his buddies, out at the racetrack or one of the strip clubs."

Megan tilted her head, remembering how Case had commented so knowingly about the effects of not having a father around the house.

"At home, he never finished a single project he started. Until I was old enough to start fixing things myself—which was about age ten—my mother had to live with holes in the walls and toilets that didn't flush. Sometimes I'd find her sitting alone in the kitchen, crying because the refrigerator had stopped running again or a new leak had appeared in the roof.

"A few years before she died, I bought her a townhouse, and it was the first time in her adult life she got to live someplace that was completely finished." He shook his head.

Megan involuntarily glanced around at the kitchen.

He saw her gaze. "It'll be finished before I bring a wife here. That's one thing I swore to myself from an early age: I'd never make my family live in a home that wasn't finished."

"How long will it take you to do this house?"

"At least a year. Probably two or three, given the time I have to devote to paying work."

"Mm." Megan dropped her gaze and sipped her coffee. "Why would your mother point out that you couldn't have fixed your childhood home?"

"It doesn't make sense."

"It probably does. We just don't know how yet." *Or you're not telling me.*

He sighed. "I'm not sure I want to know. I thought all my parents' troubles had been buried with them. I don't like this business of the dead not staying dead and gone."

Megan met his eyes. "I think you're beginning to believe."

THIRTEEN

Case tossed and turned in his bed, memories of his unhappy mother filling his mind. Her weeping over the house, over Case's father, over the loss of her own mother. Her seeking of consolation in the dishonest hands of fortune tellers and psychic counselors. She'd believed she was cursed and had lost thousands of dollars trying to free herself of her bad luck.

You shouldn't have tried to fix it.

No, he couldn't have. It had been their family that was a wreck, and the house was only a symptom. All his childish attempts to patch up the house had done nothing to cure his parents' unhappy marriage.

But why would his mother cross the Great Divide to tell him something he already knew?

She *hadn't*. That was the answer.

Megan had somehow picked up on his thoughts or pieced together from their conversations that his home life had not been ideal. Maybe he'd mentioned his mother's name at some point, and then he'd put his own interpretation to the house and hammer she mentioned, filling in the blanks for her like any eager rube during a cold reading. If his mother had really been present, she would have been so thrilled to be talking to a real medium that the séance would have lasted all night.

He was fairly sure that Megan was sincere in her belief in her powers. She was fooling herself, but he didn't think she was trying to fool *him*. She was just another in the long list of women who misinterpreted their natural sensitivity to people as being something *super*natural.

He was annoyed that for a few minutes, he'd almost believed she'd seen his mother. He knew better.

That annoyance wasn't enough to keep him from savoring the memory of Megan throwing herself on him in a sexual frenzy, though. His body got hard as he replayed it in his mind. If Eric hadn't been standing right there, he might have taken it all the way.

The knowledge of how much she'd hate him if he bought her building wouldn't have stopped him. Even his own conviction that having sex with her could lead only to a messy entanglement and eventual breakup would not have stopped him. He wanted her.

He heard her turn over restlessly, the sound carrying through the open doorway between their rooms. He heard her punch her pillow and sigh.

"Can't sleep?" he called softly.

There was silence for a moment, then she said, "No. The house is too quiet."

"You'd sleep better with slamming doors?"

"I feel like it's watching us. Like it's gathering information and plotting something horrible." She laughed. "Crazy, huh?"

"Yeah."

"It's good to know you'll always be there to reassure me," she said dryly.

He smiled in the darkness. "I can help you get your mind off the house."

"Are you going to tell me a story?"

"That wasn't quite what I had in mind."

Megan's eyes opened wide. She heard him shift on his mattress, his feet hitting the floor. "A story would be good!" she squeaked. "Tell me a story!"

She heard him moving around, and then he was in her room. "Scoot over," he said.

Frozen in place, she gripped her sheet and stared up at him. He was a dark shadow looming above her, his presence promising fulfillment of what she'd started earlier in the day.

"Go on, scoot."

She did as told, her brain going numb at the implications even as her body tingled to life. He lay down on top of the covers, and it was only then that she saw he was wearing his robe.

Doubt trickled in. Was he going to seduce her or not?

"What type of story do you want? Pirate adventure? Cowboy campfire story?"

"Fairy tale."

He grunted. "Figures. Okay, so once upon a time, there was this horny girl named Meg—"

"Hey!"

"Named Magdalen but called Meg by her friends. She lived in a mansion on a hill and was spoiled rotten by her father. He'd give her anything she wanted, ponies and ribbons up the wazoo, but wouldn't let her date until she was eighteen. He was so rich and powerful, no young man dared to get near her."

"Ponies. Do girls really want ponies? I never did. My feet would have dragged on the ground."

"It was a stallion she truly wanted, if you get my drift."

"I'm impressed by your use of literary symbolism."

He chuckled, then lowered his voice and turned onto his side, facing her. "Poor Meg was suffering. Her body was ripe and ready, but no one could touch it. All she could do was lie in bed at night, her hands stroking softly over her breasts, wishing there were a man beside her to touch her everywhere that ached."

"This is a very strange fairy tale."

"All she wanted was someone to touch her." Case lightly touched the side of her neck, then trailed his fingertips down to the neck of her gown.

Megan closed her eyes, goose bumps rising on her skin.

His fingertips brushed along her collarbone, then lifted away.

"He wouldn't tell her why she couldn't date. All he ever said was that if she let a man touch her before she was eighteen, something terrible would happen. So she was a good girl and obeyed her father, but on the day before her eighteenth birthday, she saw a young man in the garden of the house and suddenly all the years of waiting were too much for her. 'Seventeen years, and three hundred sixty-four days is as good as eighteen years,' she told herself, and slipped outside."

"Naughty thing. She's going to get what's coming to her."

"The young man didn't know who she was," Case continued. "She ran across the lawn to him, her lips parted in an eager smile." He traced the outline of her lips, then stroked his fingertips through her hair. "Her golden hair was down around her shoulders. And she was wearing her nightgown, the neck unbuttoned and showing the pale skin of her breast to the bright light of day."

Case's hand undid the top button of her gown,

then the second. His fingertips drew circles over her breast bone.

Megan's breathing grew heavy, her breasts tingling with the wish to be touched.

"The man let her throw herself into his arms, and when her mouth reached up to his . . ."

Megan felt the warmth of Case close to her and opened her eyes to see him within inches, his mouth above hers.

"He kissed her."

Megan's lips parted, her heart thudding. Case lowered his face a fraction closer, then drew away, leaving her untouched.

"And when he kissed her, she fainted dead away. This scared the crap out of him, of course, and since he was a coward, he dropped her on the lawn and got the hell out of there."

"Some Prince Charming," Megan said in frustration.

"The whole house was in an uproar, the doctor was called, but no one could wake her up. Her father knew it was hopeless; he'd been cursed years ago by an evil gypsy fortune teller."

Megan made a noise of disapproval.

"Or an angry Indian shaman. At any rate, they stuck her in a room in a tower and forgot about her."

"Bastards."

"People died and moved away, and the house fell into disrepair. Blackberry vines covered the yard, and roses wrapped themselves around the house. A hundred years passed, and property values went up, and a handsome builder bought the house."

"Of course."

"He hacked his way through the blackberry vines and the roses, suffering many injuries. Scrapes, pricks, slivers, you name it."

"Poor man."

"He climbed the stairs inside the house, higher and higher and higher, until he reached the attic and found a small doorway at the farthest corner. Through it, he found one last stairway, so narrow and twisting that he could barely fit his big, manly, muscular frame through it."

Megan giggled.

"He emerged into the tower room, the windows on all sides covered with vines that cast their shadows on the pale, perfect woman who lay upon the bed, her body still clothed in the white gown she'd worn on the three-hundred-sixty-fourth day of her seventeenth year.

"He held his hand near her face," Case said, doing the same to Megan, "and felt the warmth of her breath. And as he looked at her and drank in her beauty, he began to want to touch her. Just a little bit. Maybe right here," he said, touching her temple. "And here." He trailed his fingertips over her jawline and then her lips. "And down here."

Megan felt his touch move down her throat, down

over her breast bone, and then his hand flattened out and covered her breast. She closed her eyes, sucking in a breath.

"He knew he shouldn't. He knew she would protest if she had the chance." He massaged her breast, catching her nipple between two fingers and pressing gently. "But she was so beautiful, he couldn't resist. And then he kissed her."

Case's mouth pressed against hers, gently at first, small, nipping caresses. Then harder, taking her lower lip between his, his tongue stroking it before delving inside. His weight came half over her, pressing her down into the mattress, his hand still at her breast.

Megan wrapped her arms around his neck, pulling him closer. She felt the hardness of his arousal against her thigh and felt an answering rush of wet warmth between her legs. A low growl of pleasure rumbled in her throat, and the sound of it seemed to increase his passion. His mouth on hers became ferocious, devouring her, his hunger almost frightening. He threw back the bedcovers and pulled up her gown, his hand sliding between her thighs.

He stroked her once, slowly, with the flat of his palm, the roughness of it sending shivers of sensation through her, and then she felt his fingertip dip into her core.

The intimacy of the touch was a shock, and by reflex she grabbed his wrist, stopping him and turning her head away from his kiss. "Case, no."

He froze, his body tense against hers. "No?"

She shook her head, hating the words she made herself say. "I barely know you." But God knew she wanted to continue anyway. She could barely keep her hips from moving against his hand, still lodged between her thighs.

"You're killing me," he said, his voice tight.

"I don't want to ever have to regret sleeping with you. Let's get to know each other a little better first, okay? Make sure we like each other enough and won't regret it."

He didn't answer.

"Please don't be mad at me."

A strained laugh answered her. "It's not my place to be mad." He rolled off her and stood. "Good night, Megan."

"Good night," she said softly. "And Case?" she said as he moved toward the door. "Sleep well."

He barked a laugh and was gone.

FOURTEEN

Case got out of bed cranky and bleary. He showered and slogged downstairs, at odds with himself and the world. He got the coffee going and went outside for the Sunday *Seattle Times,* tossed in a plastic bag at the end of the driveway. By the time he came back inside, Eric was up.

"Time to check the mousetraps," Eric said cheerfully as he passed in the hallway.

Case grunted and continued toward his pot of coffee.

He was halfway through a microwavable sausage and pancake frozen breakfast when Eric popped his head in the door, his cheerfulness gone.

"Case, you got a minute?"

"Why? What's up?"

"Not much. Which is the problem. The electricity must have been doing some strange stuff last night. Can you come take a look?"

"It does strange stuff every night. If I knew how to stop it, I would."

"I've got some ideas I'd like to talk over, see what you think."

"After I finish my breakfast."

"How can you eat that crap? God knows what they make it out of."

"Pigs' eyeballs, I hope," Case said, and stabbed a sausage with his fork. "Delicious!"

Eric shuddered and left.

Case spent another half-hour getting acquainted with the day on his own terms before setting down his coffee cup and heading for the grand salon. Above him, he heard footsteps and running water. Megan had finally arisen. He pictured her naked in the shower, water running down her body, her soapy hand washing her breasts, her belly, and the deep dark valley below.

Christ. He was developing a serious case of blue balls, and it was his own damn fault. He was horny, but if she got to know him better, the way she wanted, there'd never be any chance of getting her into bed. He was well and truly screwed.

He found Eric ensconced like a medieval lord behind the crenellations of his computer equipment. "So, what's your idea?" Case asked.

"Ah, you're finally here! Come look at this footage from last night."

Curiosity at last rousing itself, Case came around the long tables of equipment to the bank of LCD screens Eric was looking at. Several of them had green-gray scenes frozen on them, and a few had screen savers running.

"This is all the input from the night-vision cameras. Some of them were set to record all night; others were triggered by motion detectors. Look at this one," Eric said, pointing. "This is the hallway outside the Smithson family bedrooms."

"Okay."

Eric hit a key on one of his keyboards. The scene stayed the same.

"Wait for it," Eric said. "It looks like the camera's not recording because nothing is moving."

Case watched and waited. A shadow suddenly moved across the screen from left to right. "Whoa! What was that?"

Eric replayed it, then froze the screen with the shadow in its center. "I couldn't tell you."

Case leaned forward and tried to make out any detail in the amorphous shape. "Can you enlarge it?"

"It doesn't help." Eric zoomed in on the image, but it became more diffuse, less easy to differentiate from the background in the grainy night-vision recording.

"Play it again."

Case felt the hairs standing on the back of his neck as the shadow moved once more across the screen. Its shape changed as it moved, like a person struggling under bulky layers of cloth. Eeriest of all was the unnatural speed with which it jerked its way across the screen, as if moving in fast-forward.

"Is this normal speed?"

Eric nodded. The screen went white, then black. A moment later, it was back again, showing the empty hallway.

"At least this camera came back," Eric said. "Some of them shut off completely."

"Could that shadow have been a malfunction in the camera?"

"It's possible it could have been pixilation. I've never seen pixilation quite like that, but . . ."

"But it could have been. Is that the only thing the cameras caught?" Case asked. There had to be at least twenty thousand dollars' worth of equipment set up around the house, and all it had caught was a questionable shadow. The hairs on the back of his neck smoothed down.

"I think that's pretty much the shape of things," Eric said, reaching again to tap keys. One by one, the screens came alive, revealing views of other parts of the house.

The screen saver on a screen to Case's right disappeared, replaced by Megan's bedroom. The sheets were mussed, her robe tossed over the foot of the bed. She must have returned from her shower. Was she just off-screen, naked? Case felt a pulse of desire at the thought.

"Eric!" Megan shouted.

Case jumped.

Fully dressed, she marched into the room and slammed a small piece of equipment down onto the table. "What the hell was this doing in the bathroom?"

"Careful with that!" Eric cried.

Case recognized what it was and turned on Eric in disbelief. "You put a camera in the bathroom?"

"In the bathrooms and all our bedrooms. It made sense, given what's gone on here."

"You should have asked!" Megan screeched. "You should have told us. You don't just stick a camera in someone's private space."

Case stared at her, wondering despite his better instincts whether her shower had been recorded. And then he realized exactly *why* she was so alarmed.

"I didn't hide the cameras. They were in plain sight," Eric was saying.

"Maybe in the daylight. But not at night, with the nonexistent lighting. You were hoping to get your own private peep show, weren't you?"

"Megan, you know this is how SPIRIT sets up investigations. You've set up the cameras yourself. How was I supposed to guess that you'd purposefully forget that?"

Case broke in. "Eric, erase everything from Megan's bedroom and from the bathroom, right now. You haven't looked at any of it yet, have you?"

"No," Eric grumbled. "What type of guy do you think I am, anyway?"

"A normal one."

Megan crossed her arms. "Go on."

Eric tapped keys. "I only set them up in case you reported that something *had* happened, like something crawling into bed with you. Wouldn't you want it recorded, if you were molested in your sleep like Case said he'd been?"

Megan leaned past Eric and tapped keys herself, double-checking that the recordings were truly gone.

"I really thought you'd remember there'd be cameras everywhere," Eric went on. "You *know* how these investigations are set up."

When Megan spoke again, her voice was heavy with suspicion. "You always have such good excuses for why you've pissed people off."

"Look, I'm not a bad guy. I didn't aim the bathroom camera at the tub. I'm not a Peeping Tom pervert. Whatever happened to innocent until proven guilty? You refuse to give me a fresh start."

"Do you really deserve one?"

Eric made a petulant sound.

"Whatever you think Megan should have already known about the cameras," Case said, "you can't deny that I should have been told where they were."

"You're right. I'm sorry." Eric looked down, his hair falling forward and hiding his eyes. "I got so caught up in tweaking the software last night, I forgot to say anything. I'm sorry."

His false deference further annoyed Case. "Your apologies come easy and fast. I wish you were less practiced at begging forgiveness. It doesn't inspire confidence."

Eric flashed him a look that was dark with submerged anger, the intensity in that momentary glare taking Case aback. It also pissed him off—he'd respect the man a hell of a lot more if instead of seething silently, Eric would tell him to shut up.

"Are you still going to help me try to fix the electrical issue?" Eric asked.

"Later. I've got some work to do." He strongly suspected that Eric had watched the video and seen him in Megan's bed. Was that why Eric was so angry? Was the guy *in love* with her?

The thought infuriated him, for no reason he could comprehend.

Christ, he was a mess. He couldn't think straight. He had to get away from everyone.

"Case—" Megan said as he moved past her, her hand reaching out toward his arm.

He flinched away from her touch.

She pulled her hand back, hurt and confusion on her face.

Case forced himself to stop and tried to smile reassuringly. "I'm sorry, what was it you wanted to say?"

She examined his face and shook her head. "Nothing. It can wait."

"Later, then."

FIFTEEN

Megan sat silently while Eric squirted blobs of contact gel onto her scalp and affixed the electrodes that would monitor her brain-wave patterns as she wore the temporal lobe stimulator.

She was too morose to care that Eric was touching her or that she was going to invite God-knew-what into her head with the helmet. She was just glad that it was finally night and the day could be considered almost over. It had been about the longest, loneliest day she could remember.

Case's mood had been the source of her misery. While he wasn't rude to her, it was also clear that he wanted to be alone today. Their cozy intimacy at the kitchen table the night before might as well have happened to different people. Apparently, sex really *did* destroy friendships.

A quick drive to Antique Fancies to fetch her box of keys led to a half-hour visit with Tracie.

Tracie said, "He's probably got male PMS."

"Give me a real answer."

"I am! He's in a bad mood. You don't know why. He may have been pissed off before you came into the room. And because he's a guy, he can't tell you why he's suddenly turned into an emotional warthog. All he can do is go to his burrow and grunt until he feels better."

"I wish he'd say something."

"No, you don't, not until the grunting is done. Believe me, it's better to wait. He'll probably forget what was bothering him, so even if it *was* you, he won't care. Guys don't have the same long-term memory we do."

So Megan had come back to the house to look for clues. She'd opened a few of the trunks and desks in the various rooms but was too self-conscious to go up to the attic, knowing that Case was on the servants' floor working. Or grunting, as Tracie suggested.

Megan hadn't opened anything in the Smithson sisters' rooms, either. Although nothing ghostly had happened all day, she didn't have the courage to stir things up in those rooms on her own. She couldn't forget the shadow in the hallway or the way the door had refused to open to her.

She spent her lunch in the library, reading over the papers that Case had collected during his initial cleaning. She began to piece together the raw facts of the Smithsons' lives. There was no real sense of who they'd been as people, except for the ledger where someone had written down their expenses for several months. There were three entries for visits by spiritualists.

Eric had been as elusive as Case all day, but she saw that as a blessing. In a house the size of this one, it hadn't been hard for three busy people to spend the day alone.

Now, having finished with the electrodes, Eric went to his computer and was tapping keys and testing the signals. The three of them met in the grand salon, Case sitting on an old Victorian chair, legs crossed in that wide-open male style with an ankle resting atop the opposite knee, a hand holding it in place.

His gaze met hers and he gave her a small, reassuring smile.

She returned it, uncertainty and hope spelled out in the fragile U of her lips.

He broke their gaze and watched Eric work, and Megan felt herself deflate. With that deflation came annoyance, with herself more than with him.

Was she getting a crush on the man?

She'd thought he was beginning to like her, too, but now she wondered if he had just been trying to get into her pants. Maybe now that she'd made it clear she didn't go for casual sex, he'd lost interest. He didn't want to get any closer to her; didn't want to get drawn into her "flaky" world.

She sighed.

Maybe she should do as Tracie suggested and stop speculating. It wasn't helping her.

"Let's move over to the chaise longue," Eric finally said, lifting up her trailing wires. It was best if she lay down during this experiment, since the helmet was heavy and she needed to be relaxed.

She sat on the edge of the couch, and Eric handed her the helmet, wires hanging from its underside like tentacles on a jellyfish. The tentacles ended in a black box, which in turn sent a cable to the computer. Megan peered inside the helmet and saw that the solenoids attached all over its surface were both smaller and more numerous than the last time. Eric hadn't been lying about refining the device.

Whether those refinements would make a difference was yet to be seen.

With Eric's help, she carefully slid her head into the helmet, trying not to dislodge any electrodes. When it was firmly in place, she lay back and covered herself with a blanket, knowing her body temperature would drop, just as it did while preparing to sleep.

Eric clipped a blood oxygen saturation and pulse monitor to her fingertip.

The helmet muffled sound, so it was a surprise when Case appeared beside her, looking down with concern.

"Are you sure about this, Megan?" he asked.

"We're not learning anything about the house without it."

"That doesn't matter compared to your safety."

"But you tried it yourself," Megan pointed out. He had done so an hour earlier, holding to the promise he'd made before to see for himself that it was safe.

"I'm not you." Case had reported an out-of-body experience and memories of early childhood with the helmet, but when Eric had altered the electromagnetic pulses to the pattern he thought worked best for visionary or paranormal experiences, Case had experienced no result.

"No, but I trust you to keep an eye on things. I know you'll shut it down if I'm in distress."

Eric made an insulted noise.

"As would Eric," Megan added.

Eric grumbled, "S'more like it."

"As long as you're sure."

Megan nodded and reached up to flip down the visor attached to the helmet. It was lined inside to block out all light, although she could still see it coming in from the bottom of the helmet. A few moments later, that light dimmed, and she knew they had turned out most of the lights.

"Okay, Megan," Eric said, "you do your trance

thing, and when I see your brain waves approaching the theta state, I'll turn on the stimulator. It should be like someone turned up the brightness and volume on your experience."

"Okay."

"We'll keep you in theta for half an hour unless you signal for me to stop. We won't question you about what you're seeing this time, until the half-hour is up. I want you to get a good, uninterrupted look around. You should have a lot more control than when you're in a trance without the helmet."

"Okay." She doubted it would work that well, but now that the helmet was on her head and they were about to begin, whatever apprehension she had left was overruled by curiosity. Just what *would* she see?

She took a few deep breaths and turned her mind to her private trance induction, sinking deeper and deeper beneath the sea. She left Eric and Case behind, glad to escape her daylong dwelling on personal relationships.

Down, down, down . . .

Her feet hit sandy bottom, and she walked through the underwater cave. As she passed through it, she felt something happening; it wasn't taking the same degree of concentration to stay in the moment. The cave walls took on a life of their own, as if unimagined by her. When she came out the other side this time, there was no charcoal void.

An endless sky of pale blue greeted her, alive with

sounds. She blinked against the light, lifting her hand to shade her eyes. The sounds became louder, a hubbub of voices and animal noises. They pounded at her, intimidating her with their pressure, making her heartbeat quicken. She struggled to gain control of the experience and, after a few moments, managed to push the sounds back slightly, giving herself space to hear herself think.

The endless blue bleached into white. Then suddenly, the scene changed, and she was standing in the grand salon of the house, furnished as it must have been at the turn of the last century. The voices disappeared, and there was no sound but her own breathing and heartbeat.

She blinked, stunned by the clarity. She'd never had an experience like this on her own and might have been frightened if not for the unreal silence and a vague feeling of being dissociated from her own body.

She looked around, recognizing a few pieces of furniture from her explorations of the house, recognizing as well that their arrangement was the same as in one of the photos. She walked to the tall windows that looked out on the garden and saw close-trimmed lawns and a formal pool, the white statue of a goddess. The trees at the far end of the garden were mere saplings, but there was no view for them to block. The world turned to a wall of white mist beyond the back wall of the garden.

She heard a noise behind her and turned around.

The man from the portrait stood in the wide doorway, his eyes wide as he stared at her.

Megan gaped back. Was he real or a figment of her imagination?

He kept staring.

A sudden thought struck Megan, and she raised her hand to her face, feeling for the helmet, thinking that was what made him goggle at her so. She felt the soft skin of her own cheek, no helmet or visor. So this was her astral self, appearing in the form she envisioned for herself.

She smiled at the man, trying to appear unthreatening. "Hello."

He glanced back down the hall behind him, then took a few hurried steps into the room, stopping several feet away from her. He leaned toward her, eyes wide. "How did you get in here?"

"I . . . couldn't really say."

"Do you know how to get out?"

"I'm not sure," she said, realizing that that was the case and suddenly feeling grateful that the power of the helmet could be shut off with the flip of a switch. With this degree of reality around her and no cave opening in sight, she wasn't confident that she could simply open her eyes and be back in her own world.

"You shouldn't stay here, if you can help it."

"Friends will come get me," she said.

He nodded. "Outside friends. Very good. I don't have any."

"Are you *trying* to leave?"

"They won't let me go!" he burst out, then glanced anxiously around and lowered his voice. "They have me locked up here like a monkey in a cage. But then I caught a glimpse of a man up in the attic. And I've seen him in the halls a few times, just for a moment. I saw you, too. You're easier to see. When the man arrived, I knew there must be a way in and out."

"You want to leave."

He closed his eyes as if gathering internal strength, then slowly opened them and met her gaze square on. "I would gladly give my soul to the devil were he to take me from this place. Even hell must offer more peace than this house."

"Who's keeping you here?" Megan asked, her voice as low as his.

"*They* are."

"Who are they?"

He shook his head. "They'll hear us if we say their names."

"Then may I ask yours?"

He looked at her in surprise, then a sunny smile broke over his face. "Forgive me, my manners have atrophied from lack of use. I am Zachariah Armstrong, originally of Cincinnati, Ohio." He gave a small bow.

"It's a pleasure to meet you, Zachariah. Er, Mr. Armstrong, I mean."

"And whom do I have the very great pleasure of addressing?"

Megan smiled, enjoying the courtliness. "Megan Barrows. Of Seattle."

"Ah, a native daughter of this fledgling city."

"How long have you been here, Mr. Armstrong?"

He blinked at her. "This is terribly embarrassing, but I'm afraid I have no clear notion of the date. The last I remember, it was July 10, 1898. Have I been here half as long as I think?"

"I don't know. How long do you think you've been here?"

"Ten years, perhaps?" He bit his lower lip, looking at her with apprehension. "Could it be as many as twenty?"

Megan grimaced.

"Oh, dear. Thirty?"

She shook her head. "I'm afraid it's been well over a hundred."

His eyelids fluttered, and he staggered backward. "A hundred years."

"Mr. Armstrong, this may seem a rude and forward sort of question, but . . . are you . . . er . . ." Megan chewed her lip. It really was a harsh question to ask someone. "Did you know that you, ah . . ."

"Yes?"

"Er. You're dead, right?"

A hurt look came into his eyes. "My dear, it is hardly a topic on which I need reminding."

"Sorry."

"I don't *show* it, do I?" He looked down at his nattily dressed self with worry. "There aren't signs of decay, are there?"

"Oh, no, you look stunningly lifelike," Megan rushed to reassure him. Time to change the subject! "How did you come to be trapped here, Mr. Armstrong?"

He brushed lint off his sleeve and blinked at her, visibly gathering his thoughts back together. "I tried to show you."

"You did? When?"

He gave her a charmingly apologetic smile. "I'm not very good with details of time, I'm afraid. But I do know that you were trying to sleep, and I asked you to come with me."

"That was you!"

He bowed again.

"You almost sent me headlong down the stairs!"

A look of horror came over his features. "No!"

"Yes!"

"My dear lady, I am so sorry! I never meant for such a thing to happen!"

She brushed away the apology. "It's all right. I thought maybe it had been a mistake on your part."

"Do forgive me! Say you forgive me?"

"There's nothing to forgive."

"I was trying to show you—"

A piercing screech cut through the room, the

vibration of it causing the very fabric of the scene to tear. The screeching came again, from more than one direction, the room shredding under the force of the sounds. Zachariah's image bent sideways and stretched, as if being sucked away.

"Don't let them catch you!" Zachariah cried, his voice distorted.

"Who are *they?*" Megan shouted over the screeching that sounded like a flock of harpies. "Tell me who *they* are!"

The last remnants of the grand salon vanished, and with it the ear-piercing screeches. Megan was back in the endless sky blue, surrounded by silence, hovering in pale nothingness. Moments passed, and then she felt rather than saw the approach of a presence.

"Please don't listen to him," a soft, feminine voice lilted close to her ear. "He has the charms and guile of a snake, and he will bring you to ruin as he has brought others."

A chill ran up Megan's arms, making the hairs stand on end. She could barely see a white face near her shoulder, hiding in the corner of her vision. She was afraid to turn and see the woman full-on. "Who are you?" Megan asked quietly.

The woman ignored her question and continued to speak in her strangely gentle tone. "Please, do not listen to his lies. Do not let him tempt you and lead you astray. You would not want the end that you would bring upon yourself."

"What did he do to you?"

"He has trapped us here with his lies and deceits. He has stolen our very lives."

"Can you tell me who you are?" Megan asked.

The white face pulled back, beyond the edge of Megan's vision. Megan slowly turned her head.

There was no one there.

The silence around her gave way to the hubbub she had heard before.

A shiver ran up Megan's spine. That white face had been so close to her, she would have felt the woman's breath if she had been alive. Megan shuddered.

There seemed to be nothing left to see, so Megan coaxed herself up a notch of consciousness and hovered there.

She heard Eric speak. "She's coming out of it." Then louder: "Megan, are you finished?"

"Yes," she said aloud.

"Did you learn anything?" Case asked.

"I learned a lot, but I have no idea what's true."

SIXTEEN

Megan pinched the bridge of her nose and tried to coax away the headache that was forming. Squinting at the screen of a microfiche machine for two hours was doing neither her back nor her eyes any favors.

She hadn't even known that microfiche was still around and still in use. She'd never used it in college; any research she'd had to do for projects was done with databases. She ordered the articles she wanted, and voila! Done.

But here at Seattle's Museum of History and Industry, the microfiche machine was the only way she could see copies of the *Seattle Times* from 1898.

The name Zachariah Armstrong was unusual enough that she'd thought it would be easy to find any mention of him in the paper. Alas, she had forgotten that punching his name into a search function was not an option. She had to scan each paper line by line, and so far, she hadn't found a single mention of him.

Instead, she saw talk of the Klondike gold rush, city development, local and national politics, and reports of fires and accidents. The classified ads offered the same questionable assortment she was used to: rooms for rent, jobs sought, men seeking women for romance and more. There were ads for quack medicines and ads for psychics. It was similar to modern newspapers, except for the old-fashioned layout with narrow columns and headlines only marginally larger than the text of the stories themselves.

People clearly stayed the same over the centuries.

She'd started with July 10, assuming that to be the date of Zachariah's death. But neither that day, nor any other day for a week afterward had offered mention of his death. There were no anonymous murder victims, no suggestive death notices, no mention of the Smithson family.

Megan leaned back and stretched. If she was going to suffer through this tedious search, she preferred to suffer somewhere more comfortable. She found the librarian, handed over the money Case had given her for making copies and buying any pertinent books, and requested June, July, and August 1898 printed out.

It was late afternoon by the time she returned to

Case's house with her thick stack of printouts. As she drove under the iron arch, she glanced up at the crest and motto.

I get what I deserve.

It had an eerie ring of similarity to the white-faced woman's warnings during the séance. "You would not want the end that you would bring upon yourself."

Megan shivered. There was something unspeakably creepy about it all.

As she drove slowly down the driveway, she saw that both Case's and Eric's pickups were gone. Lovely. She was alone at the haunted house. She parked the van and sat motionless in the driver's seat.

Had the ghostly woman been a member of the Smithson family? It seemed likely, since her words were like the motto. But if so, which Smithson was she? Mother, Daughter One, or Daughter Two?

Whichever she was, Megan wasn't eager to see her again. She was too unnerving. At least Zachariah had been charming. Amusing.

The better to tempt her to a terrible fate?

He *had* almost sent her headlong down the stairs, after all.

She didn't know what to believe.

With a sigh, she got out of the car and headed for the house. She stood for a long moment just inside the door, letting her senses reach out into the house around her. As before, she had a sense of being watched. The house knew she was there.

Her footsteps were loud on the bare floor as she made her way to the kitchen. Two notes lay on the table.

Had some work to do, and have to pick up lumber and misc. for the house. You have my cell #—call if you need anything. Back by 6:00. —C

Got called into work today. Don't let the boogey men get you! —E.

Everyone was off working as usual, and here she was in spook land. She felt a sudden pang of longing for the familiar comfort of her shop and her daily routine there.

With a sigh, she plopped down the stack of printouts and started water boiling for a cup of tea. She could hardly sneer at the promise of twenty pieces of furniture, but even that prize had somehow lost its allure.

"Maybe that's why you shouldn't do things purely for the money," Megan scolded herself out loud. It could never compare to doing something purely because it gave her joy.

She sat down and settled in with her tea, intent on getting herself up to date on current events, circa 1898.

She was midway through June 6 when the thumping began. Her gaze froze on the newspaper, her ears pricking and the hair rising on the back of her neck.

The noise wasn't as loud as when she had eaten there with Case. It was far off, somewhere above her. If the house hadn't been otherwise silent, she doubted she would have heard it at all.

Thump. Thump. Thump.

Maybe an animal had gotten into the house?

Thump. Thump. Thump.

Megan scrunched down in her chair, realizing the kitchen had grown shadowy with the lateness of the afternoon.

She glanced at her watch. Five-twenty. Another forty minutes until Case would be back.

Thump. Thump. Thump.

Megan tried to concentrate on the paper in front of her. Nothing had happened to her and Case when they'd ignored the sounds before. Surely it would be the best course to follow now.

Thump. THUMP! THUMP!

Megan jumped at the sudden increase in sound, then looked up at the ceiling, as if she could see through the floors to wherever the sound was coming from. It didn't seem to want to be ignored.

THUMP!

Goose bumps shivered over her skin.

It could be Zachariah up there. It could be the white woman. It could be the nameless *they*.

She didn't want to see any of them, alone.

Megan pushed back from the table and hurried

from the room toward the door to the outside.
THUMP! THUMP! THUMP!

She stopped, then took a few steps back until she could see the staircase. In the movies, it was always a mistake to go investigate the creepy noise on one's own. A gory death awaited every bimbo who tried it.

Megan put her hand on the banister, feeling a sick kinship with the horror-film characters. What could it do to her, anyway, as long as she didn't panic? It was just a noise. A harmless thumping noise.

Wasn't it?

She put her foot on the first step, and with that small commitment her courage returned. She climbed the stairs cautiously and stopped at the top, listening to the thumping. It was still above her.

She jogged down the hall to the servant stairs.

THUMP!

The sound was coming from the attic.

She yanked open the door to the attic stairs and flipped the switch for the lights.

THUMP!

The sound vibrated down the stairs, hitting her in the chest.

With a whimper in her throat, she forced herself up the final flight of stairs. As the attic came into sight, she saw the large locked trunk she'd pulled from the pile.

It was hovering a foot above the floor.

Megan's grip tightened on the handrail, her whole

body tensing, certain in that moment that the trunk was about to be thrown at her.

It dropped flat onto the floor.

THUMP!

Megan crouched where she was, heart thundering in her ears, the cold sweat of fear trickling down her skin.

Long moments passed. The trunk remained where it sat. The thumping sounds had stopped.

It was another minute before Megan rose from her crouch and cautiously climbed the rest of the stairs.

There were shallow dents in the floor around the trunk, where it had been dropped repeatedly. Her hand shaking, Megan reached out and touched the trunk.

A sense of wanting to be noticed passed faintly over Megan, too faint for her to know if it was her own assumption or the feeling of whoever had been thumping the trunk.

She tried the latch on the trunk. It opened with a quiet snick.

"So you want me to look inside," she said to the empty attic. "Okay."

She knelt down on the floor and lifted the lid.

The stench of mothballs lifted like a mushroom cloud from within. Megan coughed and fanned the air in front of her, sitting back until the worst of it had passed.

Inside, a top layer of trays held baby shoes, school-work done in an old-fashioned childish hand, stacks of personal letters, and mementos of parties: dance cards, feathers, pressed flowers, scraps of lace, a white kid glove. Megan lifted the trays aside and found clothing beneath: a girl's dresses from the 1880s and '90s, a couple of pairs of shoes, broken hair combs, and odd bits of beading and faux pearls that had come loose from objects long since lost.

At the very bottom of the trunk was a framed photo lying on top of a large, shallow box.

The photo was of Mr. and Mrs. Smithson on their wedding day. Mrs. Smithson looked beautiful, radiantly happy in her stunningly small-waisted, corseted gown.

Megan lifted the lid off the box and found the aged ivory silk wedding gown from the photo. It was stained in places, and the silk was tattered, but it was still beautiful enough to leave Megan staring for long minutes before she carefully settled the lid back onto the box.

Was it the dress that she had been meant to find?

The tray with the letters made a short grating sound against the floor, as if it had been bumped.

Megan stared at it. Had her foot hit it?

Probably not.

She settled down cross-legged on the floor to go through the letters.

Twenty minutes later, she'd formed a pretty good impression of the young and giggly Isabella Smithson, "Bella" to friends and family.

Most of the letters were from girlfriends; a few were letters Bella had started to write and not finished. In the margins of those, Bella had often drawn small cartoons in illustration, some of them surprisingly sharp with humor.

So Isabella was the artist who had drawn the picture of Zachariah.

One letter beneath all the others was wrapped in a white velvet ribbon, a pressed flower tucked under its bands. Megan gently untied the ribbon and set the flower aside, then unfolded the letter.

My dearest Bella,

You have captured my heart, as surely you must have guessed by now. I cannot sleep for thoughts of you. You haunt my nights as the goddess Diana, and how willingly I would let you slay my heart.

But say the word and I am yours, for now and forever.

—Z.A.

"Megan?" Case called from somewhere down below. "Are you here? Megan?" he called, his voice rising in concern.

"I'm up here! I'll be down in a second!" she hollered, and hurriedly packed everything back into the trunk except the letter.

She was certain it was the beginning of everything. Carefully holding the letter, she hurried back down the stairs. Case was waiting on the servants' floor. He visibly relaxed when he saw her appear.

"I was worried. What happened downstairs?"

"What do you mean, what happened?"

"The mess in the kitchen."

"Mess?" She'd left her teacup and the photocopies, but surely that wasn't enough to cause alarm.

"Come see."

She followed him back down, neither of them talking until they reached the kitchen.

It was covered with paper, her printouts from the library.

In the sink, on top of the refrigerator, on every inch of floor, on the shelves. It looked as if a storm had blown through. Everything was covered in drifts of paper.

Everything except the kitchen table.

It was wiped clean except for one single piece of paper, centered exactly on the tabletop.

Megan set down the letter she was holding and picked up the photocopy, a page from the July 20 classified ads. She scanned the columns, and at the top of the third one, she saw what she'd been looking for:

> Z.A.
> *Where are you? Whatever has happened, all will be forgiven. Come back.*
> B.

She read it out loud to Case.

"Zachariah Armstrong and . . . ?" he asked.

"Bella. Isabella Smithson." Megan unfolded the letter and handed it to him.

He met her eyes when he had finished. "So this is a tale of love gone awry."

"Yes. But if Zachariah abandoned Bella, how did his spirit end up trapped in her house?"

seventeen

Case blew out his candle and climbed into bed, feeling strangely contented for a man in a haunted house. Eric had been gone all evening, returning just half an hour ago, so Case and Megan had spent a peaceful time in each other's company. He'd failed to keep his mind off the feel of her breast under his hand, but he'd been a gentleman and refrained from making a second go at her.

The lights had resumed their pattern of flickering, eventually going off completely and leaving Case and Megan to dine by the light of the oil lamp. She'd taken pity on his cooking, and together they made dinner on the propane-powered stove. Afterward, they settled in the library and pored through papers, writing up the solid facts they could find on large sheets of paper that they later tacked to the walls of the grand salon. Another sheet held unanswered questions, and a third held theories.

The evening was peaceful, warm, and punctuated by pithy comments and bursts of laughter. Once he'd sworn to himself that he would keep his hands off her, Case found himself enjoying the fall of her hair across her cheek as she read, the curve of her lips when she smiled, the mischief in her voice when she asked him a teasing question. He enjoyed her periodic silences, which he began to appreciate. He didn't need to entertain her, and she didn't speak solely for the sake of making noise.

Case punched his pillow and rolled over restlessly. Did they know each other well enough now to have sex? he wondered.

He closed his eyes and listened to Megan's movements next-door. He could imagine her clearly, in her prim white nightgown, lying alone in her bed. If he knocked on her door and leaned his head in, would she smile and welcome him? Would she say *yes* this time if he climbed in beside her and tossed that virginal gown to the floor?

He felt a stirring in his loins and cursed. How was he going to get to sleep now?

He forced his mind from Megan and focused on one of the houses his company was flipping. Halfway through his mental revamping of the kitchen, he fell asleep.

He woke to a hand sliding up his thigh. Groggy from dreaming, his half-sleeping brain thought it was Megan, that he was in her bed with her. He smiled as the hand slid higher, grazing his groin and continuing on up his torso. Soft lips kissed his jaw, and he felt a naked body pressing against his side.

"You're cold, darling," he mumbled. "Did I steal the covers from you?"

The lips dotted kisses along his cheek, landing on his mouth as a cold hand descended back to his groin, clasping his sex.

"Careful, honey!" he said, flinching from the cold, and opened his eyes.

A white face with hollow black eyes stared back at him.

He let out a sound like a murdered cat. The face vanished. He leaped out of bed and crouched, eyes darting wildly around the moonlit room. He could see nothing, but seeing nothing didn't mean there was nothing.

He snatched his robe off the foot of the bed and pulled it on, then opened the connecting door to Megan's room.

"Megan!" he whispered. "Megan! Are you awake?"

There was no answer. He pushed the door open wider and edged into the room.

Moonlight showed him the covers thrown back on her bed. She wasn't there.

She's in bed with Eric.

He didn't know where the thought came from, but

he was out in the hallway in frantic pursuit before it occurred to him that she may simply have gone to the bathroom. Or to the kitchen for a snack or a glass of water.

He was halfway down the stairs before the worst possibility of all struck him: Zachariah might have returned for her.

Case froze, staring down into the shadows, looking for a crumpled form in white cotton.

There was nothing.

He closed his eyes and listened.

Again, nothing.

He descended the rest of the staircase and quietly moved through the house in search of Megan. The library and the grand salon were unoccupied, Eric's electronics dark except for the few running on battery power.

Case turned down the hall to the kitchen. There was no flickering candlelight from either the kitchen or the crack under Eric's door. Case stood motionless in the center of the hall, straining his ears for a hint of sound.

From behind Eric's doors came the grunting, gravelly snores of a man with sleep apnea. The sound was as much a relief as a terror: if Megan wasn't with Eric, then where was she?

From below his feet came a heavy sound of metal dragging and scraping.

The cellar.

Cold washed over Case. Megan would never have gone down there on her own. And especially not in the middle of the night.

On silent feet, he dashed through the kitchen and the small hallway beyond. The cellar stairs were open, and at their dark bottom he saw the moving glow of a flashlight.

Caution held him back from calling her name. You weren't supposed to startle sleepwalkers, were you? If she was not fully conscious, it could be disastrous to wake her down in the cellar, in the dark.

He padded down the wooden stairs, coming out into a cellar gone dark. There was no flash of light in that room or the next.

He inched forward, his feet cautiously feeling his way across the bricks.

A flash of reflected light caught his eye, down at floor level. It came again, still faint but definitely there and in a half-moon shape.

The darkness threw his sense of perspective out of whack, and he could make no sense of the light. Where the hell was it coming from?

He remembered the sound of dragging metal.

The drain.

"Oh, Christ," he said beneath his breath. He found the drain cover pushed to the side and dropped to all fours at the edge of the drain.

The light wasn't moving anymore, and when he peered over the edge of the drain, he saw why.

The flashlight lay on rock and dirt eight feet below. The drain was not a drain: it was the entrance to a deeper space beneath the house. An iron ladder welded to a man-sized tube extended three feet down from the floor of the cellar. From somewhere in that rock-floored room, he heard Megan whimpering.

He was down the ladder in an instant, leaping the last few feet and snatching the flashlight from the ground. "Megan!"

"No, no, no," she whimpered, tears in her voice.

The beam of the light hit her back. She was standing, swaying, staring at something in front of her. Case shifted the beam of light, looking for something in the blackness, but only found it when he cast his light toward the ground.

The ground in front of Megan opened into a chasm, five feet across and twice as wide. Black iron stubs that might once have belonged to a protective fence surrounded the hole, their ends bent back down into the earth.

Megan's bare feet were inches from the edge, and she was swaying.

Case's legs felt as if they had turned to lead, moving with the horrific slowness of a nightmare as he ran to her. A shout of denial rose in his throat.

The sound of it pierced through her awareness, and she spun around, a look of utter surprise on her face. She stepped backward, and Case saw the error he'd made in distracting her. Her foot met air, and her mouth parted in horror as she began to lose her balance. With a final burst of speed, he reached out and snatched her arm, jerking her back from the brink.

She fell into his arms, and he clasped her tight against his chest, shock at what had almost happened blocking all thought from his mind. All he knew was that she was in his arms, she was safe, he hadn't lost her.

He didn't know how much time had gone by when he felt her begin to struggle against the confinement.

"I can't breathe, you're squeezing me too tight!"

He loosened his grip slightly, irrationally afraid that if he let her go, she might head straight back to that fissure.

"Case, it's okay, I'm all right."

"No, you're not." He put his hand on the back of her head and forced her to lay her cheek against his shoulder. "You've had a fright."

"Only caused by you," she grumbled into his neck. But then he felt her arms come up around his waist, holding him in return. A moment later, she began to weep quietly, tucking her face more closely into the collar of his robe.

"Shhh," he whispered against her hair. "It's okay."

She shook her head against his shoulder, then lifted it. "This is where he died. Zachariah."

"Down here?" Case asked in surprise, then shined the light up at her face for a moment.

She nodded, squinting, and he lowered the beam. "He was beaten and then tossed into that hole."

Case shined the light at the fissure. "God, talk about convenient disposal of a body. I wonder how deep that thing is?"

"I don't know. But there are ledges, and Zachariah landed on one. He wasn't dead yet. It took him hours to die, alone in the dark. He screamed for help as long as he could, but the drain hole had been covered up, and no one could hear him. His body was too broken for him to try to climb out on his own."

"Christ. Who did that to him?"

"I think it was Jacob Smithson."

EIGHTEEN

"What does it all add up to?" Case asked, standing in front of the posters he and Megan had created, now with the circumstances of Zachariah's death added.

"Obviously, Daddy didn't think Zachariah was good enough for his precious daughter," Eric said. "Jacob is rich and above the law. He tosses the guy in the hole like a piece of garbage."

"But why not just forbid the marriage?" Megan pointed out. "Or even buy him off? It's a huge risk to kill someone, even if you're rich."

"Maybe he knew his daughter wouldn't obey him, and Zachariah couldn't be bought," Case said. "If they were young and in love, there was probably no force that could stop them."

"I bet ol' Zachariah was a gold digger," Eric said. "I'll bet he came out here when the news spread about gold in the Klondike. He gets here, starts buying gear and outfitting himself, but then begins to hear about what a lot of work it's going to be. He starts hearing the horror stories. Frostbite, starvation, the long trek through the wilderness to reach gold fields that have all already been claimed. And he figures there are easier ways for a man to make himself a fortune. So he finds a rich man's daughter to seduce. Only Daddy knows a thing or two and can smell a rat when it's eating at his dinner table."

"Okay, I can buy that," Case said. "It fits what you can see of the man in that picture Isabella drew. But then how did his spirit get trapped here? Or, if the white woman is to be believed, how did he trap others here?"

"The white woman might be Isabella," Megan said. "Only her actions seem contradictory. I was assuming she was the one who led me to the trunk in the attic and to the love letter from Zachariah. But why would she say bad things about him during the séance? And why would she keep trying to molest Case? That hardly seems the act of a faithful lover."

They were all silent, contemplating.

"It seems that for each piece of information we discover, a half-dozen more questions are raised," Megan said.

"We need to know who's lying," Eric said. "Zachariah or Whitey. One of them's full of crap."

"Maybe they both are," Megan said. "Spirits can be as deceitful or deluded as the living."

"We've got to do another session with the helmet," Eric said. "It's the most controllable way we have of getting information."

"No," Case said. "Absolutely not. If there's one thing that's clear, it's that Zachariah is drawn to Megan, and he has twice now come close to causing her physical harm." He turned to Megan. "I think it might be better if you abandoned the investigation. You should leave. Go home."

Megan's jaw dropped, the air going out of her. "You're firing me?" she squeaked.

He shook his head. "It's not a matter of firing. It's a matter of ensuring your safety."

"You're overreacting! Nothing bad has happened to me!"

"Twice now—"

"You never let things go long enough to be sure there was going to be a bad outcome. Zachariah could have led me right into that fissure, but he didn't. I was the one who walked up to the edge," she said. "It drew me, almost like . . . like a magnetic force. Or gravity. I could feel a pull that had nothing to do with any spirits."

"Electromagnetic forces," Eric said. "I've got to go down there and get some readings."

"Could it have been the fissure itself that trapped Zachariah?" Megan suggested. "Maybe that pull is harder to resist if you've got no physical body to hold you back. Maybe it's an enormous spiritual magnet or a sort of spiritual black hole."

"A vortex," Eric said.

Megan shook her head. "A vortex is a doorway. This is more of a sinkhole, or somehow it works as a prison that spirits not only can't get out of, they can't easily get in, either. Maybe that's why Case's mother sounded like she was such a long way off. She was shouting over the walls, so to speak, and couldn't risk coming closer."

"All of which is more reason for you to put your safety first," Case said. "Didn't you once ask me to take you out of here if you were unable to take yourself? You sensed that you might become trapped."

"But I'm not trapped! Case, please, believe me. I'm a huge coward, and if I thought I might come to real harm, I'd be out of here so fast you couldn't catch me."

"You can't send her home," Eric said, gathering up equipment. "We wouldn't know any of this if it weren't for her. If you want this house to ever be livable, you've got to let her stay. You know that." He looked from one of them to the other. "I'm going down to the cellar. Either of you got an issue with that?"

They both shook their heads.

Eric made a noise. "I see how highly *I* rate on the concern scale." He trundled out with his gear.

When he was gone, Case came over to where Megan leaned on the edge of a table. He met her eyes. "Are you reluctant to leave because of our bet?"

She felt absurdly hurt by the suggestion. "It's not personal gain that keeps me here."

He touched her cheek. "It's not?"

She shook her head, suddenly too shy to hold his gaze.

"What does keep you here?" he asked.

"Pride, maybe," she said, flashing a glance up at him. "I started this job, and I want to finish it."

"Pride's never a good motive all on its own."

"Then there's curiosity. And . . ."

"And?"

"It's a little embarrassing."

He stroked her cheek and ran his fingertip along her jawline, ending at the curve of her bottom lip. She felt the sensation of it all the way down to her sex.

She met his eyes but didn't have the courage to say that she didn't want to leave because she feared he'd stop pursuing her.

"This is the first time in a long while that I thought my ability was truly useful and might do some good. If I don't figure out what's going on here, I don't know how Zachariah and any others are ever going to be free. And if they aren't freed, this house will never be the beautiful, peaceful home you're striving for."

"I see."

"You almost sound disappointed."

"I was hoping you'd say you'd miss me if you left."

A flush went through her, and her heart started to pound. "I—" she tried to say, but then he slid his warm palm around the back of her neck, his thumb stroking the tender spot in front of her earlobe. Her eyes half closed in pleasure.

He bent his head down to her, and she felt the warmth of his breath. Her lips parted of their own volition, her limbs going weak.

His lips touched hers lightly. Then again more firmly. He brushed her mouth with his own, setting her nerves alight. His other hand went to her waist, and then he was kissing her full on, and she felt herself sinking into the pleasure. Her eyes closed, and she gave herself up to it, vaguely aware of her own arms going around him, her own lips moving as directed by his.

He pressed his leg between her thighs, and she molded herself against him, arching her back so that she could feel the pressure of his chest against her breasts. It seemed she couldn't get close enough to him to satisfy her needs, those needs stoked ceaselessly by his mouth on hers.

She was tingling and dazed when he finally pulled back.

"I don't want you to hate me later, so there's something I should probably tell you," he said.

"You're married?" she joked.

"No. I'm buying your building."

She blinked at him, not understanding. "My building?"

"The one your shop's in."

She pulled away from him, shaking her head, a sick dread filling her. "No. Don't say you are, Case, not after I told you how much it means to me."

"I'd already made the offer. The seller has accepted. The deal closes in three weeks."

"You're going to have to get out of it!" she said in panic.

"I can't do that."

"Of course you can! Find a flaw when you inspect it. There are loopholes if you want to use them."

"Megan, even if you did win the bet and sold the furniture, it wouldn't be enough for the down payment on a place like that. The mortgage would have crushed you. You weren't being realistic."

"I knew what I was doing."

"It was a fantasy."

"Like everything about my life, huh? Is that what you think?"

"You're not the only woman to imagine she has psychic powers."

"*Imagine!* Did I *imagine* the name Zachariah Armstrong?"

"All we've ever seen in writing were the initials Z.A. You probably came across them in the papers somewhere and filled in the full name yourself."

She shook her head, her understanding of their relationship shattering into pieces. "You don't believe in me at all, do you?"

"I believe you're well-meaning and sexy as hell."

The words struck her like knives. "That's all this has meant to you, isn't it? Sex. You don't care about me. You don't like me or respect me. You just want to fuck me."

"Megan!"

"You can't deny it, can you?"

"I *do* care—"

Cold fury rose within her. "Bastard! Liar!" She slapped him.

He grabbed her wrist, his voice going cold. "Don't ever do that again."

She yanked herself free. "Don't *you* ever touch *me* again. You're exactly the type of man I took you for when you first walked through my door: a self-satisfied, overconfident, overgrown high school jock. I should have listened to my instincts."

"Not to your psychic powers?" he retorted, his face red with anger.

"You don't have to be psychic to know a bastard when you see one!" She spun on her heel and stalked from the room, her jaw clamped tight against furious tears. Out in the hall, she hesitated, then went out the back terrace doors into the garden. No one would hear her crying out there; no one would see her falling apart.

She plunged down the trail into the overgrowth, stopping only when she found the white statue. She sank to the ground, and her fury turned to sadness. She wept, remembering Case telling her his stupid fairy tale; remembering the cozy intimacy of the night before as they worked together; remembering his tender kiss just minutes before.

It had all been a lie, and she'd fallen for it. He didn't respect her or think she was gifted. He thought she was deluded, and he only cared about his own crotch. Why hadn't she listened to herself from the beginning and stayed away from Case Lambert?

She thought of Antique Fancies and the bank account that she and her mother had filled with $150,000 in hopes of one day having the chance to buy the building. All those years of scrimping and saving had been for nothing. On a whim, Case had taken her dream away from her, and he didn't even have the grace to say he was sorry. Instead, he told her she was an idiot for having had the dream, and there she'd been, eagerly lapping up his kisses and attention. It made her stomach churn in shame and embarrassment, and she wanted to retch.

In time, she sobbed herself out and quieted. What now? She could pack up and go home and never have to see him again.

"Or I can win my damn furniture," she said to the statue. "I'll take the best in the house, and I'm *not* splitting the profits from the colonial table with him."

It wasn't much of a revenge, but it beat crawling back home with her tail between her legs. She wanted to see his face when she proved him wrong about her. She wanted to hear him grovel for forgiveness.

Well, maybe he wouldn't grovel. But seeing him admit his error and apologize would be almost as good.

And maybe then he'll respect me and want me for something more than a night of passion.

Idiot! she scolded herself for the thought. *Christ, if that's how stupid I am, then I deserve him!*

She went back to the house, surprising Eric in the hall outside the grand salon.

"Megan, you're still here?"

"Why shouldn't I be?"

"Case said he thought you were taking off."

"He'd like that, wouldn't he?" she said darkly.

"What happened between you two?"

"I found out what type of person he really is. He thinks I'm imagining everything I see, did you know that?"

"He didn't make a secret of it." Eric touched her arm, his voice softening. "You know *I've* always believed in you. I've always thought you were the most amazing woman I'd ever met. I don't think there's anyone in the world half as special as you are."

The words were exactly what she needed to hear, and she felt her heart softening toward him. "Thanks, Eric. I needed that."

"C'mere," he said, opening his arms.

She hesitated but then gave in and let him hug her. His body was soft, almost feminine, making her feel that she was getting a comforting hug from someone's grandmother.

Maybe she and Eric could be friends, after all.

"You need someone who understands you," Eric said against her ear.

But then she felt his erection forming, pressed against her thigh. She shifted, trying to break contact.

Eric's hold on her tightened with surprising strength, and his mouth slanted across her cheek and clamped onto her lips. She struggled in his grip and felt his hand grab the back of her head, holding her in place as he kissed her.

"Eric, no!" she said when she could get her mouth free. She shoved at his sides but couldn't get her arms between them to push him off. She pinched and twisted both his love handles hard, but he only held her tighter.

"Get your hands off her!" Case roared, and the next moment Eric was torn from her and thrown halfway down the hall. Case charged after his fallen prey, but Eric stumbled to his feet, turned tail, and ran.

"Let him go!" Megan cried.

Case turned and stared at her, but there was no recognition in his eyes. She saw blind fury. "Did he touch you?" Case demanded.

"You saw."

"Did he *touch* you?"

"What are you asking?" He'd seen Eric kissing her. "Of course he touched me."

Case's neck muscles bulged, his eyes going wide. "I'll kill him!" He spun on his heel and ran down the hall after Eric.

"Case! Wait!" Megan cried, running after him. "Don't hurt him. I'm okay!"

Case moved with surprising swiftness, the force of his anger seeming to carry him. A sick dread of impending violence seeped through Megan, her stomach turning.

Case outdistanced her as her legs slowed, growing heavy. Her vision blurred, her eyes unable to focus on a single point. She stopped and leaned her hand against the wall, taking deep breaths and closing her eyes.

When she opened them, the world had changed. The house was finished, the walls papered, the floor covered in an Oriental runner.

She heard running footsteps behind her and turned.

Penelope Smithson, disheveled and pink-cheeked, was running toward her with a look of intense distress. Megan flattened herself against the wall, her own eyes wide with terror at being touched by this vision from the past.

Penelope slowed to a stop beside Megan, but her gaze was forward, her lips parted.

Megan turned to see where she was looking.

Jacob Smithson was dragging a body down the hallway.

Megan sucked in a gasp of air, sweat breaking out over her body. She recognized the man Smithson was dragging by the ankles: it was Zachariah. The young man's face was bloodied, his arms trailing above his head.

Smithson turned into the kitchen doorway, bumping Zachariah around the door frame. They were almost all the way through when Zachariah stirred, grabbing the jamb and convulsing in an obvious attempt to kick free of his captor. He cast a single desperate, imploring look in their direction, fear for his life plain in his dark eyes.

Megan and Penelope dashed forward together, then stopped in unison as Smithson appeared in the doorway, bent over, and pounded his fist into Zachariah's face until he lay still.

Megan looked away and closed her eyes. When she opened them, the past was gone, and she was again in the deconstructed hallway with its string of construction lights.

From the kitchen, she heard the distant sound of male voices raised in anger.

Déjà vu washed over her, the past overlapping with the present. She had a sudden certainty that Case was going to beat Eric to a pulp and toss him in the crevice. Only this was the twenty-first century, not the nineteenth, and Case would surely be arrested and convicted as Jacob Smithson was not. Eric would be dead or severely hurt. All three of their lives would be forever altered.

Penelope—where had Isabella been?—had been either helpless or unwilling to stop her father.

Megan was neither. She gathered her strength and ran to the cellar door, rushing down the stairs with her feet barely touching the treads.

"Stop! Stop! Case, don't kill him!"

They weren't in the room. Their voices came floating up from the hole in the floor, the drain cover shoved to the side, an orange electrical cord snaking down inside. Megan threw herself onto the floor and stuck her head into the opening.

"Case!" she screamed. "Don't kill him! It's the house! The house is making you do it!"

Without waiting for an answer, she sat up and swung her legs into the opening, finding the ladder rungs and descending as swiftly as she could.

She dropped to the dirt floor and spun round.

A light on a tripod illuminated the room. The two men were standing several feet from each other, their stances belligerent and defensive, the air thick with testosterone. The harsh light cast stark shadows on the walls of the rough, uneven space.

"What?" Case asked her, giving her a glance. "Kill him?"

"Don't! It's the house making you do it!"

He shook his head, his attention reverting to the object of his loathing. "I have no intention of killing him, but I'm going to beat the crap out of him."

"Well, don't throw him in the crevice when you're done."

"Jesus, Megan!" Eric said, edging away from the gap in the ground. "Don't give him ideas!"

"I'm not a sociopath," Case said crisply, some of the anger seeming to fall away from him. "No matter how tempting it is to act like one when dealing with a slimy little bastard who richly deserves a beating."

Eric's eyes narrowed. "At least I'm not a patronizing, smug, know-it-all bully who doesn't have the wit to think before he speaks or acts and who's been running around like a stag who smells a doe in heat."

Case's eyes narrowed on Eric. "Sounds like you're *asking* me to punch you in the mouth."

"This is *my* battle," Megan said, intruding between them. "Case, leave him alone."

"You're defending him."

"Shut up and sit down, will you?"

Case's angry eyes focused on her, and then she saw confusion breaking across his features.

She sighed and sat down on a rock, feeling a headache coming on. "While you two were acting like angry gorillas," she said wearily, "I had a bit of an experience in the hallway."

That got their attention. "What happened?" Eric asked, just as Case asked, "Are you okay?"

"I'm fine. This was a glimpse into the past, I think, one of those 'recorded' hauntings I told you about, Case, and that you apparently still believe are a load of crap. But I think what was going on just now between you and Eric—and perhaps me, too—was similar enough that the recorded haunting got triggered."

"Go on," Case said, skepticism thick in his voice.

Megan explained what she had seen Smithson do to Zachariah.

"So you see," she finished up, "there's no question now that Zachariah was killed and dumped in the crevice. He didn't lie to me about that."

"I thought it was Isabella who was infatuated with Zachariah," Case said. "Why was it Penelope who was disheveled and following the two men?"

"Isabella obviously didn't know what happened to Zachariah. Not for at least a few weeks, given that ad she placed asking about him."

"She may never have known," Eric said. "Her sister may have kept it from her."

"Why? To protect their father?" Megan asked.

"Maybe Penelope was jealous of her sister."

Megan nodded. "There's something else I realized as I was coming down here to stop Case from killing you," Megan said, and turned back to Case. "The memories in this house, or the ghosts, or *something* about it might be influencing us. Our thoughts, emotions, behaviors. We might, in some way, be playing roles that were first played by the Smithsons and Zachariah more than a hundred years ago. It seems too big a coincidence, for example, that you two should take your fight down here."

"I suppose that makes me Jacob?" Case asked in obvious distaste, standing up again.

She shook her head. "I don't know. Maybe it doesn't need to be as specific as that. It's just . . ." She trailed off, searching for words. "It's the *emotions* that may be moving us. Jealousy. Anger." She paused and blinked. "Lust."

"I don't need ghosts for that," Eric said.

Megan got off her rock. "Now, if you'll excuse me, I've managed to give myself a headache." She moved toward the ladder, then turned with her hand on a rung. "I don't think you two should stay down here. It feels like something wants to happen down here."

"Like what?" Case asked.

"I don't know. That's what scares me."

NINETEEN

Megan lay in the dappled light under a big-leaf maple tree, listening to the crows and to the occasional high-up rumble of passing aircraft. In the spaces of quiet between the two, there was the rustle of leaves in the breeze to entertain her.

She lay on a blanket, a T-shirt over her eyes as a makeshift sleeping mask. Darkness soothed her headache, as did being out of the house.

In the crevice room, Case and Eric had declared themselves spelunkers. They had temporarily set aside their differences in a male way that was beyond Megan's comprehension. As she lay there, they were no doubt finishing up their system of ropes, pulleys, lights, and harnesses and preparing to descend into the fissure in search of Zachariah's bones.

Fine, Megan thought. Let them break their legs and bang their heads and be frightened by ghosts. Let them kill each other. She'd had enough of both of them.

Case, of course, didn't believe there were bones to be found, but the crevice was a mystery he couldn't resist exploring. Eric thought that bringing up the bones might help release Zachariah from the house. It usually helped in the movies.

But Megan didn't think it was going to work out that way.

No, something or someone had trapped Zachariah, or he himself had trapped others, including the woman who whispered to Megan. In either case, the question was why?

Revenge? Love? Obsession? Spite?

Or was it something about the very earth the house sat on that trapped souls?

Beside her was an armful of books she'd dug out of the house's library, intent on continuing her research into what the sisters had been up to with their séances and psychics. An hour's reading about spells and potions had been as much as Megan could stand, though. She refused to believe that sprinkling herbs around a house while drinking red wine and chanting could have any effect on the dead. The spells seemed to be meant purely for the peace of mind of the living.

Perhaps she was too strongly rooted in her own

century. She had more faith in Eric's electronic gizmos than in potions of fennel and pine and pentagrams drawn on the floor.

Megan heard someone approaching through the grass, the blades whishing against feet. She pulled the T-shirt off her face and turned her head, squinting up at the interloper.

Case sat down beside her, almost close enough for his hip to touch hers. She inched away. Was he there to apologize?

His gaze wandered over the garden. "It's really a mess, isn't it?"

"But it's so quiet that I forget we're only a handful of blocks from downtown."

He set something beside her on her blanket. "I thought you might want to see this."

Megan pushed herself up into a sitting position, staring at the item. "A gold watch. It was Zachariah's?"

"It was in the rotted bits of cloth that were once his clothes."

She grimaced. "And what else was inside those clothes?"

"Bones. Not all of them, of course. Some must have fallen deeper into the fissure, including his skull." He was quiet a moment, then touched the pocket watch with his fingertip. "Funny that I should have first met you over a watch."

"I can't say I'm enjoying the coincidence."

He crooked a smile at her, seeming uncomfortable. "But maybe it wasn't such a coincidence that I chose a watch to bring you. You said the house could be influencing us in subtle ways. Maybe it influenced me to choose that. God knows there are fifty other things in the house I could have brought to you."

"You're not talking like the skeptical Case I know," she said.

"Maybe I'm finding it hard to argue with a body hidden in a room I didn't even know existed until you found it." He nudged the watch. "You don't want to touch it, to get a reading?"

She shook her head. "I'd rather not. Not now, anyway."

They were both quiet, the watch sitting beside them, a symbol of life ended too soon. Of chances lost.

"Megan, I . . ." Case started, then stopped.

"Yes?"

He blew out a breath, ran his hand through his hair, then plunged ahead. "I feel like I owe you an apology. Not for being skeptical but for being determined from the beginning that you were a fraud and then letting that belief color my perception of you. It was unfair."

She watched him in silence, watched the nervousness in his movements. She wasn't going to let him off easy. "I cared what you thought about me, you know," she said. "It hurt when you said those things."

"I can't excuse my behavior, but you need to

understand, you weren't the first so-called medium I'd met in my life. My mother was addicted to them. I saw the whole gamut, from palm readers to faith healers to aura photographers and spoon benders." His voice grew angry at the memories. "They were bloodsucking frauds, each and every one."

"Some of them probably believed in what they were doing, thought they were helping people."

Case shook his head, a quick, angry denial. "All I know is that our phone and electricity got turned off when Mom spent all her money on psychics instead of paying the bills. So you can see that I didn't have a very high opinion of anyone in the profession."

Megan bit her lower lip, taking in what he'd said, trying to see things from his perspective. Truth be told, she didn't think much of most psychics, either, and thought even less of the ones who would take money from those who couldn't afford it. "Do you know what your mom was looking for?" she asked in a softer voice.

"Who the hell knows? Hope, I guess. After watching her, I swore I'd never fall for any of that crap. Which makes it ironic, doesn't it, that I should end up buying a house like this and hiring ghost hunters to help me."

She had thought she'd enjoy seeing him apologize, but without his skepticism, he seemed fragile and at a loss. "Maybe you bought the house because, deep down, you knew it was haunted. They say that we seek out the same problems in life, over and over again, until we learn how to overcome them."

"So, I unconsciously bought the house as therapy?" He laughed. "I don't think so."

"Do any of us truly have free will or know why we make the choices we do?"

He looked up at the house, his amusement fading. "It was love at first sight with this house."

"It has something you need, even if you don't know what that is. You may never know."

He looked back at her. "Megan, I don't want you to hate me. Can you forgive me?"

It would be so easy to say yes, but one thing stood in her way. "You're buying my building," she said quietly.

"Could you really have afforded nine hundred thousand dollars?"

Megan's jaw dropped. *Nine hundred thousand?* I thought it was only worth five or six. The place is almost a tear-down."

"You'd need at least forty percent down if you wanted to break even every month, more likely fifty. Do you have that?"

"I have one hundred and fifty thousand dollars." It suddenly seemed a pittance, as she did the math in her head. "You were right," she said, the utter hopelessness of it coming clear to her. She saw now that she *had* been a dreaming fool. "All those years of saving, of my mother and me planning what we'd do when the building was ours. It was never going to happen."

"Not unless you got a loan on your house to finance it."

"I thought of that but was afraid I'd be stretched too thin."

"You would have been. A hundred and fifty thousand, huh?"

"Yeah." She smiled sadly. "I guess I can afford to take a vacation now."

"Yeah. Or . . ." He trailed off.

She waited.

"Or I could let you buy into the building. You could afford an eighth share without getting a loan or a quarter share with a small loan."

Her heart thudded. "You'd let me do that?"

He nodded. "I don't like having partners in real estate, but I'm feeling guilty."

She put her hand over her lips to hide the trembling. "You'd do that? Partners. Really?"

"We'd fight a lot. I have ideas for the place that you won't like, and you'd have to listen to me since I'd be the majority owner."

"The building's a wreck. You can't hurt it."

"You'd still have to pay rent." He met her eyes. "This isn't a free ride."

"I know." But letting her buy into the building was a sign of respect. He never would have offered, guilty feelings or no, if his opinion of her had not changed.

She ducked her face, smiling, her heart filled with light and hope where it had been dark moments before. She slid her hand toward his on the blanket, then entwined her fingers with his. "Thank you."

His fingers tightened on hers. "Are we friends, then?"

"Of course."

He lifted her hand and kissed its back. Then he pulled her toward him slowly, the determination in his face bringing a flutter of alarm and of arousal to Megan. He tilted his head and kissed her hard. Her lips parted under his, allowing him entrance, and as he plundered her mouth, her fingers dug into his flesh. A soft cry of pleasure tightened her throat.

The next thing she knew, he was lowering her to the blanket, his body covering hers. He held one of her hands and raised it above her head, pinning it to the ground while his other hand went to her waist, finding the soft flesh beneath the hem of her T-shirt. His palm stroked her waist, then up her rib cage, while his lips moved to her ear, his tongue teasing her lobe and the small space behind it, then tracing down the line of her neck and sucking hard at its base.

His palm brushed over her breast, then again, and she felt her nipple responding through the cloth of her thin bra. He shoved the meager garment up, his palm meeting her flesh-to-flesh.

He left her breast for just long enough to grab her other wrist and raise it above her head, too, insisting she keep both hands there with a noise in his throat. She clenched her fists and obeyed, her back forced into an arch that raised her breasts. She felt a deep, primal pleasure at his sexual hunger. She instinctively understood that for this moment, he didn't want her to do anything but submit.

Her obedience was rewarded with a quick removal of her shirt and bra, and then his hands were at her jeans, unfastening and pulling them off with her panties, leaving her naked on the blanket with the gentle breeze on her skin.

He met her eyes, checking her willingness, perhaps remembering how she had stopped him when he was in her bed.

She didn't want to stop him now.

He read the answer on her face, and a devilish pleasure filled his eyes. His mouth explored her breasts while his hand stroked her hip and along her thigh. He laved her nipple, then moved up her neck, returning to her mouth, distracting her with the invasion of his tongue as his hand moved from her thigh to the mound of her sex. He cupped his palm over her, his strong fingers barely touching the folds beneath. Megan moaned deep in her throat, tilting her pelvis and parting her thighs, trying to bring herself into stronger contact with his hand.

He had no intention of fulfilling her wish. With the delicate precision of a musician, he stroked his fingertips over her folds with the gentlest, lightest of touches, a bare skimming that set her nerve endings on fire. Again and again, he barely touched her, his fingertips a mere whisper against the apex of her desire. The kiss broke off, and he lay half over her, his mouth near her ear, his breath warm in the crook of her neck. She could feel his concentration and control in the tenseness of his body, and she lowered her hands to his shoulders, gripping his shirt.

"Please," she said, arching her hips.

He pressed his lips against the side of her neck and held steady there while his fingers continued their sweet torture.

"Case, *please.*"

"My kingdom for a condom," he said hoarsely, and then, before she could respond, his hand moved lower, and his fingertips swirled in the damp opening to her sex. One strong finger gently parted her, then began to slip inside with slow, shallow thrusts.

His mouth left her neck as he slid his whole body down until his head was level with her hips. His finger thrust fully inside her as his mouth came down on her folds. His lips captured her clitoris, sucking it while his tongue moved in expert circles. His hand continued its thrusting, the finger inside her stroking up against a place she hadn't known was there, a place that seemed directly tied to the movements of his tongue on her clit.

The tension in her body quickly built, like an

ocean wave swelling in size. "Case, *oh, God,* what are you—"

He stopped, mouth and hand going motionless as she hung on the peak of the wave, every muscle in her body tight. For a long, exquisite moment, she balanced there, and then his finger moved once more inside her, his tongue stroked her, and waves of pleasure rolled through her body.

When the last of the pleasure receded, Case moved up beside her on the blanket and pulled her against his side. She lay in blissful contentment, gazing up into the green leaves of the maple, the pale blue sky in broken pieces of mosaic behind it. Then her hand inched down his flat belly to the buckle of his belt, and she gave back to him all that she had received.

TWENTY

"So!" Eric said, rubbing his hands together in glee. "Séance tonight in the subcellar, yes?"

Megan turned around from drying the dinner dishes. "Tonight?" she squeaked. "Go down there tonight?"

It was the last thing she wanted. All through dinner and cleanup, she'd been daydreaming about Case and just what they might do tonight. It had been lovely out there under the maple, but her body wanted a deeper satisfaction. She'd been counting the minutes until they could all retire for the night.

"I've got everything set up down there. Temporal lobe stimulater, EM blaster, computer, even a chair for you, Megan. Got a power cable running to a rented generator so there's less danger of losing juice. We're all set. If we can't figure this all out tonight, then we're a sorry bunch of losers!"

"Eric, the last thing I want to do is go down to that subterranean chamber of horrors in the middle of the night and put on that helmet."

"It'll be phenomenal! There's no scenario we've ever encountered that is so ripe for investigation and resolution! How can you not want to do it?"

"Quite frankly, I'm scared," Megan admitted.

"She has good reason," Case said.

Eric gaped at them. "But you've both used the helmet. You know it's safe!"

"Don't be obtuse," Megan said. "You know that's not what I'm afraid of."

"But we have Zachariah's bones. This is the moment! The iron is hot!"

"I don't want to go down there at night," she said simply. "I don't know how well I'd be able to resist whatever might happen, especially if my mind's been opened up with that helmet."

"I agree," Case said. "It's too great a risk. We'll go down there tomorrow and try something during the daylight hours."

Eric looked from one of them to the other, suspicion and disbelief mingling on his face. He shook his head. "There's no point in going down there for a séance if it's not during the night, when the total effect will be strongest. You both know that. What's the deal? You have other plans for tonight?"

Megan involuntarily glanced at Case.

Eric caught it. "What? What's going on?"

"Nothing's going on," Case said. "I think we've both spent more than enough time down there today."

"Well, it's not like we can watch TV tonight. What else are we going to do? Play Scrabble?"

"I thought I'd read through the rest of those copies from the *Seattle Times*. Maybe there's something more there," Megan said. It was the best she could come up with.

"By candlelight? Not good for your eyes."

"I've got paperwork to catch up on," Case said.

Eric blew out a breath. "So busywork is taking precedence over some active investigation." He shrugged. "Okay, have it your way! You want the ghosts to have the run of the house for another night, that's your decision."

"What are you going to do?" Megan asked.

"Same thing I always do. Tweak the equipment, review recordings. Guess I'll fill the long, lonely hours somehow." He looked from one of them to the other.

Megan pressed her lips together, refusing to be manipulated into offering to spend the evening with him.

A few hours later, Megan put the newspaper she had been reading down on the kitchen table and rubbed her eyes. Eric had been right about the candlelight.

She listened to the noises of the house: creakings and cracks, the hum of the refrigerator. No door bangings, though, or ghostly footsteps.

The last she'd seen, Eric had been in the salon. Case had worked on his laptop at the kitchen table, until the battery got low, and then he kissed her on the forehead and said he'd see her later tonight, after the house had settled down.

She remembered the feel of Case's mouth on her sex and closed her eyes as the memories of pleasure passed over her. Megan bit her lip, a moment of doubt hitting her. Was she really ready for sex with Case, when earlier in the same day she had been cursing him? Maybe the house was pushing her toward it.

She'd be glad when this was all over, *if* it was ever all over. She had no way to tell if they'd be able to rid the house of ghosts. The uncertainty of how to deal with the situation had been quietly eating at her since the day Case first tried to hire her.

She blinked, surprised by her own thought.

It *wasn't* dealing with the dead that scared her. She didn't fear what was "out there." She feared her own lack of competence.

"Well, crap," she said, taken aback. She hadn't considered that it was fear of failure that stopped her from doing things.

Was it fear of failure that kept her at the shop instead of trying something new? Even worse, was it fear that had kept her dating men she knew she could dominate, as Tracie had said?

Case scared her a little bit, despite the delicious things he'd done to her under the maple tree. There was no way to control him, no way to tame him. That thrilled her, but it made her afraid to show her whole heart to him and risk annihilation.

She was a coward. In work, in love—a miserable, yellow-bellied coward.

"You going up to bed soon?" Case asked.

Megan started. Case was poking his head in the doorway to the kitchen. "Bedtime?" she squeaked.

"It's almost eleven, but Eric is still as bright-eyed as a squirrel and running around the house with his sensors."

"Oh," she said, a world of disappointment in the sound.

"He can't stay up *all* night."

"The guy's nocturnal."

"We'll have the morning to ourselves, then," Case said with a deliberate leer.

Megan smiled.

Case stepped fully into the room. "Find anything interesting in the newspapers?"

"An ad for an elixir that promises to cure both gout and baldness, some fancy women's hairpieces for sale, but other than that, no."

He nodded, unsurprised. "So. Coming up to bed?"

"You go on ahead, get some sleep. Gather your

energy," she said, waggling her brows suggestively. "I want to tidy up a bit down here, then maybe take a bath."

"Okay. Holler if you need anything."

He kissed her forehead, then tilted her head up and kissed her on the lips. It was a soft and tender kiss, but it went right to the core of Megan's unsatisfied hunger. She kissed him back, her hand going around his neck to bring him closer. She was rewarded with a low moan in his throat, his arm going around her and starting to raise her out of her chair.

A loud *thump* in the hallway startled them apart. They both stared at the empty doorway, waiting, Megan's heart tripping.

"God *damn* it!" Eric said from the hall, his butt appearing as he bent over, half out of sight. A moment later, he was upright and looking in at them, a piece of broken equipment in his hands. He held up the thing in his hands. "Can you believe it? Flew right out of my hands. If I didn't know better, I'd say the ghosts did it. But they're not going to outsmart me so easily, oh, no, not if I have to stay up all night."

"Good for you," Megan said, and didn't mean a word of it.

Case lay awake in bed, listening to the muffled, barely audible sound of the generator down in the cellar, to Eric's occasional swear words from down the hall near the sisters' rooms as he struggled with disobedient equipment, and to the faint hints of movement that told him Megan was taking a bath.

She was so close, so naked, so willing, and so completely out of reach as long as Eric was prowling the halls. Case blew out a breath of frustration. He should stop thinking about her naked body, her hands soaping her breasts, the sheen of water on her buttocks . . .

He rolled onto his side and shut his eyes, willing his exhaustion to overcome his lust. *Nixon. Think of Nixon!*

And for God's sake, don't make another move in this house without a condom in your pocket.

He had reached a light sleep when, like so many times before, he felt a hand sliding up his thigh.

Only this time, the hand was warm.

His eyes popped open, staring straight ahead into the darkness of the room. *This was real.* Elation and surprise mixed together, keeping him motionless as she made her move.

He felt the covers lift behind him, then the mattress shifted with Megan's weight. She snuggled up behind him, her nightgown between her soft body and his back.

"Hi," he said softly, feeling his arousal stir.

"Hi," she said, her voice a hoarse whisper. He felt her breath on the back of his neck and then her lips pressing against the skin at his nape. Her hand slid around his pelvis and reached for his groin, finding his sex and cupping it.

Something suddenly seemed not quite right.

Her hand was big. *Too* big. And her arm—surely it couldn't be that heavy?

The hand encircled his penis and began to move up and down in a well-practiced motion. At the same time, Case felt a nudge against his buttocks. A type of nudge he had never felt before but had undoubtedly given to women in his bed.

Understanding dawned, and in a sudden frenzy of motion, Case scrambled out of bed, the covers tangling in his limbs. He fell to the floor with a thud and was as quickly on his feet again.

"Darling," the whisper came out of the dark. "Darling, what's the matter?"

"Eric! God damn it! What the hell do you think you're doing?" Case shouted.

There was a soft giggle from his bed. "I'm not Eric, you silly," the whisper said.

The hair rose on Case's skin. "Then who are you?"

He heard the rustle of movement, the squeak of the bed. "I'm the one you've been dreaming of," the voice said.

In the faint light from the window, Case saw a tall shape moving toward him. Horror crept up his spine, terror flushing through his blood and making his ears ring. It moved toward him, the dark shape of its arms rising as if to embrace him.

Without thinking, Case hauled back and punched the thing where he thought its face was.

His fist met solid flesh. The shape grunted and dropped to the floor, the force of the fall shaking the floorboards.

The connecting door flew open, light spilling into the room. "Case! Are you okay?" Megan cried.

Case's gaze went from Megan to the shape lying at the foot of his bed. It *was* Eric.

And yet it wasn't.

Megan's eyes followed his. "Holy mother of—" she whispered. And then, her voice too flat to be bemused, "So that's what happened to my nightgown."

Case barked a laugh and felt his muscles trembling with adrenaline. He sat on his bed, fearing his legs would give out beneath him. He grabbed a corner of the sheet and pulled it up over his bare lap.

Megan inched forward, holding the candle over Eric's supine form. "He got into my makeup, too." She looked at Case as he bent forward, examining Eric's crudely made-up face. "Is that lipstick on the back of your neck?" Megan asked.

His hand went to where he'd felt Eric's lips and rubbed viciously at the spot. "Would it be asking too much of life," he said dryly, "if once—just once!—when I woke up in the middle of the night with hands on me, they were the hands of a living woman?"

He looked up at Megan.

She blinked at him. "Eric—"

He shuddered. "Yes." He frowned down at the unconscious man. "What the hell got into him?"

Megan cocked her head, examining Eric herself. "Maybe not what. Who."

Eric moaned, his eyelids fluttering. Megan knelt down beside him in her bathrobe. "Eric?"

Case grabbed his pants and quickly put them on. There were times when a man wanted serious clothing between himself and the world around him.

"Eric, can you hear me?"

Eric blinked his eyes open. "Megan? What's going on?"

Case and Megan helped Eric into a sitting position. The nightgown was rucked up around his thighs, perilously close to his goods.

"Eric, do you remember what happened to you?" Megan said.

He looked from her to Case, then gingerly touched his jaw. "I feel like I was punched in the face."

"You were," Case said.

Concern pinched Eric's features. "I don't remember being in a fight."

"There wasn't a fight," Megan said softly. "You got into Case's bed and kissed him."

Eric's eyes widened, his mouth falling open. Then he blinked rapidly. "Like hell I did!"

Megan put her hand on his shoulder. "Eric, you're wearing my nightgown and makeup."

He looked down at himself and sucked in a breath. His wide eyes lifted to Case. "Jesus Christ, man. You know I'm not—"

"Yeah, yeah, I know," Case said, wanting him to shut up. He didn't want to rehash the situation.

"What did I—"

"Never mind! What was the last thing you remember?"

Eric lifted his arm, staring at the white cotton covering it.

"Eric, what do you remember?" Case asked. "The last I knew, you were down the hall, messing with your equipment."

Eric stared into space, a small frown between his brows. "Yeah, I remember that. Then I went down to the salon to go over some data, and while I was there, I thought I saw something on one of the live monitors. The one for the sub-basement. I left a camera down there, working on generator power like the rest of my equipment."

"What did you see?" Megan asked.

He shook his head. "I don't know. It was just a white blur of movement. It was being digitally recorded, of course, so I replayed it. Slowed it down. Still couldn't see what it was. So I decided to go check it out." He blinked at Megan, then at Case, helplessness in his eyes. "I don't remember anything after that. I got down there, and . . . and here I am." The corners of his mouth quivered and pulled down, his eyes squeezing shut. "Oh, God, oh, God . . ."

Case slapped his hand down on Eric's shoulder, making him jump. "You'll just have to chalk this up as one of the lousiest nights of your life. Come on, get up," he said, standing himself and grabbing Eric's hand, tugging him upward. "Go wash that crap off your face." Case nudged Eric ahead of him toward the door, pausing only to light his own candle off Megan's. "You make a god-awful ugly woman, you know that?" he said to Eric.

Megan gaped at him. He gave her a reassuring wink. "He'll be fine. Go on back to bed. We can talk about this tomorrow."

She nodded and turned to go back to her own room.

Case led Eric toward the bathroom, shaking his head as the magnitude of what had happened sank in. There'd been a shift in the game the ghosts were playing; it was hardball now.

The score in this new game was Ghosts 1, Living People 0.

It was time to even up the score.

Twenty-One

"That was it!" Megan said, her fingers working on one of Eric's keyboards.

"I missed it."

"Here, let me play it again."

On-screen, the fissure room sat empty. Through the speakers came the rumbling *chugga chugga* of the generator in the cellars above. Megan put her finger to the screen. "Watch right there."

Something wide and white blurred across the screen, the sound from the speakers turning to static for a brief moment. And then the white was gone, the generator chugging along as normal.

"Christ, I can't believe he went down there," Case said.

"You remember how impatient he was last night."

"Is he brave or an idiot?"

"I really couldn't say," Megan said, and tapped the keys again, setting the recording back to play. "Let's see what he does."

They watched the screen in silence, waiting for Eric's appearance. A minute went by. Then another. Almost five minutes passed before bright green glowed and wavered at the edge of the screen: Eric, coming down the ladder with a flashlight.

The light steadied, the scene thrown into sharp black and pale green relief. The camera auto-adjusted to the change in light level, evening out the contrast.

Eric moved into view.

He stood, staring into the fissure, then turned around and reached for something on the ground. Megan couldn't quite see what it was.

The screen flashed white, then went black.

Nothing.

"Shoot," Megan said under her breath. "It went dead." She fast-forwarded, but there was nothing to see.

"That's suspiciously convenient," Case said.

"Convenient for whom?"

"The ghosts. Or Eric. That could have been a power cable he reached for. He may have shut it off himself."

Megan shook her head. "To what end? Nothing is real to him unless it's recorded."

"I'm not saying I can see a reason. But it's possible."

"Or the ghosts could have shut it off, so we couldn't see what happened."

"That sounds like premeditation. If you wanted to look at it that way, then Eric was lured down there."

Megan rewound the footage to the white blur, freezing the image on-screen. They both stared at it.

"It seems elaborate, for a ghost," Megan said. "Using technology to lure someone? It speaks of an understanding of how the cameras work and that Eric is watching from another room."

"It's the same thing as them slamming doors on other floors," Case said. "Only this time, they refined the act. Unless Eric doctored the footage and shut off the camera himself."

"And purposefully put on my nightgown and makeup and got into bed with you? I don't think so. You're cute, but not that cute."

"Is that a compliment or an insult?"

"Neither. Eric's not gay."

"Bi?"

Megan shrugged. "Not that I know of. I suppose he could surprise me, though. You think this was all an elaborate scheme on his part, so that he'd have an excuse to get into bed with you?"

Case was silent, mulling it over, then shook his head. "The guy was too upset after he woke up. He flinched when he saw himself in the bathroom mirror. I thought he was going to start crying again."

Megan sat back, trying to piece it all together. "Tell me again what he said to you in your bed?"

Case repeated what had happened.

"It does seem that the simplest explanation is that he was possessed by the spirit that's been visiting your bed. But how did it get hold of Eric?"

"Maybe the same way that dark entity got hold of you a couple of years ago," Case suggested. "Maybe it was the helmet that Eric was reaching for when the camera went out. He might have gone down there thinking he was going to communicate with whatever had flashed across the screen."

"Which was exactly what the spirit wanted," Megan agreed. "Eric wouldn't have any psychic defenses, especially not down there, where everything is magnified. The ghost got inside him and took the chance to lay her hands on you for real. After making herself pretty with my things, of course. The better to seduce you."

Case grimaced. "She's a horny old hen, I'll give her that."

Megan felt a smile tug at the corner of her mouth. "She didn't seem to like being punched in the face, though. It chased her right out of him. Who knows how long it's been since she felt real physical pain?"

"A little more of it might be a good thing for her."

"I wonder if it's Isabella," Megan mused. "She seems to have been a passionate woman in life. I'm fairly certain that she had to be the one who led me to the letters in the trunk. She wanted me to know that Zachariah loved her." Megan chewed her bottom lip, thinking of her vision in the hallway, of Zachariah's murder. Penelope, disheveled, watching it happen. Isabella not being told for several weeks.

"I wonder if Penelope tried to steal Zachariah away from her sister," Megan said. "Maybe Penelope got herself into a compromising position with Zachariah and was discovered in the act by her father."

"Maybe Zachariah tried to rape her?" Case suggested. "That would infuriate any father to the point of murder."

"Maybe. Or maybe he assumed his daughter had to be a victim, not a seductress."

" 'I earn my fate,' " Case quoted. "Did Zachariah earn his?"

"Or was it the sisters who somehow earned theirs, spending their lives together in this house, spinsters to the end?" Megan tapped her bottom lip, thinking. "Do you suppose they hated each another? Supposedly, they went everywhere together, but maybe that was just because they didn't trust each other. Maybe the day they died, Penelope wasn't trying to carry Isabella to safety. Maybe she was trying to dump her out at the curb like a piece of trash."

"That's a bit too harsh to believe."

"I suppose if she hated her that much, she probably would have found a way to hurt her much earlier."

"I suddenly find myself hoping it was Isabella who was in my bed. Under this theory, Penelope was a piece of work."

"But it's still just a theory." Megan's stomach rumbled, and she looked at her watch. "It's nearly noon, and Eric's still not up. Last night must have drained him."

"Let the guy sleep. I'm sure he'd just as soon put off remembering last night."

"Despite myself, I feel kind of sorry for him," she admitted.

"You have a tender heart."

"I never thought I did. But to have your whole body taken over by something else . . . I couldn't wish that on him."

He took her hand and squeezed it. "Promise me one thing?"

"What?"

"Never wear that helmet again."

"I can handle it better than Eric."

His hand tightened on hers. "I don't want you to have to try."

"You're not afraid of *me* crawling into your bed at night, are you?" she teased.

"I don't want you there if it's not really you. It's not just your body that I want."

"Glad to hear it."

He laughed and stood, releasing her hand. "How about lunch?"

She rose from her chair. "Lunch, yes." Where she could digest the fact that they hadn't had the wild sexual romp of a morning that she'd been hoping for. *Gee, thanks, Eric, for making sex the last thing on Case's mind!* If Eric weren't in such sad shape, she'd have punched him again herself.

By three o'clock, Eric still hadn't gotten out of bed. Megan poked her head in his door to check on him and was greeted by a loud snore. The gray light of the overcast day, creeping through the windows, had not been enough to wake him.

"Eric?" Megan called in a whisper. "You awake?"

More snores.

She gently shut the door and left him to it. Last night must have taken a lot out of him, and he was probably sleep-deprived to begin with.

Earlier, Case had gone outside to do some physical work. "It clears my mind," he explained. Now Megan went outside to see what he was up to.

She found him a half-dozen feet from the front gate, digging at the base of the wall. A heap of greenery was behind him.

"Gardening?" Megan asked, walking up the drive to him.

He looked up from his work. "De-gardening. I'm pulling off the ivy. Nasty stuff, not native. Rats love to live in it."

"Ugh."

"Eric up yet?" he inquired.

She shook her head. A chill passed over her skin, and she crossed her arms, rubbing the backs of them with her hands. She raised her eyes to the gray sky. "Looks like the weather is turning."

He balanced his forearm atop the shovel, looking upward himself. "My guess is it'll start raining within the hour. The breeze has been picking up." He took a step back to admire his handiwork. "Not much more to go. Looks better, doesn't it?" he asked, grinning.

"Much." Megan tilted her head, looking at the wall. "That iron fence on top is a little strange, isn't it?"

"I've seen walls done like this before. Not quite in these proportions but a similar idea."

"It might look better without that iron. It's sort of prisonlike, don't you think? And it somehow doesn't look quite right."

"You think I should take it down?"

The wind gusted, and Megan felt a sprinkling of cold rain. "I wonder if the fence was part of the original wall or a later add-on. It might be truer to the original house to take it down."

"One of those old photos might show you."

She perked up. "You're right! I'll go look."

"I'll be in soon," he said, and went back to work.

Megan hurried back toward the house, casting another look skyward. A crow coasted by, almost low enough to touch. Surprised, Megan skittered sideways, but it flew on to join its cronies in the maple. She regained the shelter of the house and went to grab a sweater before heading to the library to go through the photos.

Rain pattered on the glass of the library window by the time she found an old photo with a good shot of the wall.

There was no fence on top.

What had possessed the Smithsons to put up the fence? The wall was much more pleasing without it. Inviting, friendly.

Had that been the problem?

Maybe Isabella and Penelope had put it up, two aging spinsters afraid of the big bad city outside their walled cloister. Maybe they'd had a break-in.

She took the photo and an umbrella and went outside to find Case. The wind had picked up during the short time she'd been inside, a storm obviously blowing in from off the Pacific. She dashed down the drive toward the gate but stopped when she saw that Case wasn't there. His shovel leaned against the wall, but he was nowhere to be seen.

Cold wind pushed at her back. Her attention was drawn to the gates.

The rocks propping them open to either side were gone, and they swayed in the wind. The one on the right squeaked, and then, in one long, slow movement, it swung to the center of the arch and shuddered to a halt against the small steel stop in the drive.

Go, something whispered in her ear. *Go now, hurry, while you can!*

The gate on the left began to swing shut, then opened again, its hinges as creaky as its twin's.

Go! Hurry! It's your last chance!

The same feeling of dread and being trapped that she'd had upon her arrival at the house overwhelmed her now. She could feel the very earth around her reaching up to grab her, to pull her down into the cellar, down into the fissure, where it would keep her forever.

The gate swung again, this time closing all the way. Megan's heart jumped, panic flooding her.

The gate bounced open a couple of feet and hovered there.

Go! Go! Hurry! Last chance!

Terror rushed through her, obscuring all else, promising only that if she didn't obey it, it would swallow her into the damp darkness where the spiders lived.

Megan dropped the umbrella and dashed toward the gate like a spooked horse.

Out, out, I have to get out! her mind screamed at her. *Now! Now!*

She was almost to the gate when her eyes fell again on the shovel. She skittered to a halt, her heart jackhammering in her chest.

Case! Where was Case? She had to take him with her.

She whimpered, looking madly around the empty garden. Where was he? Where *was* he?

The gate creaked, swaying.

"Case!" she cried out. "Case! Where are you? Case!"

"Here! Megan, I'm right here!"

Megan yelped and turned around. He was jogging toward her from where his pickup was parked. "Case! Let's go! Go!" she cried, running to him and grabbing his arm, pulling him toward the gate.

"Megan, what's going on?"

"We have to go! Now!" She got behind him and put her hands on his back, pushing.

"Okay . . ." he said, letting her push him toward the gate.

The opening was still there, still two or three feet wide. Still enough to get through. Megan's vision narrowed to that one spot as she peered around Case's back. That one opening through which they would escape was all that mattered.

They were almost there. She pushed Case toward the opening, but before he so much as put one foot through it, the gate creaked, and, with surprising swiftness, slammed shut. The clang of metal on metal had the ring, to Megan's ears, of shackles locking home.

"No!" she cried, letting up on Case's back. "No!"

"Megan! Megan, calm down! It's not locked!" Case grabbed her shoulders. "It's not locked! We're fine!"

Rain trickled down her forehead and into her eyes. "We're trapped!"

"No, look." He reached for the gate.

A sudden, overwhelming instinct hit Megan, and she grabbed his arm, stopping him.

He met her eyes in surprise.

"Don't touch," she whispered, her body trembling. "Don't touch it."

He slowly lowered his hand. "Why not?"

She shook her head. "I don't know. But don't."

As they stood there, they heard the distinct sound of a lock turning.

"It's locked now," Case said, his face losing a shade. And then a realization of some sort washed over his face. He turned slowly and looked back at the hole where he'd been digging out ivy roots. "Come look at this," he said softly, and took her hand.

She followed and looked down into the shallow hole. Something dark and straight cut through the bottom of it.

"I think it's an old power line of some sort," he explained. "It's coated in insulation. See that tiny shiny part, there?" he asked, pointing. "That's where I hit it with the shovel. I went to grab my ohm meter to test if it was live."

Megan's eyes went from the cable in the ground to

the closed gates and then up to the fence along the top of the wall. "Electric fencing."

"I never felt it when I propped open the gates."

"Maybe they weren't electrified then." She pointed to the metal stops in the drive. "Maybe that's the connection." Her eyes went up to the archway that connected one side of the gateway to the other, iron fence to iron fence.

In a mental flash, she saw the iron stubs of a fence around the fissure, their ends bent back down into the earth.

"They would need a helluva lot of power to keep electricity flowing through that much fence," Case said. "There's resistance in all that iron."

Megan shook her head, her eyes closing in understanding, her knees going weak. "They didn't need much. Just enough to reinforce the circle with the same electromagnetic energy the fissure generates, to make sure their captive couldn't escape."

"Who's *they*?"

"Isabella and Penelope. Do you know why people used to put small iron fences around graves?"

Case shook his head. "To keep dogs out?"

"To keep spirits in. They thought that a spirit couldn't escape a pen of iron."

Case looked up at the wall above them. "So the fence—"

"Is an enormous pen for one dead man." Megan's grip on his arm tightened. "Isabella and Penelope weren't trying to get rid of Zachariah's ghost all those years. They wanted to let him out of the basement and into the rest of the house, where it would be easier to play with him. But they didn't want their pet to escape the grounds and disappear into the ever after."

"And when they themselves died?"

"Trapped in their own net." Megan frowned. "No, that's not quite it. Penelope was trying to drag Isabella beyond the gate. She didn't want Bella dying on the grounds, because if she did, Bella would be alone on the Other Side with Zachariah. Penelope was trying to throw Bella out of the cage before she died—a cage that both keeps spirits trapped here on the estate and prevents outside ones from coming in. But now they're both there with Zachariah."

"Poor son of a bitch." Case turned his gaze to the shut gates. "And now they want us to come join them."

TWENTY-TWO

"Where the hell is the power coming from?" Case asked for the third time, pacing back and forth in the kitchen. "There has to be another source. It was shut off to this house for years, but I'd bet my truck that fence was still humming, however quietly."

"They must have set up a pirating system off of city power," Eric offered weakly, slurping coffee. His eyes were still glazed with sleep, despite having been awake now for half an hour.

"Obviously. And obviously it's been buried. That bit I dug up is just an arm of the octopus."

Megan had watched as Case chipped out enough of the stone wall to confirm that the cable went up inside the wall, not out to the other side.

"So, where's it connected? How do we unplug it?"

"You'll have to ask them," Eric said.

"It's the last thing they'd tell us!" Megan said.

"Zachariah would tell you. I'm sure he wants out of here."

"Out of the question," Case said. "I won't put Megan at that type of risk."

Eric shrugged and slurped. "Suit yourself. We're stuck here, but suit yourself."

"We're not stuck," Megan protested, her gut churning at the thought. "Not really. It's just a gate. We could drive through it." She looked at Case. "Couldn't we?"

"Not quite through. But I'm certain we could get it pried open enough to walk out."

"If your truck will start," Eric said. "They can mess with electricity, remember. You need your battery to start."

Megan's eyes went from Eric to Case, her worry ratcheting up a notch. "He's right, isn't he?"

"We're in the middle of Seattle, not the Olympic Mountains. I have neighbors. We can stand by the gate and yell until someone calls the fire department or the police."

Megan's eyes went to the kitchen window, where the day had turned to darkness and rain beat against the glass. No one would hear them yelling. Case's neighbors were at least half a block away and facing the other direction. Their homes were large, set back from the street, and well insulated against sound. And no one would be walking by on a night like this.

"Megan, please don't worry," Case said. "They can't hurt us."

Lightning flashed outside, followed almost immediately by a crashing boom that shook inside Megan's chest.

"What if they could harness that?" Eric mused, undisturbed.

"Then God help us." Megan drew her feet up onto the edge of her chair, her knees high in front of her, and wrapped arms around them. "Case, I don't know that we are safe as long as we're inside this fence. All their noises and mischief of the past, that was all to play with you. To scare you off, and if that didn't work, then to indulge their sexual appetites. But we know their secrets now. I don't know what they might do to keep us from destroying the world they spent their entire lives building.

"They locked the gate," Megan continued. "They know we'll eventually be able to dismantle the pen. The only way to stop us . . ."

"Is to kill us," Eric finished.

Megan swallowed.

"They weren't murderers," Case said.

"Not while they were alive," Megan agreed. "But they're dead now. It's probably not such a big deal to them now when people die."

Case ran his hand through his hair. "If we all stay right here until morning, we'll be fine."

"We'll get sleepy. Our mental guard will go down. We'll be vulnerable, and they're determined now. It's just past dusk; they'll only get stronger as the night progresses."

"Megan," Case said, pulling out the chair next to her and sitting down facing her. He put his hand on her knee. "You can't open yourself up to them in hopes of finding answers. That's probably exactly what they want, and then they'll take advantage of you as they did Eric, perhaps with worse consequences."

The concern in his eyes warmed her and at the same time undermined her. With each caring word, she heard, *You will fail, you can't win, you're not strong enough.*

A slow anger at herself boiled in her gut.

What kind of freaking useless medium was she?

She was sick of it. Sick of it! She wanted to be the hero for once. She wanted to test herself against the enemy and come out victorious. She was bored to death with running when scared.

She unfolded her legs and let her feet settle on the floor. She sat up straight, then pushed back from the table and stood. "Eric. You up to this?"

He looked up at her and brightened. "You bet your sweet ass I am! It's time they got a taste of their own medicine."

Megan turned to Case. "You can't stop me. Even if

you physically barred me from going down those stairs, you can't stop me from going into a trance."

"Don't do this, Megan," he said, standing. He put his hands on her upper arms, looking into her eyes and holding her gaze. "The house doesn't matter. *You* matter. I'll give up the damn house if that's the only way to keep you safe. You hear that?" he suddenly shouted to the room. "You hear that? The house is yours! Take it! We'll leave in the morning!"

Nothing happened.

"This isn't just about the house for me," Megan said softly. "It's not about ownership of my building or picking out twenty antiques and selling them. It's about who I am and who I want to be."

And who I want to love without fear.

If she could face this challenge that awaited her beneath the cellar, she'd never fear any other challenge in life. She might fail, she might get hurt, but she would have learned not to let fear paralyze her or send her screaming into the night.

"I don't want to see you harmed," Case said, brushing his fingertips along the side of her face.

"It would harm me more to sit here helpless through the night."

He nodded, although it seemed to pain him to do so. "It's your decision."

She smiled, trying to reassure him, even as she felt her own bravado quaking with the realization that the path was now open for her to go down to that fissure and face the dead on their own grounds. "The helmet will help me," she said. "In some ways, it opens up my defenses, but in many other ways, it helps me. I have better control of my gifts, and they're stronger. I'll be a match for the Smithsons."

"More than a match, I hope."

She smiled faintly. "I hope so, too."

"Oh, for God's sake," Eric said, moving past them with a flashlight at the ready. "She's not departing on the *Titanic*. We're going to the basement."

Lightning flashed again, the thunder simultaneous with it. The lights flickered and went out, leaving them dimly illuminated in the light of the oil lamp on the table.

When the rumble had rolled away, Case took her hand, and together they followed the bobbing light of Eric's flashlight.

"It's just a basement," Megan said under her breath as they descended the stairs. "Nothing here to fear but us spiders."

TWENTY-THREE

Case watched in sick trepidation as Megan prepared herself for the helmet. "What about the EM blaster?" he asked, seeking some alternative. "Isn't there something we could do with that? Send a blast into the fissure—maybe that will break them apart. At the very least, it could disrupt the electrical flow."

"I have it right here," Eric said, nodding toward the piece of equipment on the ground. "I'll have it powered up and ready. One way or the other, it's time to put an end to this."

Megan slid the helmet over her head and sat on the ground, leaning against a boulder for support. She flashed Case a reassuring smile and lowered the dark visor over her face. "Ready or not, ghosties, here I come."

Eric's laptop was perched on the boulder, behind Megan's head. He tapped keys, and the screen filled with line graphs of brain waves. He picked up the EM blaster and stood beside Megan's sitting figure as if standing guard.

Case's hands were clenched into fists, helpless to do more than stand by and watch.

The first day he'd met Megan, if he'd known that this is what his proposal would have brought her to, he would have walked out of her shop and never bothered her again. His stomach turned at the thought that she was doing this because he had been so obsessed with the house and making it into the perfect haven he envisioned for the future.

A future that would mean nothing if he had no one with whom to share it.

"I see someone approaching me," Megan said, her voice breaking into the quiet anticipation of the room.

"What's she doing?" Eric asked.

"She's hesitant. I don't think she's the one who talked to me before. She looks . . . yes, she looks like Isabella Smithson, as a young woman."

Megan fell silent, and Case's muscles tightened yet further. He knew from before that she might now be holding a silent conversation with the spirit, but anything could be going on inside that helmet, and there was nothing he could do to protect her.

He glanced over at the laptop screen. The brain-wave patterns seemed erratic. "Eric!" Case whispered. "Eric, is that right?"

Eric glanced at him and then to where Case pointed. "It's fine."

"I don't remember it like that last time."

"It's nothing, just a fluctuation." Eric got a better grip on the EM blaster and checked its settings.

"Shouldn't you be monitoring the patterns?"

"I am! And trying to make sure the one weapon we have to defend ourselves with is in working order. If you don't mind?"

Case scowled but held his peace when he looked at Megan and saw that she appeared perfectly relaxed. She looked almost Buddha-like, cross-legged with her wrists resting on her knees.

"She's coming closer," Megan said. "Slowly closer. Like she's scared to."

"Closer, Isabella," Eric said in a high-pitched whisper, moving closer to Megan, the EM blaster held steadily in front of him at hip height. "A little closer, Bella."

A sound moved past Case's ear, like an insect buzzing by. He jerked his head and swatted reflexively.

The buzzing pass came again and a flash of movement in the corner of his eye. He turned around, seeking explanation in the darkness.

"A little closer," Eric whispered.

Stop them, a male voice said in Case's ear.

He jerked around, eyes seeking the source. In the corner of his vision, a face appeared at his shoulder, indistinguishable except for two dark eyes. *Stop them,* it said.

"Stop who?" Case asked.

Save her!

Her. Megan?

Case turned quickly around. Eric had the EM blaster pointed at Megan's head, the wide cone almost touching the side of the helmet.

Save her! the voice demanded.

"Closer, Bella," Eric whispered in a falsetto.

The hair rose on the back of Case's neck. It was the same falsetto he'd heard last night in his bedroom.

"There you go," Eric said, and his finger moved toward the trigger.

"No!" Case cried, and launched himself over Megan, knocking her over as he tackled Eric, knocking the blaster away from the helmet.

Eric screamed and fought back, struggling to bring the blaster back around toward Megan. Case fought him for it and in the struggle knocked it away from him. It skittered across the dirt and rock floor to the edge of the fissure.

"No! No!" Eric cried, and lunged for it.

Case threw himself over Eric and hit the blaster with his fist, trying to knock it over the edge. His fist made contact, but it was the trigger that was the point of impact. Case felt it give way under him an instant before the blaster fell over the edge.

The construction light blew in a flash as Eric rolled out from beneath Case, reaching for the blaster that was no longer there. "No!" Eric cried.

Utter darkness fell upon them, not even the light from the laptop surviving the electromagnetic blast.

"Megan!" Case yelled, in terror for her soul. He'd triggered the damn thing himself! God damn it! "Megan, are you okay? Can you hear me?"

"Worry about yourself," Eric said, and Case suddenly found himself engaged in a battle for his life, the edge of the fissure invisible in the darkness. "Meet the end you deserve!" Eric shrieked in a female voice utterly unlike his own, a preternatural strength powering his muscles as he grappled with Case.

Case knew it wasn't just Eric he was fighting; it was one of the sisters. "I deserve better than you, you self-ish bitch!" Case grunted out, struggling in the dark to get a hold on his insane adversary.

They rolled across the floor, Case feeling the helmet hit up against his back.

Megan. Oh, God, what had they done to her?

A fist hit awkwardly at his head. Case shoved the heel of his hand hard against the underside of Eric's jaw, snapping his head back.

Eric's grip on him loosened, and Case took advantage of the weakness, shoving him onto his stomach and making a grab for his nearest hand, trying to force it up behind his back. The two of them shoved and struggled back up to the edge of the fissure, Eric suddenly slipping loose and rolling away. Case quickly rolled in the other direction, knowing better than to stay in the same position in the dark. He was disoriented, but the fissure was a landmark, and he moved to where he thought Megan should be.

His hand touched the helmet, on the ground. Ah, Christ, she still hadn't moved or made a sound.

His hand moved down to where her shoulder should be . . . and felt nothing.

She was gone.

Down! the male voice said in his ear, with the faintest of shoves on the back of Case's neck.

Case obeyed automatically, and something metal struck the rock behind where his head had been, sparks flying. Animal instinct took over, and he threw himself at the only place Eric could be, flesh meeting flesh. Case felt something hit his shoulder and knew that Eric was trying to beat him with the light stand.

In life and death, there were no fair fights. Case brought his knee up in a powerful jerk.

A screech left Eric's throat, the eerie sound of a woman coming from a man who has just had his balls smashed for the first time.

Case followed that knee with another to Eric's gut and a punch to the face. Eric fell to the ground and Case dropped on top of him, pinning him down with his knees, grabbing his hands and bringing them up behind him. Case reached around in the darkness until his hand fell on the cord to the light stand. He jerked it toward him and used it to bind Eric's hands.

As he worked, a faint blue-white light began to illuminate the room. Case looked up.

It was coming from the fissure. Silhouetted against the light was the tall figure of Megan.

"Megan! You're all right?"

She didn't answer.

Case finished tying Eric up and stood. "Megan?"

The glow in the crevice grew brighter, its light spreading across the room, gradually increasing until the entire space was bleached with it. Case squinted against it, holding his hand up to shade his eyes.

Megan hadn't moved. The wires from electrodes trailed from her hair, and he could see now that her eyes were closed. He approached her with caution, and as he did so, her eyes opened, staring straight ahead. His gaze followed hers. Two figures hovered over the gap in the ground. One was male, one female.

Behind him, Eric made a noise. Case glanced back at the trussed man, then did a double take. Eric's body was blurred by an image laid over it—the image of a young woman, lying as he was with her hands behind her back, her face turned to the side, superimposed over Eric's own.

Both Eric and the woman opened their eyes and cast Case an evil glare.

He looked back at Megan. There was no double image to her. Relief coursed through him.

She was still herself.

As he watched, Megan raised her arms to her sides. The light in the fissure grew somehow denser, as if drawing on hidden reserves.

"Isabella, take her!" Eric cried.

Isabella moved forward, but Megan's forefinger flicked, and Isabella stopped as if she'd been hit in the chest. *I can't!* Case could barely hear the woman say. *Penny, I can't! She's too strong!*

The male figure did nothing, and as the light grew denser, so did the figures, until Case could clearly see the face of Zachariah, smiling faintly as if with a disbelieving hope.

"She's going to spoil it all!" Eric said. "Bella, she'll send you onward. Don't leave me, Bella!"

A beam of light shot from the fissure to Megan, and with a tearing, sucking sound, the entire column poured into Megan's chest.

Case shouted and reached for her, but some force he couldn't see repelled his hand.

Zachariah was sucked into the beam, his image warping as it was pulled into Megan, and then Isabella's shape began to bend with the force of the pull. *Penny!* she cried, reaching out.

With a sudden movement, Eric rolled toward the fissure, and before Case could pull him back, one leg went over the edge and into the column of light. Isabella dove into his leg and disappeared, and Case dragged Eric away from the fissure.

Eric looked up at him. Two feminine faces merged and separated above Eric's own. "Thank you," he said, and simpered.

"Down!" Megan shouted.

Case dropped to the ground.

The last of the light disappeared into Megan, and the room went dark. An instant later, a crack of lightning split the darkness, the crash of it slamming through Case's body. The jagged bolt shot from Megan to the metal stairs hanging down from the ceiling, racing up them and out.

Above them, the entire house shook as if it had been shot. They were plunged into darkness again.

Case stood in the dark, his own breathing loud in his ears. "Megan?" he asked again.

He heard the breath of a sigh.

He reached out for her in the darkness, his hand finding her arm. He pulled her toward him. She came easily, wrapping her arms around him and resting her cheek gently against his shoulder. They stood that way, silent, for a long time. He stroked her hair.

"Do you know," she said quietly, "I think I've gotten over my fear of the dark."

He laughed under his breath. "My dear, I think it's now the dark that has things to fear from *you.*"

He felt her smile against his neck. His hold on her tightened, and he bent his face to her neck and closed his eyes, thankful with every ounce of his being that she was alive and in his arms.

TWENTY-FOUR

Megan zipped up her suitcase and set it by her bedroom door, then sat down on the bed. Though she'd only been there about a week, it felt like a lifetime's worth of experience.

Blue sky glowed outside the window, and a pink rose was opening against the glass. The day had dawned clear, with only puddles of rainwater as evidence of the storm that had blown through the night before. Puddles and an unnatural hole a foot in diameter, burned through Case's house from the cellar straight up through the floors and out the roof. If it had been normal lightning, the entire house might have burned.

But of course, it hadn't been normal lightning. It had been electricity transformed into spiritual energy, conducted, through her, out of the house and up to God knows where. Zachariah had passed through her and been freed.

It was the EM blaster going off while she wore the helmet right next to the fissure that had done it. Instead of allowing Isabella to possess her, as Eric/Penelope had plainly intended, those three combined forces of fissure, helmet, and blaster had created psychic superpowers in her, if only temporarily.

Perhaps temporarily. She rubbed her thumb and fingertip together, feeling the crackle of spiritual electricity between them.

Things had not gone so well for Eric. Both Penelope and Isabella were in him now, refusing to let go. All three were struggling for control of Eric's body.

Unable to control Eric in any manner better than tying him up, Case had finally been forced to take him to the emergency room for evaluation, telling the staff that he was a danger to others in his present state of mind.

Once Megan figured out how to use the new strength of her powers, she'd find a way to help Eric rid himself of the Smithson sisters—assuming that they hadn't tired of him and moved on. How much fun could two squabbling sisters have in one male body, anyway? *Plenty.* They'd treat his private parts like toys, fighting over them, abusing them, experimenting with them. Megan grimaced at the thought of just how much mischief they could get up to. Sooner or later, she hoped, the novelty would wear off and they'd abandon Eric and go looking for Zachariah, thus finding their own escape from the traps they'd laid for themselves in this life.

Case rapped on her door and pushed it open. "You sure you don't want to take any of the furniture right now?"

"I'll come back for it, if you don't mind."

"Of course, I don't mind. You more than won the bet," he said, coming into the room. "I almost had a heart attack when that lightning shot out of you."

"You sure it wasn't a panic attack you felt coming on?" she asked, but without much enthusiasm. They still hadn't consummated their relationship, although she tried to tell herself that was for lack of time, energy, and appropriate mood. One didn't go for the gusto immediately after packing a friend off to the ER, after all.

But still, there'd been time this morning. In her mind was the niggling worry that she'd convinced Case a little too well of her abilities, and he didn't want to sleep with someone who blasted holes in his house with spiritual energy. Sensing ghosts was a harmless parlor trick in comparison.

"I thought you might like to see this," he said, and handed her a piece of paper.

It was a page from the photocopies of the *Seattle Times*. "What did you find?"

"Center column, halfway down."

"It's Jacob Smithson's obituary," Megan said. "From late August."

"He died of a 'nervous collapse.'"

"Guilt?" Megan wondered.

"Or tormented to death by his daughters. I feel for the guy. What a pair! He probably drank himself to death."

Case sat down beside her as she read. Her gaze skimmed over the bare facts of Jacob's business life, his upbringing in New York, his standing in the community. The part she cared about was at the end:

Mr. Smithson is survived by his daughters, Isabella and Penelope, to whom friends say he was devoted. "It is a tragedy, the ill luck that has befallen that family," Mrs. Harold Greenway said. "Mrs. Smithson died of childbed fever shortly after Penelope's birth, and Jacob's heart was broken. I do not believe he ever recovered from the loss. Mary was such a pretty young thing, so gay and lively. He used to say she was his sunshine against the rain. The only thing that kept him going after her death was those two little girls. He'd have given his life for them, poor dears."

"The sadness in the master suite," Megan said, meeting Case's eyes and feeling tears start in her own. "That was Jacob Smithson, missing his Mary." Her throat tightened against the thought of it; a thought she wouldn't have completely understood before meeting Case and being able to imagine losing him. It was a different kind of loss from losing a parent.

Case took the paper from her and set it aside, then took her hand in his own. "Do you still want to take his bed?"

She shook her head. "It belongs here."

"You're leaving me with his sorrows?"

She smiled. "The bed needn't be sorrowful forever. There are simple ways to be rid of that sort of haunting."

"Ways like?"

"Recording happy times over it, until the sadness has no choice but to fade away. There's no point in allowing mourning to continue forever."

"How am I going to record happy times, alone in this gutted house?" he asked. "Do you remember during the first séance, my mother spoke to you?"

Megan nodded. "She said, 'You shouldn't have tried to fix it.'"

"I always pretended to myself that it was the house that made her sad. As a child, I told myself that if I could fix it, she'd be happy." He squeezed her hand and stared out the window. When he spoke again, it seemed as much to himself as to her, and she wondered if it was hard for him to share things close to his heart.

"She didn't care about the holes in the walls," he said, "Or the dripping faucets. None of that would have mattered, if only she'd been sure of my father's love. But she wasn't, and each flaw in the house became a reminder that he didn't care enough about her—about either of us—to provide a comfortable home." He glanced at her, a sad smile on his lips. "I knew that, even as a child. So I've been wondering why my mother would cross the Great Divide to tell me something I already know. 'You shouldn't have tried to fix it.' That wasn't news to me.

"Only, in some ways, maybe it was. Look at this house," he said, gesturing around him. "Why on earth would I take on a job like this and plan to start my future family here, if not to fix it for once and for all? Maybe I really did buy this house as therapy." He snorted. "Apparently, I signed up for the fifteen-year psychoanalytic approach."

"Is it working?"

"Hell if I know. And maybe that was part of my mother's message: not to keep fixing a house in hopes that it will fix my life. Maybe I need to let things go."

"Are you thinking of selling the house?" Megan asked in surprise.

"I don't want to put my personal life on hold, waiting for it to be finished. What do you think? Is it too awful a place for a woman to come and live in, before it's completely finished? If there was a proper kitchen, a living room, a bedroom that was more than bare walls and floor, would it be unbearable?"

"It depends on the woman," Megan said carefully, her heart beginning to pound as she hoped he would say the words that were in her own heart. "If she knew she was loved and cared for, I don't think she'd mind one bit about the house."

Case met her eyes. "Do you think you ever might be willing to live here, if you knew you were loved?"

Megan felt tears sting her eyes. "If I knew I was loved, yes."

He touched her face, as if touching a fragile piece of glass, his fingers betraying the slightest tremble. "You would be happy?"

"Yes. If I knew I was loved, with all my flaws and . . . oddness."

He pulled her into his arms. "Then know that you are," he whispered against her ear. His hand at the back of her head, he pressed a kiss deep into the crook of her neck, then quickly moved to her mouth, finding her lips and taking them with his own.

Megan's body melted into his embrace. His hunger fired her own, his touch opening up a need in her that was greater than mere physical satisfaction.

She pulled away from his kiss for a moment. "Do you think we could find a mattress to fit that big bed?"

He looked at her in surprise, then laughed. "Darling, we'll go buy one today. But let's give this one a try, for now."

"It's about bloody time. You'd better have a condom with you, or I swear I'll—"

"You'll what?"

"I'll be very difficult to satisfy, that's what. It'll be hard labor in the salt mines for you, boy-o. If you get my drift."

"I'm impressed by your use of literary symbolism."

She laughed, and he undressed her and went to work as if he did not have three Trojans hidden in his pockets.

His technique was different from before, his hands slowly exploring her body, his mouth following. Long, massaging strokes punctuated by nips and high-pressured swirls of his tongue in unexpected places—behind her knees, on her sides, in the small of her back.

When he tossed his own clothes to the floor, she returned the favor, her hands tracing over the broad planes of his chest, her fingertips trailing down the line of hair to his groin. His cock stood at attention as she stroked his nether hair and gently cupped his balls. When her hand at last brushed against his staff, its thick hardness bobbed against her. Her fingers instinctive closed around it, leaving the silky skin of the head exposed, presenting a temptation her mouth could not resist.

"Christ, Megan," he said, and his fingers dug into her hair. "Oh, God. You've got to stop."

In answer, she swirled her tongue over the head, then took him even deeper into her mouth, her fingers tight around the base of his shaft.

With a long groan, he gently but firmly made her release her hold on him. "We're not ending it that way, this time. Not if I have anything to say about it."

With a quick shift, he reversed their positions, and now it was her turn to be tortured to the brink of release by his mouth. She could feel it coming, the breaking wave only a lick or two away, but she'd lost all capacity to stop him. He read the tensing of her muscles and stopped a bare moment from the end, holding her motionless for long moments until the intensity receded.

He stood beside the bed and pulled her toward the edge, lifting her legs up around his waist, stopping only when her hips were at the end of the mattress. With one arm supporting him on the mattress, he bent over and kissed her, hard and deep. She felt his cock at her entrance, the head sliding over her moisture a few times before pushing through, stretching her, as she raised her hips harder against him, her body hungry to have him deep within her. His tongue plunged inside her mouth, rubbing rough against hers as his thrusts found that same magic spot inside her that he'd found while they were under the maple. He broke the kiss and stood up straight, helping to support her legs with his hands, using his hold on her to pull her harder against him with each thrust.

The pleasure built inside her, but slowly this time, and she knew he would be done long before she was halfway there. She was resigning herself to that when he abruptly stopped, deep inside her, then lay down on her and rolled both of them over until she was on top. She parted her lips in surprise.

"It'll be better for you this way," he said.

She grinned and straddled him and, after a brief moment's embarrassment, reached down to touch herself as she began to ride him. Case reached up to touch her breasts, and she threw her head back in abandon.

Case groaned. "Oh, God. You'd better hurry."

She looked down at him. "Hold on," she said softly. "Hold on . . ." One final thrust, one final stroke of her fingertips, and her pleasure spilled over the edge. Case felt it and, with a moan, found his own release.

Megan bent down and kissed him. A few moments later, she was lying tight beside him, her arm and leg thrown over his body. They drifted off together in a doze.

"You don't have any plans today, do you?" he said at long last, when they both stirred. "You don't *have* to leave."

"No, I don't have to."

"Not today," he said. "Not ever."

She smiled and gave herself over to the promise of a life where she would always have someone she loved by her side.

EPILOGUE

One year later

"Just about got it . . . *there!*" Tracie said in satisfaction, and got up from the floor where she'd been kneeling, putting one last finishing stitch on the hem of Megan's dress. "A work of art, if I do say so myself."

"It's beautiful," Megan said, looking at herself in the mirror that stood in the corner of the master suite. "I feel like a virgin princess."

"Well, I know you aren't, but it doesn't hurt to look like one on your wedding day."

Megan laughed, then surprised Tracie with a hug. "Thank you."

"Hey, it's what I do."

"No, for more than that. Thanks for being here. For playing Mom to me and helping me get ready."

"You'd be a nervous wreck if I didn't. Now, enough dawdling. There are guests waiting for food and alcohol, and the only way they're going to get it is if you move your butt down there and get yourself married."

Together, they walked down the finished hallway, with its freshly plastered walls and polished floors, then down the stairs, past the table in the foyer stacked high with gifts.

"Did Eric send one?" Tracie asked.

"A frying pan that was on the registry. His note said I should beat Case with it if he ever misbehaves."

Tracie frowned. "Is he . . . okay now?"

"I think so. The electroshock therapy got rid of the Smithson sisters, as far as we can tell. I invited him to the wedding, but I suppose it's no surprise he didn't want to return to this house."

"I'm thinking of moving in myself. You have enough spare rooms. I'll take the third floor, if you don't mind."

Megan laughed and stepped out into the sunshine on the back veranda. The garden spread out below her in its green manicured summer finery, the marble statue returned to glowing, pristine glory. Along one side of the statue's reflecting pool were the white folding chairs set up for the wedding. Her uncle Charlie was there, and her cousins and her friends.

Zachariah was there, too. She and Case now knew

that without the sisters there to torment him or the fence to pen him, he had decided the house wasn't such a bad place to spend eternity. He stayed out of their way for the most part, leaving only small, friendly clues to his presence, like the coffee maker starting a few minutes before they woke up. They'd seen him once on a late afternoon, sitting in a lawn chair, his hand on the glass of Scotch that Case had left behind.

Tracie sighed. "You couldn't have asked for a more beautiful day. Or a better guy." She put her arm around Megan's waist and gave her a squeeze. "I'll cue the music," she said, and ran off, leaving Megan alone to walk down the aisle.

Megan closed her eyes, missing her mother in this moment more than she ever had. Then a feeling of warmth and love washed through her, and she turned and opened her eyes.

Her mother stood to her left, smiling gently at her.

"Mom?"

Her mother didn't answer but, instead, turned and looked out into the garden.

Megan followed her mother's gaze to Case, talking to one of the guests. "You approve, don't you?"

But when she looked back at her mother, Megan found herself alone.

The violins and cello started up, and she watched as the last of the guests took their seats. At the end of the aisle between the chairs, Case took his place and turned toward her, their gazes meeting across the distance.

Megan's lips curved into a smile, and she stepped toward the future.

POCKET BOOKS
PROUDLY PRESENTS

The
Erotic Secrets
of a
French Maid

LISA CACH

Available in trade paperback
from Pocket Books
February 13, 2007

Turn the page for a preview of
The Erotic Secrets of a French Maid. . . .

"These are your instructions."

Russ took the typed sheet that Emma handed him. "Instructions?"

"For our 'entertainment' tonight."

Instructions. Great. He scanned the sheet, his attention catching at the script in the middle. "You want me to say that?" he asked in disbelief.

She nodded, her face serious. "Please."

He scanned the rest of the sheet, growing alarmed. "You're sure about this?"

She nodded.

"I don't want you to get hurt."

"I won't. And look, see there?" She reached over the top of the paper and pointed to one short sentence. "That's our 'safe' word: *Apple*. If I say *apple*, then we stop."

Hell's bells. He'd never engaged in sexual activities that required a safe word. It was on the tip of his tongue to ask her to forget this crazy plan and just have good, plain, old-fashioned sex. But then he met her eyes and saw the uncertain, hopeful expectation there, and he remembered that she'd worked so hard on her plans for this evening. "Okay, let's give this a go."

She smiled and turned him toward her bedroom, giving him a small shove. "You go lounge on the bed while I get ready. And there's something there for you to put on."

Oh Lord. He could hardly wait to see.

The bedroom was again lit softly with candles, and this time the bed had been turned into the divan of a pasha. Jewel-toned fabrics with gold prints covered the mattress, the pillows, and lumps that were probably heaped blankets serving as the arms and back of the exotic love nest. In the center of a swath of royal blue fabric sat a red satin turban, complete with fake diamond in the front, a small gold feather sticking straight up from behind it. It looked like the turban that Johnny Carson wore whenever he played Karnak the Magnificent.

Russ sighed and glanced again at his instruction sheet:

You are the sultan of a small country on the Mediterranean, and have bought a young English noblewoman from pirates. Your other concubines have been training her for your service, and tonight is the first night you will have her. When the eunuchs deliver her to your room, follow the script below.

He lifted the turban and went to the mirror, where he settled the turban onto his head. It was heavy, straining his neck with the effort of keeping his head up when there was the least hint of imbalance.

He looked like a clown. She couldn't possibly find this sexy.

With a shake of his head he went to the bed/divan and tried to make himself comfortable, spreading his arms out over the "back" and stretching his legs out in front of him, crossed at the ankles.

The turban pulled his head back, and he let it go until a pillow bumped up against the back, shoving it forward and down lower over his brows, but also helping to support it.

He just knew that self-consciousness was going to prevent him from performing sexually. There was no way he could get aroused while dressed like this, speaking those words on the paper.

He closed his eyes and tried to ignore his surroundings, picturing how Emma had looked when she opened the door to him this evening, her hair done up loosely with tendrils hanging down, her tight light green T-shirt showing the outline of her bra and clinging faithfully to her shape. She was wearing a short pleated skirt that had offered no resistance when she straddled him during dinner.

He felt a faint tingle of life in his loins.

A strain of music drifted to him from the living room, and he almost recognized it. A few bars later he had it: "The Young Prince and Princess" from Rimsky-Korsakov's *Scheherazade*.

The tingle of life died away, as he was reminded of this harem scene in which he had to play his ridiculous role.

"Unhand me, you filthy cad!" Emma shrieked in a fake English accent that sounded more like Cockney Eliza Doolittle than a gently bred young lady.

He opened his eyes just as she threw herself into the bedroom, landing on all fours in front of the bed. For a moment he thought she had dumped a basket of laundry over herself, but then she raised her head and he saw that she had a scarf covering her face except for her eyes, her dark hair spilling in disarray around her shoulders. The rest of her getup came into focus: a dark pink bra-and-panty set with a dozen silk scarves attached all around, both top and bottom.

She turned and looked back over her shoulder, addressing her imaginary captors. "Ye brutes! When me faither gits ahold o'ye, ye'll be paying with yer hides! Ye'll not fergit that it was Lord Oakley's daughter that ye did this to."

She turned to him and narrowed her eyes, slowly rising from the floor until she stood before him, her chin raised in defiance. "Ye'll not be taming me, sirrah!"

He gaped at her.

She scowled and nodded strangely with her head. "Sirrah! Ye'll not be taming me!"

"Oh! Oh, sorry!" He grabbed the paper and scanned down to the script. "You'll part your thighs for me, wench, and you'll like it," he read stiffly.

"Never! Ye shall never sully the rose o'me virginity, ye scurvy dog!" She lowered her voice to a stage whisper. "Put some emotion into it, Russ!"

He cleared his throat and lowered his voice. "Your rose is mine to pluck, saucy wench."

She put her hand on her hip and tossed her head. "It'll be me thorns yer tastin', not me precious petals."

"You're mine now, and the sooner you submit to me, the happier you'll be."

"Never! I'll die first!"

There was a line of stage direction. He paused to read it, then declared, "First, you'll dance!" He clapped his hands in the air. "Dance for me, wench, as my concubines have trained you!" He clapped again. "Dance!"

"I will not!"

"Dance, or I'll give you a taste of the bastinado. You'll not like to have the soles of your feet beaten, my comely wench. Dance! Or feel my wrath."

"You would beat me?"

"Disobey me once more, and you will feel the cruelty of my anger. Dance!"

She put her hands over her veiled face and pretended to sob.

"And call me 'Master,' " Russ threw in for the hell of it.

She peeped over her fingers, a questioning look in her eyes.

"Why do you stand there, wench?" he ad-libbed, abandoning sanity and going with the absurd drama Emma seemed so determined to play out. "Dance!"

"Yes, Master," she said, and dropped her hands, her gaze fixing on the floor as if in shameful submission.

The Rimsky-Korsakov piece had just started to repeat itself. Emma swayed gently to it, the scarves—veils, he supposed she meant them to be—following her movements and reminding him of the floppy rags that shook themselves over your vehicle while going through a car wash.

She lifted her arms and rose up onto her toes, still swaying, and started to move around the room in some perversion of ballet moves, from the looks of it. His momentary amusement began to fade and a faint embarrassment crept in. She wasn't a particularly graceful dancer, nor an erotic one, and his imagination simply couldn't transform her panty set and scarves into a harem girl's sultry silks.

She pranced in a circle, then stopped in front of him and seesawed her hips up and down. She snaked her arms in the air and moved her torso in an undulation that looked like nothing so much as a boa constrictor swallowing a large animal. Good God, had she made this up herself, or had she paid someone to teach her to do this?

He was gathering courage to tell her that Master wanted something different, when she plucked the first scarf off her costume and let it flutter to the floor. It revealed one cup of the bra—which had a slit down the center of the cup, allowing the nipple to poke through.

His gaze attached to that revealed nipple, pinched in the slit of dark pink fabric, and he forgot about asking her to stop.

Another veil fell to the floor, revealing a length of thigh. A curve of back appeared. A buttock. She danced between each revelation, her movements seeming saucy taunts now, teasing him, prolonging the unveiling of her lithe body. Soon she was wearing nothing but her undergarments, the veil over her face, and one scarf tucked into the top of her panties, hanging down over her loins. His gaze flitted back and forth between her nipples and that last piece of flimsy fabric, unable to decide which was more enticing.

At last she plucked the final veil from her panties and let it fall to the floor. There was a tiny bow down low on her mound, and he realized that they were split-crotch panties. One tug on the end of the bow and they would open wide. Her hand brushed down over her panties and he held his breath, waiting for her to untie them.

Her hand moved away, leaving the bow still tied.

He was hard and ready, and the bow was now a fixation. He wanted her to untie it. Wanted her to part the lacy fabric and straddle him, lowering herself onto him and riding for all she was worth. He wanted to suck on her nipples, lapping at them through their slits, and have her arch her back and moan.

Instead, her dancing slowly stopped and her hands fell to her sides. She looked at the floor. " 'Tis all I know, Master."

She couldn't stop *now*! "Untie the bow. Now."

She slowly reached for it, grasping one end. She began to pull, the loop of bow shrinking. When it was almost at the point of release she stopped, her hand falling away. She turned her hips slightly away from him, as if in modesty. "I cannot! I will not shame meself!"

What was he supposed to do now? He snatched up the script and scanned down. Where were they? Ah, here it was. He read through the remainder of her instructions and just as when he'd first read the script, doubt assailed him.

He looked up and met her eyes. She was watching him, waiting. He raised his brows in question. Barely perceptible nodding was her answer, and he thought he saw the shadow of a smile beneath the veil over her face.

It wasn't his type of thing, but for her sake he'd go through the motions. He was going to feel like a fool, and already felt his excitement dying.

He put the paper aside and cleared his throat. "I told you, wench, that you'll not disobey me. Untie that bow!"

"No, sirrah!"

"That's 'Master' to you, wench."

"You'll never be my master!"

Oh, Lord. He really wasn't enjoying this. "Come here."

She inched closer to him, standing a foot away.

"Closer."

She took a small step forward.

He reached out and tugged at the end of the bow. She stood motionless, letting him. It came undone and he pulled the ribbon completely free of the lace. He dropped it and brushed his fingertips lightly over her lace-clad mound. He could feel the damp heat of her exertions. He brushed over her again, feeling for the edges of the lace.

He glanced up at her. "Part your thighs."

She hesitated, then moved her feet apart a few scant inches, just enough so that he could slide two upturned fingers between her legs. She rocked forward against his hand, her breath catching. He found the center of her heat and gently pressed upward, teasing his fingertips back and forth to part the lace. It opened and one fingertip slipped in, stroking against her entrance, the pad of his finger barely parting her.

He could hear her breathing, and her excitement revived his own. He gently massaged his palm over her mound, his fingertip still against her opening, and felt her hips move in response. She made a soft noise deep in her throat and then pushed away from him, scampering several feet away.

He pushed up off the bed, grabbing the turban to keep it from falling off, and went after her, as her written instructions had dictated. She dashed away, his fingertips grazing her bare side as she exited the room.

He caught her in the living room, arms coming around her soft waist from behind. She held still for a moment, her breathing rapid, and let him slide his hand up her rib cage to one breast, where he gently pinched her nipple between his fingertips. His other hand slid downward to cup her sex. She leaned back against him, tilting her hips against his hand. He reached inside the slit of her bra and stroked the tender skin of her breast, then pulled down the strap that held it up, baring her breast entirely.

She pulled away from him again, dashing across the small room, freeing her arm from the trapping strap. She turned around and faced him, one breast bare, then feinted to one side. He went that way, and she switched directions. He let her go by, putting his hand out to brush along her as she passed by and scampered toward the bathroom.

He pursued, grabbing her around the waist before she could reach its sanctuary. She twisted around in his arms and pushed against his chest in a mock struggle to get away. He held her more tightly, one hand going down to cup her buttock and pull her against him. With his other hand he pulled down the remaining strap, then reached behind her and unhooked her bra. It fell free, falling off her arm. She leaned away from him, arching her back, and he saw that the pale skin of her breasts was marked in pink vertical slashes where the lace slits had pressed against her skin. He lowered his mouth to one breast and laved tenderly at its silky surface. She struggled and raised her knee beside his hip as if trying to climb out of his grasp, in the process giving him access to her from below. His fingertips found her dampness, slipping between the strips of lace. This time he plunged an inch of finger inside her.

She went rigid, the hands that had been pushing him now clenching tight in the fabric of his shirt. She raised her veiled face, her dark eyes wide as they sought out his own. He looked into her eyes as he gently thrust his fingertip inside her, in and out, never more than an inch deep. He could feel her heart beating rapidly and watched as her eyes slowly closed. He felt his own arousal building, the exertion of the chase intensifying it.

She released his shirt and, fists clenched hard, shoved him firmly away. They struggled for a moment, but her efforts were harder this time and fear of hurting her made him let her escape.

She darted into the bedroom and started to close the door. He got himself in the path of the door before she could, his turban getting knocked off in the process and thumping to the floor behind him. He reached for her and she dashed away, picking up a scarf from the floor and throwing it at him.

He caught it and advanced on her, both of them breathing heavily now. With her veil, she was almost a creature unknown; a woman he'd never met. With her breasts bare beneath the hem of the veil and that hint of panty her only garb, she was a temptation he had no reason to resist. He'd become absorbed in the game, the primal instinct to hunt and capture fully aroused. Conscious thought was all but erased, the silk scarf in his hand the only reminder of what he must do before he could penetrate her.

Emma felt a flush of adrenaline as Russ stalked her, the silk scarf in his hands. Something near panic rushed in her blood and she felt the instinct to flee—the reflex of the hunted. She knew it would take but a single word to make him stop, but there was something delicious to being chased. She *wanted* to be frightened, overpowered, and taken, all within the safety of this play they had constructed.

He moved toward her, the intensity of his expression that of a wolf cornering prey. She gasped and darted past him. His arm caught her around the waist and swung her around, lifting her off her feet. She struggled within his grasp, the strength with which he held her sending bolts of alarm through her muscles. He was so much stronger than her, she couldn't break free unless he allowed it.

The security of his grip pushed her panic too close to the edge and she struggled harder, elbowing him. He released her and she darted from the room. She stood in the hall, panting, poised for further flight, waiting for him to chase after her and scared that he would. It took a moment for it to sink in that he *had* released her.

When he still didn't emerge from the doorway she crept back toward it, moving silently on the balls of her bare feet. She couldn't see him in the room, and couldn't hear him above the music and her own heavy breathing. She crept closer, leaning forward to peer into the room.

Still no sign of him.

She looked over her shoulder, suddenly certain he'd gotten behind her. As she did, her wrist was grabbed and she shrieked in surprise. He tugged her into the bedroom, and before she knew what he was doing he had bound her wrists together with the scarf. She made a token tug of resistance, and he scooped her up into his arms and carried her to the bed. He dropped her onto the pillows and put his hands to work on his belt buckle.

Emma flipped onto her stomach and crawled toward the far corner of the bed, over the mounds of blankets and pillows. She felt his hand on her ankle, pulling her slowly back toward the edge. She reached forward with her bound hands, trying to find something to grab to slow her slide, but the brass bars of the bed were beyond reach.

He pulled until her legs were half off the bed, and with a few quick tugs he stripped her panties off her. Emma lay still, her cheek against the mattress, her arms stretched out in front of her. Her hair obscured her vision, and all she could see were shadows in the candlelight and the pillows near her.

His hands slid up the backs of her thighs, then up over the mounds of her buttocks. His palms explored her lower back, her hips, the place where her buttocks met her thighs. He brushed his hands along the insides of her thighs, rising up to but not quite touching her sex. He pulled her farther over the edge of the bed, until she had to bend her knees to keep from being unbalanced. The edge of the bed hit her at midthigh now.

She felt him gently parting her legs and obeyed the silent command. Cool air touched her most intimate area and then she felt his hands against her pushing to the sides, causing her flower to unfold and her entrance to part its lips. She closed her eyes, embarrassed, and tucked her nose and chin into the side of her arm.

He released her flesh and a moment later his hands were on her hips, urging her upward. He helped her onto her knees with her legs together, her forearms still on the mattress. She felt the blunt head of his rod against her opening, rubbing back and forth, its path becoming slippery with her moisture. He parted her thighs slightly and slid himself along the folds of her damp sex. His hips came up against her buttocks and he reached around to her front, his hand pressing downward on her mound as he slowly thrust between her slick folds.

She moaned deep in her throat as each thrust brought his head into contact with the nub of her pleasure. She rocked against him, joining his rhythm. His other hand cupped her breast, massaging it.

He pulled away, then pushed a big pillow under her and had her lie down on top of it, her hips raised up. Then he was parting her thighs and she felt him slowly enter her, thrusting in gradual, deepening strokes. Taking her without words, as if they were strangers.

When he'd made it halfway in he leaned forward, bracing himself on his rigid arms. She could feel the tension in him as he breathed her name and slowly thrust the rest of the way, embedding himself deep within her.

Emma instinctively wrapped her lower legs behind his back, her feet touching each other as she pulled him more securely to her.

"Emma," he breathed again, and began to thrust, his angle bringing his rod in contact with that one sensitive spot inside her passage. She mewled in her throat and tried to move with him, but it was nearly impossible. She could only grip him with her legs and let him take her as he would.

For the first time in her life, she felt an orgasm approaching from penetration alone. She dug her fingernails into the silks, her body clenching and urging the passion upward. She squeezed her inner muscles, wanting to grasp all of him that she could, and a second later felt him slow.

"Oh God, Emma," he said, and grabbed her hip with one hand, pushing her down against him as he slowly completed his final thrust and held motionless. His stillness was followed almost instantly by a pulse she felt at her entrance, and she knew he was done.

She dropped her legs from his back and he eased

down on top of her. She could still feel the pulsing expectation of her own desire, of her body seeking its own fulfillment. Russ's breath was warm and heavy against the side of her face, and within a minute it became heavier still.

Emma scowled. He'd fallen *asleep?*

She wiggled slightly. He murmured and lay one arm along her own, gripping her wrist for a moment and then subsiding.

Her unslaked desire roused a flame of annoyance. She'd been so close! This was the second time they'd had sex, and the second time she'd had to go to bed hungry for an orgasm.

She wiggled harder, and then shifted to slide more of his weight off her back.

He came groggily awake. "Oh, sorry." He pulled the pillow out from under her and then turned onto his back. She moved to get up, but he caught her arm. "No, come lie with me."

"I have to get a towel," she said, not wanting to give in to the sleepy comfort of a postcoital snuggle. It wasn't post-anything for *her*.

His lips tightened, and the sleepiness began to clear from his eyes. "I should go clean up."

Her annoyance warred with her liking of him, and liking won out. She pushed against his chest, making him lie back again. "Don't be silly. I'll be just a moment. Stay here."

She cleaned herself up and removed her veil, then warmed a washcloth in hot water and carried it back to him, cleaning him of the vestiges of their lovemaking. She set the cloth aside and climbed up onto the bed with him, letting him settle her against his side. She pulled lengths of silk up over them and then rested her palm and cheek against his chest.

He reached over and stroked his hand down her side. "You need to have your turn."

She closed her eyes and shook her head. "That's not what this is about."

His hand moved over her hip and down to the edge of her sex. "I'll enjoy it more if I know that you enjoy it."

It was what she'd wanted five minutes ago, not now. Her mood was gone and some perverse part of her wanted to wallow in the injustice of the orgasm score. "I do enjoy it. Very much," she said, with a hair less conviction than might have been believable.

"Don't do that."

She tucked her face against him, knowing what he meant but asking anyway. "Don't do what?"

"Say things you plainly don't mean. Be honest with me, Emma. You've nothing to lose by telling me the truth."

She opened her eyes, staring at the hairs on his chest, and gathered the courage for honesty. "I do enjoy it. But I was very close to enjoying it a lot more—if you know what I mean."

He squeezed her arm. "Tell me when it's like that, so I can do something about it. Will you tell me?"

She nodded, but it was so much easier to try to please someone else, rather than ask another to please you.

"Promise?" he asked.

"Promise."

It was a promise she didn't know if she could keep.

EXPERIENCE PASSION, SEDUCTION,

AND OTHER **DARK DESIRES** IN BESTSELLING PARANORMAL ROMANCES FROM POCKET BOOKS!

PRIMAL HEAT SUSAN SIZEMORE
Can a heroic vampire protect his clan from
danger—and save himself from burning desire?

TOUCH A DARK WOLF JENNIFER ST. GILES
In the arms of a shapeshifter discover
the most dangerous love of all...

DARK PROTECTOR ALEXIS MORGAN
How many times must this immortal warrior die before
he can claim the heart of the only woman he desires?

Discover the darker side of desire
with bestselling paranormal romances from Pocket Books!

Master of Darkness
Susan Sizemore
She thinks he's helping her hunt vampires.
She's dead wrong.

The Devil's Knight
A Bound in Darkness Novel
Lucy Blue
A vampire's bite made him immortal. But a passionate
enemy's vengeance made his hunger insatiable....

Awaken Me Darkly
Gena Showalter
Meet Alien Huntress Mia Snow. There's beauty in her
strength—and danger in her desires.

A Hunger Like No Other
Kresley Cole
A fierce werewolf and a bewitching vampire test the
boundaries of life and death…and the limits
of passion.

Available wherever books are sold
or at www.simonsayslove.com.